PRAISE FOR

"[One of] the two most acclaimed South African novelists of the past twenty years [along with Coetzee]... Mda's greatest gift is his Dickensian social range, his ability to generate characters from diverse backgrounds, colluding and colliding across the barriers erected to divide them."

—Rob Nixon, *New York Times Book Review*

"For a long time, white writers dominated South African literature—Paton, Brink, Gordimer, Coetzee. Post-apartheid, Zakes Mda, looks like the great South African novelist of his generation, a writer rich in both imagination and ironic political attitude."

—*The Philadelphia Inquirer*

"A voice for which one should feel not only affection but admiration."

—*The New York Times*

"In novel after novel, Zakes Mda seems to have cultivated a mode of writing in which the realistic and the magical co-exist with unruffled ease."

—Harry Garuba, *Independent*

"Zakes Mda is among the most acclaimed exponents of a new artistic freedom. His fiction has a beguiling lyricism and humour, revelling in the beauty of aloe-covered mountains or Cape marine life."

—Maya Jaggi, *The Guardian*

This edition first published in Great Britain 2019 by
Jacaranda Books Art Music Ltd
27 Old Gloucester Street, London WC1N 3AX
www.jacarandabooksartmusic.co.uk

Originally published in Southern Africa by Umuzi, a division of
Penguin Random House South Africa

A CIP catalogue record for this book is available from the British
Library

ISBN: 9781909762770
eISBN: 9781909762787

Cover Design by Rodney Dive
Typeset by Kamillah Brandes

Printed and bound by CPI Group (UK) Ltd, Croydon, CR0 4YY

LITTLE SUNS

ZAKES MDA

JACARANDA

To my father who made the present possible,
Ashby Peter Solomzi Mda

MONDAY DECEMBER 7, 1903

There were others before him. But we start with Malangana because that is where our story begins. For him, though, it is really the beginning of the end. He is hobbling on twisted crutches made from branches of *umsintsi*, known to the TrekBoers as the *kafir-boom*—the tree of the non-believers—and as the coast coral tree to the colonists. Everything about him is twisted: his face, his lips, his arms, his waist, and his legs. Especially his legs. They are like dry stumps of grey wood with knees forming twisted knobs that knock against each other as the crutches try to find their way down the escarpment among the rocks and shrubs. For generations thousands of feet paved a path from one village to the next where nothing grows and smooth pebbles are embedded in the ground to massage the tired soles of travellers. Yet his feet are beyond massaging. They are granite-hard and have lost all sensation. His erratic gait cannot keep to the path. He staggers and stops to catch his breath and curse the man he has become, and then stumbles on again.

He has a long way to go. How long, he does not know. He does not care either. His journey will stop only when he fulfils his longing. Or when he dies, an eventuality he is not prepared to entertain. Not yet. He will walk from destination to destination—little destinations that seem never to have any finality. He can see his next one already, across the valley and the stream, and up the hill. He can see the whitewashed buildings of the mission station, and the smoke billowing from the houses of the school people surrounding the station. It is something that started even before he left, this practice of surrounding mission campuses with homesteads of school people as a buffer between the missionaries and the hordes who are apt to cut a white man's throat without any provocation at all—there is a lot of pacification that still needs to be done. A senior regional magistrate has decreed that only natives who conform to the rules of the mission and do not practise immoral heathenish customs should be granted land around the mission centres. Traders and Government officials have adopted the same laager-style settlements, the wagons this time being the houses and gardens and kraals of *amakhumsha*, the school people.

He is confronted by goats. About five of them including a kid. They stand directly in front of him and refuse to give way. '*Ziyadelela*,' he says to himself. *They look down upon me.* They are, in fact, looking up directly into his eyes. They do not even blink as he raises his arms to shoo them away. Even the kid is obstinate. Malangana stares at them, and they stare back unflinchingly. He cannot outbrave them so he shoos them away once more. The billy goat in front raises its forelegs as he lifts his hands. It stands on its hindlegs challenging him directly. His crutches drop and he falls flat on the pathway, face down. He lies sprawled on the ground, and the goats give him one last contemptuous look and go their way. He is struggling, trying to rise from the ground, but is unable to.

A man comes riding a horse.

'Where are the boys who are supposed to look after these goats?' he asks.

He dismounts and helps Malangana to his feet.

'I can give you a ride on my horse,' the man says as he helps him with the crutches. 'I am going to the mission station.'

'I can manage,' says Malangana. 'I have my own two feet to walk with.'

'If it suits you, *khehla*,' says the man and mounts his horse.

'*Ukhehla ngunyoko!*' Malangana shouts after him as he rides away down the escarpment. *Don't you dare call me an old man; rather give that label to your own mother!*

The man looks back in astonishment, decides a crippled man is not worth his trouble and rides on. He has no way of knowing that Malangana is not just a cantankerous old man who woke up with a grudge against the world. Malangana refuses to see himself as an old man. In his mind nothing has changed. The world is as it was twenty years ago. He has returned to continue exactly where he left off. Except he cannot continue alone. Hence his quest.

A woman comes riding a pony. She has pulled up her skirt above the knees in the most immodest manner, so that she can ride astride like a man. She controls the pony with the snaffle rein with one hand and pulls a bridled mule with the other. She is, he surmises, one of the *amakhumsha* judging by the European dress and the lack of decorum. Obviously Malangana is ignorant of the ways of *amakhumsha*. It is not because she is a school person that she rides astride with thighs on full display like a maiden's. *Amakhumsha* do not even allow their women to ride horses at all as it is ungodly for them to enjoy the highly suggestive movements of a horse. And when they have to ride, perhaps because of some emergency, they must sit with both of their legs hanging on the same side and the skirts covering the legs down to the ankles. This is the etiquette that the English have introduced from the land of their Queen Victoria.

This woman opted for a comfortable riding posture in defiance of the sacred dictates of missionaries.

Once she has greeted him and asked after his health—which according to his indifferent response has never been better—she offers him a ride on the mule. He turns down the offer because he has his two feet to walk with.

'Four feet,' says the woman, chuckling.

He scowls.

'The sun will set even before you cross the river. Soon it will be dark.'

'Am not a child. Am not afraid of the dark.'

'I can't leave you alone here. God will not forgive me if anything happens to you.'

She alights from her pony and helps him to mount the mule. He does not resist though he is mumbling his defiance, something to the effect that it would be a wonderful world if people learned to mind their own business. She merely exclaims, '*Hehake!*' and makes sure he is settled on the bare back of the mule. And then she hands him his crutches and mounts her pony.

She'll be much slower this time as the old man seems rather fragile. Also he is not holding the reins because she is using them to lead the mule. He is clutching his crutches instead and bobbing and swaying uncomfortably.

'Where is this road taking you this afternoon, *bawo*?' the woman asks.

He pretends that he did not hear. She decides to mind her own business.

Darkness is falling when they cross what she referred to as a river which is really a stream to a man like Malangana who has crossed real rivers such as Senqu, named the Orange River by the colonists, and Telle.

They are even slower when they climb the hill. The stars are twinkling by the time they enter the village, and a sliver of a scythe-shaped moon tries to be inconspicuous among them.

'Perhaps now you will tell me where you're going,' she says. 'You may leave me right here,' he says.

'Right here? Who have you come to see?'

'I'll be fine here.'

He gestures that she should help him dismount.

'*Heyi hayi ke!* I can't just leave you here at this time.'

That's how Malangana finds himself piled like dry wood on a stool carved from a *garingboom* trunk sharing a meal of samp and beans with a family of *amakhumsha*. Ever the first to grab with both hands the things of the white people, they would be maize-eaters, wouldn't they? He, of course, would have been more at home eating the corn of his ancestors, sorghum. If he had any inclination to eat at all. Perhaps with cowpeas. And pumpkin. Or with the *amasi* soured milk. But then as a stranger he can't be a chooser.

He is a strange stranger, not just for the reason that he has never been seen in these parts before, but because his hosts find him odd and baffling. People generally open their doors to strangers; hospitality is an obligation of each household. In return a stranger goes through the ritual of introducing himself, his village, his father's name, his clan, and even his mother's clan. He elaborates on the purpose of his travels, on the ravages of the weather, on those who are sick and those who are dead, and on any titbits he has gathered in the villages through which he travelled. That is how news travels. Itinerant strangers are the media. But this one is different. He's been silent from the time he was ushered into the house by the woman. This however does not unduly surprise the woman, and the husband takes his cue from her. A strange looking man like this cannot be expected to behave like a normal stranger.

Malangana's next observation is that although the school people are called *amakhumsha*, which means 'those who speak English', this family's conversation is not in English. From their dialect he concludes that they must be amaMfengu. He has heard that in his absence the land of amaMpondomise was overrun by amaMfengu, many of whom had been converted to the religion of the white man and fought on the side of the British during the last war. Perhaps amakhumsha speak their own language when they are among themselves, and only communicate in English with Government. And also with those traders and missionaries who have not yet mastered the language of the people. He wonders how much English he has left. He used to speak the language *ngempumlo*, as his people derisively called the nasal accent of the British. He learned it almost twenty-five years ago when he, as a prisoner of Her Majesty the late Queen Victoria, cleaned Magistrate Hamilton Hope's quarters and tended his garden. Granted, he may have forgotten a lot of the language since he had no opportunity of using it during his years of exile. But things that you learned as a young person don't flee en masse from your head. On his way from exile he tested it in Palmietfontein, Sterkspruit and Kingwilliamstown and the white people could understand him very well.

Malangana decides he does not like these people. Not only for the reason that they are amaMfengu, a people who played a decisive role in Mhlontlo's defeat at the Battle of Tsita Gorge, but because they are too kind to him. The woman especially. At least the man sits there chewing loudly and ignoring him. The woman is eager to make conversation as she walks in and out of the *ixande*—the four-walled tin-roofed house that is typical of *amakhumsha*—tending the three-legged pot on the fire outside and engaging in another exchange with the boys and girls sitting around the fire. She is able to switch automatically from one exchange to the other without missing a beat: immediately as she exits she admonishes the children for some transgression committed during the day, and as soon as she enters her attention is on Malangana and the purpose of his travels.

'I must go now,' Malangana says, putting his enamel plate on the floor. There is some food left, but no one comments on his lack of appetite.

'*K'seb'suku.*' *It's night*, she says as she takes the men's plates and walks out.

Malangana can hear her outside instructing the girls to wash the dishes. And then she is back inside again telling him he will leave tomorrow.

'Where does he want to go at this time?' the husband asks his wife, not Malangana.

'I don't know,' says the wife.

'I thought you would know. You brought this old man here.'

'I am not an old man,' says Malangana to the woman. 'I may even be his age.'

'Then what happened to him?' asks the man.

'The world has beaten him to a pulp,' says the woman. 'We can't let him go at this time.'

'We can't stop him if he wants to go,' mumbles the man as he lights his pipe.

Soon the room is full of smoke and the pungent smell of home-grown tobacco.

'Where are you going exactly?' the woman asks.

He gives in. He can't be stubborn any more. Maybe they will leave him alone if he tells them. Maybe they will stop smothering him to death with their kindness and will let him go in peace.

'To the mission station.'

'The gates are locked at this time,' the man says. 'No one will open for him.'

'In any case the priests have stopped their acts of charity. Because of all these wars there are shortages of supplies.'

Malangana is offended.

'I am not a beggar-man. I haven't come for charity,

yours or the priests'. I have come for my Mthwakazi. The *umkhondo* places her at this mission station,' he says, talking of the trail he has been following.

Husband and wife look at him curiously. They expect him to expound, but he doesn't. Instead he reaches for his crutches and stands up to leave.

'I will sleep at the gate. I'll walk in as soon as they open in the morning.'

'Please sit down, *bawo*,' says the woman. 'Perhaps we may help you to find the woman you are looking for. Did they say she is here? What's her name?'

Malangana knows only that she was called Mthwakazi, which merely means a 'woman of the abaThwa', the people who are called the Bushmen by the English. The Khoikhoi disparagingly call them San, which in their language means 'scavenging vagabonds' because they own no cattle and are hunter-gatherers. amaMpondomise call every Bushman woman Mthwakazi, so it will be difficult for anyone to help Malangana find his specific Mthwakazi. Even if he had a way of identifying her, these people never stay at one place, they are always on the move hunting and gathering.

The woman explains that she works at the mission station washing clothes for the minister and his family, while her husband is a lay preacher and a teacher of the Sub A class.

'Occasionally there are bands of abaThwa women who come by selling ostrich eggs or doing piece jobs for the missionaries. Where did you meet this one and how did she disappear from you?'

Malangana does not respond.

'How does he think we'll help him if he is sullen like a

pregnant goat?' the man asks the wife.

'It goes to show that your husband knows nothing about goats,' says Malangana. 'A pregnant goat is never sullen.'

'The father of my children is right; there is no way we can help you if you don't tell us anything.'

'I do not think Mthwakazi is anyone's problem but my own.'

Still he opens up; he does need help after all.

He first saw Mthwakazi at the Great Place of King Mhlontlo of amaMpondomise. He was one of the young men who were sitting by the kraal waiting for the *inkundla* to start. He does not remember what case they were going to hear, but it must have been one of those petty matters where someone's cow had grazed in someone else's sorghum field. Mthwakazi was with two old women well known for their prowess in the field of medicinal herbs, though they were not fully fledged *amagqirha* diviners.

At first Malangana mistook Mthwakazi for a child as she pranced along the pathway that led to the house of Mhlontlo's senior wife—the Great House, *Indlu Enkulu*, as it was called. She was puny. But soon he noticed she was not a child, her breasts pointed perkily towards yonder mountains. The young men told him she was a special nurse to Mhlontlo's ailing wife, the senior queen who was Sarhili's daughter, king of the amaGcaleka people, also known as amaXhosa. They gossiped about the stories they had heard about her: her knowledge of herbs and her stubbornness. She was known to argue with the doctors about which roots were effective when boiled with which berries to cure which ailment.

As Malangana listened to the young men, and as he watched Mthwakazi disappear into the Great House, he remembered that almost two years had passed since his return from the school of the mountain where he was circumcised and initiated into manhood. Thanks to time served in the white man's prison he was still a bachelor. It was high time he took a wife.

Even before Malangana can finish his story the woman interrupts him.

'I know who you are talking about,' she says. 'I know this Mthwakazi you are looking for.'

The woman tells Malangana that immediately he mentioned a woman of the abaThwa people who was a nursemaid to Mhlontlo's wife she remembered a weather-beaten woman who worked as an *impelesi*, or nanny, to the children of the missionaries. She stands out in her memory because she was different from the other abaThwa who are set in their wild ways. And she wore golden earrings at all times. She never spoke about herself. But when she suggested some remedy for an ailment that was eating one of the preacherman's children to the bone, and the woman wanted to know how the Bushman woman got to know so much about curative herbs, she confided in her that she was once a nurse to the queen at King Mhlontlo's Great Place.

For the first time Malangana's eyes shift excitedly from the man to the woman and then back to the man.

'Where is she? Take me to her right away!' he says. 'I do not care if the gate is locked. I will break it open.'

'With what?' asks the man of the house. 'How is he going to break the gate open?'

'She is no longer here,' says the woman of the house. 'I could not keep the secret to myself... the secret that in our midst was a woman who knew Mhlontlo personally and had worked at his court.'

She told other school people.

A few days later she left. In the deep of the night the woman of the abaThwa people jumped over the gate and disappeared. She was afraid that the news of her association with Mhlontlo's Great Place would reach the missionaries. And maybe even Government. When people talked of Government (rather than the Government) they meant the resident district magistrate and his minions. She feared she would be locked up in jail. The name of Mhlontlo sent fear and loathing into the hearts of the white people.

The *umkhondo* was getting warm. And then all of a sudden it gets so devastatingly cold! But Malangana vows he will find his Mthwakazi again, just as he found her that first time.

Gcazimbane was full of tricks. He had this habit of taking off at full gallop, neighing and swishing his tail from side to side in mock irritation. Malangana knew that it was all part of a game. He just wanted his groom to run after him. And then look for him when he disappeared down the gorge. Gcazimbane enjoyed playing hide-and-seek. Malangana, on the other hand, was exercised by this kind of behaviour because it was the cause of Mhlontlo's annoyance with him whenever the king needed his horse and Malangana could not locate it.

'You can't even look after one horse,' Mhlontlo would say. 'The white man's jail has made you stupid.'

Malangana should have been angry, walking the wilds looking for the horse. But who could stay mad at a fine Boerperd specimen like Gcazimbane for any length of time? He was hiding somewhere among the boulders down the hill. And the bounder did it on purpose, just to cause a problem for him.

He whistled as if calling a dog. Gcazimbane sometimes responded by whinnying back when he thought it was time to be found. He didn't this time. Malangana did not know what direction to take so he wandered aimlessly.

Suddenly the air was filled with a strange combination of whirling and chirping and buzzing and humming sounds. The sky had been blue all along with nary a cloud, but without warning Malangana was walking in the middle of deep shadows. Above him was a dark cloud of swarming locusts flying in the direction of Sulenkama.

Malangana marvelled at their stupidity—invading a month before the planting season instead of waiting till the fields were green. Their folly saved the land of a maMpondomise from famine.

Unless they were the harbingers.

At that moment Gcazimbane came cantering up. He was neighing with his head held high in search of his groom. He was obviously agitated by the sudden darkness and his tail was swishing violently from side to side.

Malangana burst out into a belly laugh while Gcazimbane nuzzled and blew.

'I thank the locusts for routing you out, you silly nag,' said Malangana.

He began to walk back to the village with the horse following him.

On the outskirts of Sulenkama, children, maidens and young women were spread all over the veld. Malangana knew at once that the locusts had landed and were feeding voraciously on the grass. When he got closer he saw that the people all had containers of different sorts, ranging from clay pots and grass baskets to enamel basins. They were picking up the locusts that had formed a thick carpet on the grass, and were stuffing them into the containers. They were all

singing and beating rhythmically on their containers. The
children were laughing and giggling and prancing about on
the hapless creatures. In the evening the whole of Sulenkama
would be feasting on stiff sorghum porridge and savouring
fried or grilled locusts.

Locusts were destructive in the fields. But they got their
comeuppance by becoming a juicy meal for the day and a
sun-dried snack for weeks to follow.

Malangana could see Mthwakazi among the locust
gatherers. He made a point of passing her way, though it
was a detour from his path to the Great Place. He stopped
next to her and gave her a mischievous look, folding his
arms across his rippling bare chest and leaning against
Gcazimbane's head. Mthwakazi surveyed him from toe to
head and then back to toe, one arm akimbo and the other
holding a basketful of locusts. She looked cheeky in her
tanned-hide back-and-front apron, a single-strand ostrich
eggshell necklace gleaming on her bare chest.

He suspected she was impressed with his European
trousers, though the turn-ups were frayed—most young men
in his age-group wore loin cloths. He knew immediately that
she was different from other girls. An ordinary Mpondomise
maiden would have cast her eyes on the ground shyly.
But this Mthwakazi was staring back at him. And she was
giggling to boot, as if there was something funny about him.

'I've seen you before,' said Malangana. 'You're the
Mthwakazi who nurses our queen.'

'I know you too,' said Mthwakazi. 'You're the man whose
buttocks were shredded by the white man's *kati*.'

He chuckled. That was his claim to fame, the fact that he

was lashed by Hamilton Hope with a *kati* or cat-o'-nine-tails. And the magistrate had done it himself, personally, instead of assigning the task to a policeman. After that he had summarily sentenced him to imprisonment. Malangana had served almost one year in prison in Qumbu. He had only just been released, and yet his reputation had spread. He knew that women pointed at him when he passed and whispered to one another: 'That's the man who was in a white man's prison.' Part of the fascination was that the whole concept of locking up transgressors in a building was new to the amaMpondomise, and Malangana had been among the first inmates of the new jail in town. The proud pioneers, so to speak.

Gcazimbane nuzzled him at the back, pushing him until he staggered. He wanted them to leave, but Malangana resisted.

'I do have a name though,' he said. 'I'm Malangana.'

'Little Suns? Ha! Your name means Little Suns!' she said in the language of the abaThwa which he did not understand.

'What did you say?'

'There's only one sun,' she said in perfect isiMpondomise.

'*Uyabhanxa*,' he said. *That's silly.* 'There's a new sun every day. It rises in the east and crawls across the sky until it hides itself behind those mountains in the west.'

'It is the same sun, you silly man!'

'Silly Mthwa girl, did you see it go back?'

She did not.

'There are many suns,' he said, driving home his victory. 'Each day has its own. Some are small, some are big. I'm named after the small ones.'

He walked away from the daft girl. The horse followed him.

She was stumped for a moment, but soon enough she was struck by a new idea.

'Come back here, silly boy. It is the same sun. When it sets behind those mountains it gets into the ground and then burrows its way back to the east where it rises once more in the morning.'

He had no answer to that except to mutter to himself, '*Iyaqweba ke ngoku lenkazana.*' *This girl is improvising a story.* He knew there was something wrong with her theory, but was not skilful enough to come up with a rejoinder.

Gcazimbane was getting impatient. He knelt down on one foreleg while stretching the other one forward. Malangana jumped on the horse and rode away bareback. He needed no reins and no saddle on Gcazimbane.

Malangana did not say goodbye to the annoying girl. He was fuming. *There are many suns!* Stupid Mthwa girl! Surely his parents were not mad when they named him Malangana—Little Suns. *There are many suns!* Indeed, he was not the original owner of the name. He was named after an ancestor, the leader of abaMbo from whom amaMpondomise descended. The patriarch who led them during the epochs of great migrations, and who was famous for his mystic powers and his prowess in the art of hunting people of the forest, as leopards were called.

From the time Malangana was a little boy he was taught to recite the genealogy of his people spanning some three hundred years or so. To the rhythm of the gentle movement of the horse he sang and chanted it, mixing it with his own

praises that he had composed as part of the graduation ritual
from the initiation school of the mountain.

Gcazimbane trotted until he stopped at the entrance
of the Great Place. As he dismounted Malangana cursed
Mthwakazi once more. She would need to be straightened
out about the number of suns out there. He would not be
defeated by a girl that easily.

SUNDAY DECEMBER 13, 1903

This thing they call *umkhondo*, it works in different ways for different people. For the abaThwa, reputed to be the best trackers in the world, it works through the eyes. They are able to see the trail where no one else can. Even on the grass or on the most luxuriant foliage or on dead leaves or on rocky terrain they can see footprints as if they were left on soft wet sand. Dogs, on the other hand, do not depend on their eyes but on their nostrils. They can sniff *umkhondo* and follow it until they catch their quarry. Malangana is neither of the abaThwa people nor of the dog clan. He has to use other instincts to follow *umkhondo*. He does not know how it works but he gets a feeling when the trail gets warm on the tracks of Mthwakazi. When his bones begin to rattle he knows that the trail is getting warmer.

Sometimes he can smell Mthwakazi's aura. Especially when the wind is blowing from the hills. Yes, he smells the aura, though he can't describe to anyone what an aura smells like. It is one of those things that you only know when you feel it or, in his case, when you smell it. Sometimes it becomes so strong that it forces him to stand alone in the veld and wail like a woman who has just been informed of the death of her husband. He shivers like one standing naked on the snows of uLundi, and his bones rattle. And this happens despite the warmth of spring or the heat of summer.

His rattling bones have led him to this place. He stands under a peach tree at the edge of a corn field. The branches cast their shade on the footpath between the fields. The peaches hang like small balls and their smell of greenness wafts towards him intermittently, depending on the direction of the fickle breeze.

A few yards away five women are hoeing. They pay no attention to him. Occasionally they break into humming a song, one of them in split-tone. Another one tells a joke. They all break into boisterous laughter as they ruthlessly attack the weeds between immature maize shoots.

Malangana just stands there staring at them. He knows that field. It used to belong to his family. Or more accurately to his mother, one of Matiwane's very junior wives—she of the Iqadi House whose main function was to support the Great House. Matiwane was Mhlontlo's father. Malangana was therefore Mhlontlo's brother from the junior house. Of course, according to the customs of the governing English, Malangana was Mhlontlo's half-brother instead of brother. As the first-born son of the Great House Mhlontlo was the king of the amaMpondomise people and Malangana was nothing more than Mhlontlo's servant. Malangana was nevertheless proud of the royal blood that flowed in his veins.

Now strangers are hoeing the field. It no longer belongs to his family. Nothing belongs to his family any more. There is no family.

'Allow me to ask a question, women of the amaMfengu

people,' yells Malangana after watching their antics for a while.

They do not hear him. He repeats his request, this time louder. It is a strain to shout. He remembers the days when he could stand on top of a hill and his voice would carry across the valley, reverberating to the next hill. He picks up a green peach from the ground and throws it in their direction. The women stop and glare at him.

'*Hehake, yintoni ngelixhego?*' says one of the women. *What is wrong with this old man?*

'Sorry, I did not mean to harm you. I thought one of you was Mthwakazi.'

'*Yho!* This *xhego!* Do we look like abaThwa?'

He is getting used to being called *xhego* or *khehla*, *old man*. He doesn't protest any more. He has come to the conclusion that it is stupid to protest when people choose to give you a label that comes with honour and expectations of wisdom.

'No, you don't. It's just that *umkhondo* led me here, and I couldn't see you properly. Some of you are short enough to be mistaken for abaThwa from a distance.'

They laugh.

'I did not mean it as a joke, women of amaMfengu. Mthwakazi is not a laughing matter.'

'He is insulting us, calling us amaMfengu,' says one of the women.

'*Masimyek'enjalo,*' says another. *Let's leave him with his own foolishness.*

'We are not amaMfengu,' says a third woman adamantly. 'We are amaHlubi and amaBhele. We shouldn't allow these people to continue insulting us with this amaMfengu label.'

Malangana should have remembered that these inter-
lopers who have taken over the lands of amaMpondomise as a
reward for fighting on the side of the British hate to be called
amaMfengu, which means refugees.

A horseman in a black suit, bowler hat and brown riding
boots comes galloping and wielding a whip. He ignores
Malangana and rides straight to the hoeing women. They
drop their hoes as, screaming, they run off helter-skelter. He
does not lash them with the whip though, but cracks it at
their heels.

'It is the day of the Lord, you heathens,' he says.

He does not pursue them further but rides back to
Malangana under the tree.

'They must respect the Sabbath,' he says as he brandishes
a Bible. 'It says so right here in the book of books.'

'I'm not a person of the book,' says Malangana.

'No work is permitted on the day of the Lord. It is the
day reserved only for praising his name.'

What a vainglorious man this Lord must be, reserving
one whole day in a week for people to do nothing but praise
him. What a needy man! What a self-aggrandising man! But
Malangana does not voice these thoughts. He just stands
there looking up at the man sitting pompously on the finest
beast since Gcazimbane.

The thought of Mhlontlo's horse forces a tear down
Malangana's cheek despite himself. He is angry that he cannot
hold it back and that a man of the amaMfengu people sees
him in such a shameful state. The man, on the other hand,
just looks at him curiously. And then he dismounts and gives

him a handkerchief. Malangana shakes his head and withdraws his hands to his chest.

'Something is eating you,' says the man. 'Perhaps your own sins. It looks like the world has not been very kind to you. You must come with me.'

'Nothing is eating me,' says Malangana, and he tries to hobble away on his crutches. The man stands in front of him.

'It is for your own good. I am the preacherman and I am on my way to a church service. We'll pray for you and perhaps, if the spirit moves you enough, you will testify and be saved from whatever has been eating you to the extent that you're nothing but bones.'

'I'm not one of your church people and I am not about to start now.'

Malangana tries to fight him away, but the man is too strong for him. He bundles him on to his horse, almost at its neck, and mounts the saddle behind him. Malangana succumbs in humiliation and the horse canters away up the escarpment to the village. Malangana looks back and can see the women at a distance walking back to the field to resume their hoeing. The man can see them too but decides their souls are not worth the trouble at this moment, there are more urgent things that need his attention, particularly the rousing sermon he plans to deliver.

The preacherman assures Malangana that he will be fine and will regain his humanity as soon as he accepts the Lord. Malangana's mind is more preoccupied with the object of his search than regaining the humanity he never knew he had lost. How did Mthwakazi's aura get there if she has not been there recently? He begins to doubt what he believed to be *umkhondo*. Perhaps it is the aura that Mthwakazi left when she was here once, maybe months or years ago. If that is the case then it certainly will complicate his mission.

Even as the horse approaches the church, a sandstone building with a red corrugated-iron roof, a boy hits the gong that hangs on a pole. He does so repeatedly and the people walk into the church. Many of the women are wearing their *manyano*—the Mothers' Union—uniforms of black skirts, red shirts, white bibs and white hats. They remind Malangana of the Red Coats against whom he fought the war that resulted in his exile. He could see them in his mind, they and their amaMfengu policemen in khaki uniforms, destroying his family's crops with fire and confiscating amaMpondomise cattle.

The preacherman helps him dismount and asks another man to look after him.

'He is our guest,' says the preacherman. 'He has come to find the Lord.'

This Lord who must be found, is he lost? Why should it be his responsibility to find him? But again Malangana does not utter these questions. He hobbles behind his minder into the church.

The preacherman leads his congregation with a hymn. His voice is booming and his eyes threaten to pop out of their sockets. *Noyana, noyana phezulu? Are you going, are you going to heaven?* This question excites the congregation and they dance in their places, clapping their hands or their hymnals and Bibles. Malangana's minder is seized by the ecstasy of the moment and does not notice him hobbling out of the church. The preacherman does see him because he is facing the congregation and the door, but there is nothing he can do about it. He cannot leave the pulpit to stop this one sinner from escaping from the Lord. Anyway, it is the sinner's loss. He did his best to save him.

The sinner wanders aimlessly on a footpath away from the village. There is no longer any *mkhondo* to follow, but he will walk on and on. He will ask the people he meets, especially the older ones who might have known Mthwakazi when she lived here at Sulenkama during the glorious days of King Mhlontlo. He will not get tired of asking even if sometimes he is answered with insults. Ultimately somebody is bound to remember the Bushman girl who nursed the queen.

It is early evening when he walks into the town of Qumbu. He has walked all the eighteen miles from Sulenkama on his crutches and was not even aware where he was going.

Three men are sitting on the veranda of a general dealer's store drinking brandy. Being Sunday evening, the store is closed. One of the men is the nightwatchman and the others are his friends helping him while away the night. Malangana stops to look at the ruins of the building next to the store. He knows the place very well. He lived here for a number of months, a time he does not remember fondly. This used to be the jail where he served his sentence. Apparently it was never rebuilt after it was set on fire during the war.

'What help do you need, *khehla*?' asks one of the men.

They insist that he joins them.

'*Ngcamla nje ezinyembhezi zikaVitoli*,' says the

nightwatchman. *Share with us Queen Victoria's Tears*. That was the term of endearment for brandy. The last time Malangana had that burning taste in his mouth was years ago when he was still in exile in the mountains of Lesotho. It was sheer luxury for any black man to drink brandy instead of the usual sorghum beer.

'His daughter's hand has been asked in marriage,' says one of the men by way of explaining the bottle of brandy. 'It was part of the *lobolo*.'

Soon Malangana finds himself relaxing among these men and even laughing at their jokes. He has not laughed for a long time and he is attacked by guilt and shame for doing so with such abandon even though he has not found his Mthwakazi. He vows to himself that he will shut his mouth and carry himself in solemn dignity. But the brandy is merciless. It tickles his brain and he breaks out laughing.

Malangana is drunk out of his wits. He stands up and wobbles around on his crutches and falls to the ground and laughs while kicking his legs in the air. The men are much entertained. They give him a standing ovation. One of them helps him up.

'Sit down, *xhego*,' he says, laughing, 'otherwise you'll break your bones which are already rattling.'

Malangana points at the ruins.

'That was my prison,' he says. 'I was as drunk as a little bird twirling in the sky after drinking the juice of the *garingboom* flowers when I was arrested.'

Once more he breaks out giggling. And then the giggles become guffaws. He laughs for a long time until tears run down his cheeks. Not just the one drop he shed earlier today at the memory of Gcazimbane. Tears gush like rivers drenching his shirt. Horror maps the men's faces: how can so much water flow from so dry a body?

MONDAY JANUARY 6, 1879

Hamilton Hope's Report

1. *The Chief Umhlonhlo is the hereditary paramount chief of the Pondomise Tribe; and since the subdivision of the country into separate districts, has been at the head of the portion of the tribe which I have had the charge since the 1st July, 1878. He is a brave and warlike man, and far more out-spoken and straight forward than most other native chiefs; and as natural consequence he is somewhat impatient of control. I believe that before I came here he had not unfrequently offered a good deal of opposition to Government authority; and when I was installed as magistrate of the district he expressed great dissatisfaction at my appointment: but I am glad to be able to say that after one or two feeble attempts at opposing me at the first, he accepted the position I allotted him as in all things subordinate to me, and he has since then rendered me cheerful, and I may say prompt obedience in all matters, and has not only ceased all open opposition, but has greatly assisted*

me by advice and example to the people, in bringing about some sort of order and respect for Government authority in the district.

2. *Crime—I am sorry to say it is frequent here, many cases of theft, and assault, of a more or less serious nature being reported to, and punished by me, during the six months I have been here; and I am at least glad that whilst I am aware that so many of these crimes are committed a large proportion of them are reported to me, as it shows that the people have confidence in the Government, and prefer their trying the cases to taking the settlement of them into their own hands. I do not, however, imply that all cases are reported to me. With regard to civil suits, I have as many cases to hear and decide on each Court-day as I can get through. And even Umhlonhlo has himself been a suitor, and has on three occasions appeared as a plaintiff in my Court; and I find that I have now seldom to take any active steps to enforce my judgments, for in almost every case, whether civil or criminal, the amount of the judgment is paid at once.*

3. *Hut Tax—I find that few, if any, people have paid their tax for 1877, and none for 1878, and even for 1876 many are in arrear. I intend, however, to enforce the payment of all arrears up to date.*

4. *Licences—There are only four trading-stations, of a very inferior class, in this district; but I have hopes that some*

merchant from the Colony may be induced to open a respectable and extensive business here, as it is much needed.

5. *Timber Licences*—A small revenue is annually derived from this source, but I have reason to believe that for want of proper supervision, timber is frequently cut and taken away without licences. I shall, however, take steps to prevent this for the future.

6. *Roads*—The roads in this district are for the most part good; and if a reasonable sum is expended upon putting them into thoroughly good order, it will require but a very small annual expenditure to keep them in repair.

7. *Ponts*—Two ponts are urgently required, at the Tsitsa and Tina drifts respectively, for as both these rivers are frequently impassable for weeks at a time during the rainy season.

8. *Socially*—I am afraid not much improvement has taken place amongst these people, who are wedded to all their old traditional customs and superstitions, and they appear for the most part to have profited but little from the few advantages they possessed; although in fairness to them, it must be said, that their position has been isolated, and they have, until lately, lived in such a constant atmosphere of strife, that they have not had many opportunities

of seeing the advantages that are to be gained from civilization.

9. *Religion—It is, I fear, still a sealed mystery to the majority of the tribe, who look upon it as an eccentricity of the missionaries more than anything else; but the energy and good example of the Rev. Mr. Davis, of the Wesleyan Society, who is Resident Missionary at Shawbury, are doing much towards breaking down the prejudices of these people.*

10. *Education—The Rev. Mr. Davis has several teachers actively engaged with infant schools at various places in the district; and at Shawbury there is, besides the usual school, a large girls' seminary, where girls of all ages from five or six to eighteen are making considerable progress in the various branches of education: and I think that Mrs. Davis, and her able and accomplished assistant, have every reason to be satisfied with the progress they are making.*

11. *Generally, I have reason to feel hopeful for the future, as I find, the people far more docile and amenable to reason than I expected.*

HAMILTON HOPE, *Resident Magistrate, District of Qumbu.*

SATURDAY FEBRUARY 8, 1879

Malangana was as drunk as a little bird that overindulged on the nectar of *garingboom* flowers. He sat on Magistrate Hamilton Hope's bench giggling and belching. Occasionally he shouted 'Silence in the court' and hit the bench with a gavel. He paged through the Book of Causes and pretended to read the names of culprits, their crimes and their sentences as enumerated in the book. But the blue squiggles from the magistrate's nib did not make sense to him. He had learned to speak some of the white man's language, but not to read it.

The Tears of Queen Victoria were burning in his belly and sending tingling sensations to his head.

It all started when he arrived in the morning to clean the House of Trials. It was his weekly assignment as a prisoner to sweep, scrub the floor and dust the furniture in the courtroom. On weekdays he did the same at The Residency and also tended the garden, comfortable jobs that were envied by the rest of the inmates of Qumbu Jail who had to dig quarries and haul rocks for stonemasons. A man who worked at the home of the magistrate was likely to see bits and pieces of delicacies find their way into his stomach, courtesy of maids and nannies. Or to get tipsy once in a while if the master had been careless enough to leave his brandy lying around.

And that was what had happened today. When Malangana walked into the courtroom followed by a Mfengu warder armed only with a baton, Hamilton Hope and Major Scott, a fresh-faced blond soldier in the uniform of the newly minted Cape Mounted Riflemen, were sitting at the desk of the Clerk of the Court in front of the bench. They were arguing spiritedly while drinking *Inyembhezi zikaVitoli* that Hope kept on pouring into enamel mugs from a hip flask.

'You'll change your tune when you've been here long enough,' Hope was saying. 'The natives will keep you on your toes and you'll sing a different song, my friend.'

The white men paid scant attention to him as he dusted the magistrate's bench. The warder wandered away. Malangana belonged to that class of prisoners that didn't need to be guarded all the time. Why, sometimes he was released early from his chores, walked all by himself back to prison and banged at the gate with his fists until the warders let him in.

'Pacification in British Kaffraria is far from being attained,' added Hope. 'We must undermine traditional power.'

'I do not dispute that,' said Scott. 'But I think the best way to undermine it is to win it to our side first and then subdue it.'

That was the problem with these upstarts fresh from military academy. They thought they knew more than the faithful servants of the Queen who had years of field experience. Hope did not really like Scott but had to tolerate him because he was sent by the new prime minister and colonial secretary, Gordon Sprigg, to plan the development of suitable defence systems. Granted, he had been part of the team that led the militarisation of the Frontier Armed and Mounted Police into the more efficient Cape Mounted Riflemen. It irked Hope no end to admit how brilliantly that task was accomplished. What irritated the magistrate most was the young man's lack of modesty about his academic achievements; he never forgot to write B.A.. (Oxon) after his name, even after his signature. And here now he was impudent enough to argue with him on how to deal with the natives.

'While suppressing insurrections against the Queen we need to address the insurgents' legitimate concerns,' said Scott.

He took a swig from the mug and then grimaced as if he had just swallowed poison. Malangana kept stealing a glance at him and shook his head; this fire-water burned the throats of powerful men and made them wince, and yet they continued to drink it. He himself had become partial to it when he was still a free man. Oh, how he would like his throat to be burned by the tears of the great queen of the white man!

'What legitimate grievance could there be when we have brought the native civilisation?'

Obviously Oxford and Sandhurst had made Scott stupid.

'Still we need to deal with these half-civilised races tactfully,' he said.

'These were wholly savage tribes,' said the magistrate, pounding the desk with his fist. 'Magistrates like me are responsible for that half-civilisation you're talking about.'

Who was he to teach him about tact? Malangana could see irritation written all over his face.

Hope was an expert at dealing with the natives. That was why he was posted to Qumbu among the amaMpondomise from Lesotho where he had subdued Moorosi, the so-called king of the Baphuthi people—the natives re-imagined their chiefs in the guise of kings, another important thing Hope needed to correct. He knew what he was doing and didn't need lessons from someone who was in nappies when he started serving in the colonies. His expertise was born of hard-earned experience, not of some anthropology degree from Oxford.

Tact? He was a master of tact. He was so tactful he made friends with their chiefs. He had even dined with Mhlontlo on occasion.

'According to Callwell, we'll only subdue the native if we address his grievances,' said Scott, turning red. Malangana could not say whether it was from the brandy or from the debate with a dismissive magistrate.

'What are you looking at?' Scott snapped at Malangana.

'Oh, leave the bleeder alone, Scott. It's not his fault you've lost your marbles.'

'Callwell says...' said Scott turning to Hope.

'I know, I know, you never tire of reciting Major Callwell's small-wars theory of counter-insurgency,' said Hope, chuckling derisively. 'What you and Callwell need to understand is that tribesmen don't follow any theories. They are apt to be seized by madness and break into war at any time.'

Hope abruptly stood up and made to go. He limped towards the side door.

'You're still new,' he added before exiting. 'Soon you'll learn.'

Major Scott would not give up that easily. He rushed after him, leaving the flask and the mugs on the table.

Malangana could see the two men through the window walking towards The Residency, still arguing. He tiptoed to the desk and poured himself a shot. He pressed his eyelids together tightly as the burning sensation slid down his throat. He coughed drily, and then took another swig directly from the flask. He took the flask to the bench and perched himself on the magistrate's own throne. He paged through the Book of Causes between swigs.

His name was there too. As were the names of the other men who were fellow prison inmates. If only he knew how to read them. He pretended to read in the nasal accent that amaMpondomise associated with the English.

He was Hamilton Hope.

He read out the names of the men from Sulenkama who had been sentenced to a year in prison for torturing a man who had been smelled out as *igqwirha*, a person who harmed others through the use of witchcraft. And there in the Book of Causes another squiggle representing the diviner who was in charge of the witchcraft-smelling ritual, now also an inmate of the Qumbu Jail. He recited the names of those who had been sentenced to various terms for housebreaking, for stock theft, for assault, and for the non-payment of hut tax. The latter was a major grievance of the amaMpondomise people. Though the tax was not introduced by Hamilton Hope but by those who came before him, the new magistrate was enforcing it with gusto since his arrival seven months ago. He was collecting arrears dating back to 1875, and a number of men were in prison as a result. Malangana surmised that more than half his fellow inmates were there because of the hut tax.

And then he came across his name. It had to be his name. The squiggles were shapelier and were in black ink instead of the blue that was used on the rest of the pages. The rest of what followed must be his record—the whole story of how one Sunday morning he woke up with a thirst that could only be quenched by gourds of sorghum beer and a craving for something salty that could only be satisfied by an open-fire-roasted chunk of beef. He knew immediately those desires were pointing him to Gxumisa's homestead, Mhlontlo's uncle who had organised a feast for the boys who had graduated from the school of the mountain and were entering manhood with poetry, songs and dances. He had participated in the slaughter of a fattened ox the previous evening and he reckoned this morning the women would have already prepared and boiled the head—the part of an animal that was reserved only for men—and the men were already gathering to sink their teeth into it.

He was sitting under a tree with five other men, basking in his own freshly minted manhood—he had graduated a month or so before—the ox's brain melting in his mouth when a group of mounted policemen came to quell the festivities. Hamilton Hope had banned drinking on Sunday and therefore a feast of this nature was illegal. It was tanta-mount to a riot in the eyes of the Government. Gxumisa must have known this, and yet he organised a feast in defiance of the law.

Malangana read in the Book of Causes how the men of the amaMpondomise had grumbled while obeying Hope's orders and how he, Malangana son of Matiwane, had stood up in front of the leader of the policemen and told him that no British magistrate had the right to interfere with the customs and traditions of his people.

'It is an insult to *uTat'u*Gxumisa, the king's uncle, to come to his homestead and tell him that he cannot hold a feast,' he shouted at the Qheya sergeant.

'You are drunk already,' said the sergeant. 'If you don't join your tribesmen and leave we'll have to arrest you for drinking on Sunday.'

'I am a Mpondomise man,' said Malangana. 'I refuse to obey laws that do not come from my king.'

The policemen laughed. Surely the man was drunk to think he could stand in defiance of the Queen of England. They grabbed him, handcuffed him and frogmarched him in front of their horses. Not a single man of the amaMpondomise lifted a finger to help him nor raised a voice to protest against his treatment. They just walked away from Gxumisa's homestead, their heads bowed in shame.

The graduates in their new loin cloths of many colours, cotton handkerchiefs and chiffon scarves fastened on white or red blankets with *iziqhobosho* pins and round mirrors reflecting the sun on their chests, cowered near the kraal.

Though these policemen were black men except for the Qheya sergeant, Malangana decided they couldn't be amaMpondomise. They must have been recruited from other nations. Otherwise they would not have scoffed at the customs of amaMpondomise and insulted the king's uncle.

The policemen were going to deposit Malangana in the holding cells until the next day when he would appear before the magistrate. But as his misfortune would have it, when they entered the town of Qumbu they chanced upon Hamilton Hope on a horse ride with two of his trusted aides, Warren and Henman.

'What do we have here?' Hope asked.

'This native was drunk and rowdy on Sunday,' said the sergeant.

Malangana yelled back that he was not rowdy. No man would tell him he could not drink on any day of the week when he wanted to drink.

Hope dismounted.

'*Paqama*,' he said, asking Malangana in Sesotho to lie on the ground face-down. He had not yet learned the language of amaMpondomise.

Malangana stood before the puny man defiantly. The magistrate's nostrils flared, which reminded Malangana of Gcazimbane. Two policemen forced him to the ground. Hope's eyes protruded and his lips twitched, making his full beard vibrate as he gave Malangana a few lashes with a cat-o'-nine-tails.

Malangana would not flinch. He would not give this white man the pleasure of his screams. After all, he had graduated from the school of the mountain where he had been trained to take pain like a man. Hope's face reddened as he lashed out with greater vigour. He would not let an impertinent native destroy his reputation which preceded him even before he assumed the magistracy at Qumbu. He had acquired it when he was the magistrate among the Baphuthi people of Lesotho. Their King Moorosi had told his close friend Mhlontlo about Hope's cruelty and penchant for flogging grown men, even chiefs, with his trusty cat-o'-nine-tails. When the amaMpondomise first saw him they didn't think the tiny man with a deformed leg could be capable of any cruelty. Soon they learned that the king of Baphuthi knew what he was talking about.

Still Malangana would rather die than give him satisfaction. Hope instructed the sergeant to lock the rebel up in jail and bring him before the magistrate for trial first thing in the morning.

The next morning, still boiling with resentment, Malangana was brought to the House of Trials where Hope summarily sentenced him to a year in prison as a lesson to all those natives who were disrespectful and stubborn. But he tempered justice with mercy. There was the option of a fine: ten pounds.

As he paged the leaves of the Book of Causes Malangana recalled how Mhlontlo refused to pay the fine. Malangana was an impetuous young man, he told the messengers. He had no business picking a fight with Hamilton Hope. He should therefore take his medicine like a man.

'He has betrayed me,' said Malangana. 'My king and 46 brother has let me down. Tell him when I am released from the white man's prison I will pack my things and seek asylum from Mditshwa.'

Mditshwa ruled over a rival branch of amaMpondomise across Itsitsa River in Tsolo, about nineteen miles from Qumbu.

By the time the warder returned to take Malangana back to the Qumbu Jail the hip flask was empty, he had become bored with the Book of Causes and was staggering about pretending to be dusting the furniture.

The warder was not blind. Malangana readied his buttocks for an impending encounter with the cat-o'-nine-tails.

'I would have kept quiet if you had shared those Tears of Queen Victoria with me,' the warder said repeatedly. '*Ngoku awulibonanga!* You will bear the consequences.

47

SATURDAY SEPTEMBER 25, 1880

The chiefs and elders were already gathered outside the Maclear Magistracy when Mhlontlo arrived accompanied by Gxumisa and Malangana. The latter was there specifically to act as Mhlontlo's interpreter. The three men were on horseback, with Mhlontlo riding in the middle on Gcazimbane. They were resplendent in European pants, riding boots and white beaded blankets, and the two older men carried knobkerries while Malangana carried an assegai and a shield, more as accoutrements than as weapons of war.

Despite the drought that the elders said was the worst in living memory, the horses still looked fresh after almost two days on the hilly terrain from Sulenkama to Maclear, a distance of about forty-five miles. They had rested at each stream they crossed so that the beasts could drink and graze, and the men could nibble a bit on the *iinkobe* boiled sorghum kernels and sun-dried beef that they carried in their rock-rabbit-skin bags as provision—thanks to Mhlontlo's wife of the Iqadi House. Most streams had run dry, but the riders moved on until they reached the ones that had some water.

'The King of amaMpondomise has arrived,' announced a policeman.

Hamilton Hope glared at the policeman. Mr Welsh, the magistrate of Tsolo, smiled. He knew that Hope was very particular on how the native rulers were to be addressed. They were chiefs and nothing more. At best they were paramount chiefs if they—like Mhlontlo—had other chiefs owing allegiance to them. They could not be kings or queens. There was only one Sovereign, Her Majesty Queen Victoria. The natives ceased to be kings and queens when they were graciously ushered into the civilising fold of the British Empire.

Mr Thompson, the magistrate of Maclear and convener of this meeting, beckoned Mhlontlo and indicated that he should join the other elders seated on the ground in front of the magistrates and their aides. There must have been a couple of hundred men gathered that day, and Mhlontlo could see among them a number of amaMpondomise military leaders who had left Sulenkama in the night and arrived at Maclear that morning. They were there to bear witness and to support their king.

The three magistrates, Welsh, Hope and Thompson, were sitting on the chairs, with the convener seated in the middle. A group of white men was standing behind them, leaning against the sandstone wall of the Magistracy. Malangana could recognise three of them: Warren, Henman and Davis. Warren was a Captain in the Cape Mounted Riflemen and Henman was a clerk of the resident magistrate of Mthatha currently seconded to Hope. Davis was also a Captain in the Cape Mounted Riflemen and Adjutant in Qumbu. He was known as Sunduza among amaMpondomise and was popular mostly because his brother was a highly regarded missionary based at Shawbury Mission, but also because he spoke isiMpondomise as if he had suckled it at his mother's breast. That was almost the case because, from the time he was a baby, he was brought up by amaMpondomise nannies and grew up playing with native children. He therefore spoke the language of the black people long before he could master his mother tongue.

Malangana got to know these men when he was a prisoner. From Sunduza, particularly, he had learned what he knew of the English language.

Malangana placed his assegai and shield on the ground and took his place next to Gxumisa.

Mhlontlo did not immediately take his place but stood to survey the delegates sitting on the ground. He knew some of the chiefs and elders besides those who came from Sulenkama. Among them were Lehana and Lelingoana, chiefs of Basotho clans. But there were many others who were strangers. Protocol therefore demanded that he introduce himself by reciting his genealogy, which dated back to the great migrations of the 1400s and 1500s. It was a ritual the magistrates found tiresome, but because they wanted the cooperation of the natives they indulged them.

'I greet you all, children of abaMbo. I am Mhlontlo, King of amaMpondomise,' he said in a singsong voice. His body moved rhythmically and he gently hit his open palm with his knobkerrie as he mentioned the name of each ancestor. 'I descend from Sibiside who led abaMbo from the land of the blue lakes. Sibiside begot Njanya, Dlamini and Mkhize. Dlamini is the one who founded amaSwati people; Mkhize is the father of those who later merged into a nation that became known as amaZulu. Njanya begot the twins Mpondo and Mpondomise, and Xesibe. Mpondo branched off to found his own nation called amaMpondo and Xesibe originated amaXesibe. Mpondomise established amaMpondomise.'

'I'm sure your fellow chiefs know all those stories already,' interrupted Thompson. 'We don't have all day.'

You don't interrupt a man in the middle of reciting his genealogy. Malangana shook his head; *the white man never learns.*

Mhlontlo ignored Thompson and continued.

'Mpondomise begot Ntose, and Ntose begot Ngcwina. Ngcwina begot Dosini, Ngqukatha and Gcaka from the Great House, and Nxotwe from the Right-hand House. Ngcwina also begot Cirha from the Iqadi House, and that was where the dust-storm began. Cirha's mother was a Bushman woman, Manxàngashe, yet still Ngcwina insisted that he be the heir to the throne even though he was from a junior house. Ngcwina felt that the rightful heir, Dosini, was an imbecile who would disgrace the throne. It is where our praise-name, *Thole loMthwakazi,* began.'

Thompson was losing his cool; the meeting should have started already. He was about to interrupt with much firmness this time, but Welsh stopped him.

'We need the natives' cooperation,' he said to Thompson between his teeth. 'Let's show them that we respect their protocol. It's a small price to pay.'

'Cirha begot Mhle,' continued Mhlontlo. 'Mhle begot Sabe. Sabe begot Qengebe. Qengebe begot Majola, the one who was born with the snake, setting a tradition of snake visits to all babies descending from him. Majola begot

Ngwanya. Ngwanya begot Phahlo. Phahlo begot Ngcambe, Ngcambe begot Myeki. Myeki begot Matiwane. I, Mhlontlo, am of Matiwane's testicle.'

There was silence for a while, as if the men were digesting the four hundred years of begetting.

To the white men whose patience had been taxed this was just a litany of names that meant nothing, but to the delegates sitting on the ground, as Sunduza was at pains to explain to the magistrates and their aides, they were stowage of memory. Each name connected to a story of heroism or villainy, once told by bards at the fireside or at special ceremonies. Indeed, some of the people on the ground found some of the names linking snugly in the chain of their own ancestries. That's how history was preserved and transmitted to the next generations—through the recitation of genealogies and of panegyrics.

Malangana, on the other hand, was digesting the omission of Mamani in Mhlontlo's recitation of the genealogy. She was supposed to feature between Phahlo and Ngcambe. She was Phahlo's daughter who, on the death of her father in the middle of the eighteenth century, insisted on taking the throne even though she was a woman.

'I'm the first-born child of Phahlo's Great House. I should therefore be king of amaMpondomise.'

Men had objected. It was unheard of for a woman to be king. The oldest of her younger brothers from the Great House qualified for that position. If there were no brothers from the Great House then the oldest of the males from the Right-hand House would be king. The search would proceed even to the Iqadi House, which is the most junior house whose function was normally to support the Great House.

But Mamani would have none of that. She took over the throne and had those men who objected executed.

Even before these events people had suspected there was something wrong with Mamani. She had refused to marry and had turned down suitors long after her younger sisters were married. One of her younger sisters, Thandela, was married to King Phalo of the amaXhosa nation and became the mother of Gcaleka. Now that Mamani was a king—no one would dare call her a queen—she sent emissaries to get her a bride. Mamani married Ntsibatha, the daughter of Nyawuza from the land of amaMpondo. People had never seen a woman marrying another woman and wondered how they would copulate and bring forth heirs.

The heir to the throne of amaMpondomise was Ngcambe, Malangana's and Mhlontlo's great-grandfather, born of Mamani's wife Ntsibatha from the seed of one of Mamani's younger brothers.

Although Malangana chuckled to himself at Mhlontlo's omission of Mamani's name he understood completely. No Mpondomise man worth his manhood talked proudly of Mamani. His mother once told him years back, 'We don't talk of Mamani, my child. She disturbed the natural order of things.'

Malangana thought the omission of any ancestor in the genealogy was dishonest. After all, some of the men in the list were villains of the first order. He would not omit Mamani when it was his turn to recite the genealogy.

The digesting continued for a few moments until Lelingoana broke the silence by making a joke about

Mhlontlo's pedigree, or lack thereof.

'I could see from your stubbornness that you are a progeny of abaThwa,' he said.

Everyone on the ground laughed. The white men on the chairs maintained their puzzled yet stern expressions.

Malangana's mind wandered to his own Mthwakazi. That was how he thought of her. As his own. Even though nothing had happened between them in the twenty-two days since they argued about the number of suns in the heavens. He had been counting as each day passed very slowly and his yearning mounted. He was seen loitering outside the Great House at the Great Place. No one suspected that Mthwakazi was the object of his desire. Usually when he went to the Great Place it was for Gcazimbane. And indeed Gcazimbane became his excuse for dawdling around. Even when he was grooming the horse at the kraal his eyes kept darting to the path that led to the Great House.

Mthwakazi was nowhere to be seen. She remained inside the house for most of the day helping the herbalists and diviners who were trying to save the life of the Queen of amaMpondomise. The story was doing the rounds from one household to the next throughout the land that she was getting worse by the day.

Occasionally Malangana spotted Mthwakazi rushing from one hut to another, or beating the drum for a line of diviners lilting to yonder hills to dig for more curative roots. Malangana vowed to himself that he would bide his time and soon he would get the opportunity to be with her and win her over.

After straightening her out about the suns, of course.

A roar of laughter brought Malangana to the present, to the meeting of the traditional rulers and the magistrates. A policeman called for silence.

Magistrate Thompson stood up to address the meeting. Sunduza stood next to him to translate.

'I have called this meeting to discuss the Basotho uprising,' said Thompson. 'Without wasting further time I will ask Mr Hope to give you the details of what we need from you.'

After Sunduza's interpretation Mhlontlo looked to Malangana for confirmation of its accuracy. He liked Sunduza, but still when he was among his fellow white men he was a white man.

'*Uyichanile*,' said Malangana. *He got it right.*

Of course, Mhlontlo wouldn't have known that Sunduza was much more proficient in isiMpondomise than Malangana was in English.

Hope did not stand up to address the chiefs. Instead he shifted for more comfort on the chair and leaned forward. He began by making his usual threats towards those who had not paid taxes; the chiefs would be held responsible if their subjects continued to dodge their civic responsibilities. The men on the ground grumbled that they had not travelled through the night to be harangued about taxes. Sunduza translated what he could catch of their murmurs to the magistrates.

'Taxes are important, but they are not the reason we called you here,' interjected Welsh.

Hope's eyes and smile could have frozen Itsitsa River in the middle of summer, but he did not even glance in Welsh's direction.

'I begin with taxes because everything flows from them,' Hope said, glowering at the men on the ground and shaking his head. 'Without the taxes nothing would be possible, including the expedition we plan to undertake. But as Mr Thompson said, the reason for our meeting is the war that Basotho rebels are waging against the Government, and the decisive manner in which we must respond.'

It was not lost to Malangana that Sunduza did not interpret Welsh's interjection. He could read in it and in Hope's expression the uneasy relations between the two magistrates assigned to the rival regions of amaMpondomise. He whispered this to Mhlontlo, who agreed with him that white men were good at covering each other's nakedness in front of the subjugated people.

Hope continued, 'You, as the subjects of the British Empire, are required to be part of that response.'

The stubborn Basotho people were refusing to hand in their guns, Hope explained, defying the Peace Preservation Act enacted by Parliament in Cape Town in 1878 which required all the native peoples to surrender their guns and ammunition to the Government.

This law was not informally known as the Disarmament Act for nothing. amaMpondomise had already felt its effect. Unlike the Basotho, who decided to take up arms against the British instead of surrendering them, a number of amaMpondomise men had already handed in their guns and ammunition to the magistrates. The wealthier men had even given up the Snider-Enfield firearms that they had acquired covertly from enterprising officers of the Cape Mounted

Riflemen when the latter changed to the Martini-Henry rifle. Malangana remembered how he caught Gxumisa shedding a private tear when he had to part with his Snider-Enfield which he prized more as an ornament and a collector's item than an instrument of death. He wondered why the old man had decided to obey this law when quite a few other men had hidden their guns. Perhaps he wanted to avoid humiliation because those who were discovered to have done so experienced Hamilton Hope's cat-o'-nine-tails on their bare bottoms.

Mhlontlo had heard of the rumours of the disgruntlement among the Basotho people about the Disarmament Act, but had not been aware that a full-scale war had broken out that very month until Sunduza mentioned that Mr Hope had received a telegram the day before informing him of what the Basotho called *Ntoa ea Lithunya*—the Gun War.

'They want us to fight against our own friends,' whispered Malangana to Mhlontlo.

'Why don't they get amaMfengu to fight for them and leave us alone? After all, amaMfengu are Government people,' asked Mhlontlo.

'I don't know.'

'Ask them.'

Malangana did.

Sunduza had to reinterpret Malangana's English before the magistrates could grasp what exactly he was asking. They broke out laughing at the way Malangana had pronounced some of the words, making it difficult for them to understand such a simple question.

'The Fingoes are wise for they cooperate with the

Government,' said Hope. 'They will therefore continue to benefit from the bounties of British civilisation. Many of them already serve the Government as policemen, clerks and aides to military officers. Indeed they will all be part of this war. But we need more men. The Cape Mounted Riflemen alone cannot fight the Basotho people. The CMR is thinly spread in all the rebellions of the natives. That is why every able-bodied man in our jurisdictions must be part of this expedition.'

Some of the younger men seemed enthusiastic about the prospect of going to war while the elders mumbled their objections. They all looked to Mhlontlo to speak but he just sat there with a scowl on his face.

Malangana was a young man fresh out of the school of the mountain and his blood was spoiling for adventure. But he felt strongly that this was not his people's war.

'Who exactly are we fighting?' he asked.

'*Awuvanga na mfondini? Silwa nabeSuthu,*' said Sunduza. *Didn't you get it, man? We are fighting Basotho.*

'That still does not answer Malangana's question, Sunduza son of Davis,' said Gxumisa. 'Are we fighting Chief Lelingoana's people? They are Basotho too.'

Lelingoana chuckled and said, 'Do you think I'd be here with you if they were fighting my clan?'

'You know very well that Lelingoana's clan lives in our territory and is our ally,' said Thompson.

'Oh, so we are fighting the Basotho of Lesotho?' asked Gxumisa.

'We have no intention of going into Basutoland,' Hope explained. 'The Basotho in Matatiele under Chief Magwayi are fighting in *our* territory. We had better go there and look.'

Mhlontlo, Gxumisa and Malangana exchanged glances and shook their heads at the mention of Chief Magwayi. Hope and Mhlontlo once quarrelled about Magwayi. The Mosotho chief was refusing to pay taxes and Hope was threatening to hold Mhlontlo responsible for that defiance because Magwayi was a vassal chief in Mhlontlo's territory, which was in Hope's magisterial jurisdiction. Malangana admired Magwayi for being the stringy meat that was stubbornly resisting being picked out of Hope's teeth. Anyone who irked the magistrate was bound to find favour with Malangana.

'We'll follow the men whose ears radiate the rays of the sun,' said Lelingoana, expressing his willingness to be led into war by the white man against his fellow Mosotho chief.

'I am only Lelingoana's puppy,' said another chief who went by the Christian name of Joel. 'I will follow him to war against Magwayi.'

But the magistrates were not satisfied. They fixed their gaze on Mhlontlo.

'*Thetha kaloku, Nkosi-e-Nkulu yaMampondomise,*' said Sunduza, smiling at Mhlontlo. *Say something, Paramount Chief of amaMpondomise.*

'Tell the white man that I cannot speak on the matter because amaMpondomise are not here,' said Mhlontlo.

Hope would have none of the delaying tactics. The man was here with his advisers. He could and should make a decision that day.

'The magistrates demand an answer now,' said Sunduza.

Without a word Mhlontlo stood up. Gxumisa,

Malangana and the other amaMpondomise men did likewise and followed their king. They walked for some distance and stopped when they thought they were out of earshot. They sat on the rocks and watched distant sheep and goats grazing on the parched grass and young shepherds frolicking among the aloes on the banks of Mooi River. Boys could frolic at the worst of times.

'I do not want this war,' said Mhlontlo.

'But what choice do we have?' asked Gxumisa, lighting his pipe.

'Our king is not a boy. He is the King of amaMpondomise. If he says he does not want his people to be dragged into a war that has nothing to do with them who will force him?' asked Malangana, also lighting his pipe.

Soon all the men were puffing on their pipes and the air was filled with the pungent smell of home-grown tobacco.

'We placed ourselves under their protection,' said Gxumisa resignedly. It was clear to Malangana that he wanted to give in.

'I was against that protection right from the beginning,' said Mahlangeni, a man Malangana admired because he shared his views on defying Government orders. 'When we asked them for their protection we allowed them to rule us.'

This was still a sore point with the older generation of amaMpondomise, especially those who had objected when Mhlontlo decided to seek British protection through the then magistrate Joseph Orpen, after being advised to do so by the missionary Bishop Key. Mahlangeni, then a young man newly graduated from the school of the mountain, had been in the forefront of those who opposed Mhlontlo's move. Even today as a married man with two wives his head was still as hot as if he were of Malangana's age.

'We didn't ask them to be our masters,' said Mhlontlo, shifting uncomfortably on his rock. 'We asked them to be our allies.'

'Well, they are our masters now,' said Malangana, flaring his nostrils like his charge Gcazimbane often did when agitated. 'Our king is not even allowed to fine transgressors for blood crimes. Only Government can.'

'Our *inkundla* doesn't have a final decision even in settling minor disputes,' added Mahlangeni. 'People can appeal to Government and the magistrate often overturns our decisions. And now we want to go and fight for the white man?'

'We haven't made that decision yet,' said Mhlontlo.

'But it's leading to that,' said Malangana.

'What does my young nephew think we should do?' asked Gxumisa.

'Fight,' said Malangana. 'No, not Magwayi. Fight and defeat Hope.'

He looked at Mahlangeni as he said this, hoping he would join the call. But he did not. He avoided his gaze as he puffed on his pipe.

'We can't fight the English because they are now the masters of all nations, even those we are afraid of,' said Mhlontlo. 'Forming an alliance with them is essential for the survival of our people.'

Malangana was no longer sitting down but was pacing the turf.

'Settle down,' said Mhlontlo. 'You always allow your

blood to boil until your head cannot think properly. That is why the white man gave your buttocks a taste of *kati* and locked you up in his jail for almost a year.'

Mhlontlo shouldn't have reminded him of that. He walked down the hill away from the men. He sat on an anthill and buried his face in his hands.

All the bitterness he harboured against Mhlontlo flooded back and filled his chest to the extent that he was finding it difficult to breathe. Mhlontlo had betrayed him. He had not come to his aid when he was whipped by Hamilton Hope and then locked up in jail. He had refused even to pay the fine, forcing him to stay in prison for all those months. Instead he had accused him of recklessness. He was saving Hope's face at his expense. Malangana had vowed that when he left prison he would pack all his belongings on a sleigh and drive the few oxen and cows that he was trying to accumulate across the Itsitsa River to Tsolo to join the rival kingdom of amaMpondomise under King Mditshwa. But he just couldn't go ahead with that plan because of Gcazimbane. He couldn't bring himself to desert Mhlontlo's horse. So he kept on postponing his departure. And then a few months later he met Mthwakazi. That had decided him. He would not leave. At least not until he had conquered Mthwakazi's heart. His bitterness dissipated until it was gone. Or so he thought. Until today when Mhlontlo opened an old wound he thought had healed.

'Oh, to be young and hot-headed,' said Mhlontlo.

'He is of Matiwane's testicle, that's why,' said Gxumisa. Matiwane was the late king, father to both Mhlontlo and Malangana, albeit from different Houses.

'Let him sulk,' said Mhlontlo. 'He thinks we are foolish old men. He'll come to his senses when he grows older.'

'Growing old is a privilege that many will not experience, thus we carry age with pride,' said Gxumisa.

The men deliberated without Malangana. After a lengthy debate Mhlontlo came to a decision.

'We'll join the white man's war,' he said.

There were exclamations of shock and astonishment.

'Provided the white man supplies us with arms,' he added.

'They have just taken our guns,' said Gxumisa. 'Do you think they will agree to those terms?'

There was a glint in his eyes at the prospect of getting his prized Snider-Enfield back.

'If they don't give us guns then we don't go to war. We cannot fight the formidable Basotho with assegais.'

He sent one of the men to call Sunduza and they briefed him on their decision. While Sunduza conferred with the magistrates inside the Magistracy the men gathered outside waiting eagerly for their response.

Malangana returned and joined a group of brawny Basotho youths standing a short distance from the elders.

'What is happening?' he asked.

'The elders have decided to join the white man's war against Magwayi,' said one of the young men.

Malangana clenched and unclenched his assegai, eyes wide open and nostrils flaring like Gcazimbane's. He thrust his assegai through the window of The Magistracy. Two other young men did the same with their assegais and sticks while laughing and enjoying the spontaneous rebellion.

Mhlontlo yelled at the young men as the magistrates and their aides rushed out in blind panic.

'What do you think you are doing, you fools?'

He went on to accuse the culprits of irresponsibility and demanded that they apologise to the magistrates. The Basotho looked blank and avoided meeting his eyes, while Malangana only sneered and shrugged his shoulders dismissively.

'Of all the native chiefs Mhlontlo is the most responsible,' said Hamilton Hope. 'I will recommend to the Government that he be considered as the head of all chiefs assembled here.'

'We'll follow you,' said Mhlontlo to Hope. 'Where you die, we'll die.'

As for the young men, the policemen frogmarched them into one of the rooms. Mahlangeni protested aloud to the amaMpondomise elders, 'You cannot allow them to take our men away.'

One of the policemen turned to him and dragged him off as well.

'Perhaps you should join them too,' said the policeman. 'You talk too much.'

The elders assembled outside could hear the men scream in pain and beg for mercy as Hope's kati ate into their buttocks.

'You can be sure that none of those screams are from Malangana,' said Gxumisa.

'*Unenkani lamfana*,' said Mhlontlo. *That young man is stubborn.*

Malangana was silent all the way from Maclear to Sulenkama. Not only was he seething inside, his buttocks smarted every time they touched the saddle. He had to ride standing on the stirrups. He wondered how Mahlangeni was feeling as he rode back to Sulenkama much earlier with the main party of amaMpondomise. He felt bad that Mahlangeni went through such humiliation trying to save him. This time he would not forgive Mhlontlo. Or Gxumisa. Once more he had experienced Hope's *kati*, administered by Hope himself, all because his brother and his uncle were spineless.

He kept aloof even when they stopped to camp under the willow trees by the streams to let the horses graze and drink. The older men let him be and carried on with their conversation.

'Do you think Hope will really give us the guns?' asked Gxumisa.

'If he doesn't keep his promise we do not go to war,' said Mhlontlo. 'I doubt if Government will allow him to give us guns. They would be going against their law of disarmament. So what does that tell you, my uncle?'

'We are not going to fight in the white man's war, my nephew!' said Gxumisa.

They broke out laughing.

Pangs of shame attacked Malangana. He had not been aware of Mhlontlo's strategy. He was not aware that the elders had agreed to go to war on condition they were given guns. He had acted too rashly when he heard from the Basotho youths that the elders were in agreement with Hope without first finding out the details. But he kept his shame to himself. Instead he palliated it by transporting his mind to Sulenkama, to the place where Mthwakazi was.

As Gxumisa and Mhlontlo discussed Hamilton Hope, Malangana was frolicking with Mthwakazi on the mountainside, helping her dig the roots and collect the herbs that would heal the Queen of amaMpondomise, and chasing her among the bushes and boulders. Her shrieks of excitement reverberated in the cliffs and the valleys.

Malangana was so absorbed in the world of Mthwakazi that he caught only snatches as Mhlontlo told Gxumisa how Hope's obsession with taxes led to a full-scale war with the Baphuthi people which resulted in the brutal murder of their ruler, his dear friend King Moorosi, only a year before.

Hope had issued writs against the Baphuthi people who had not paid tax, particularly those in Doda's territory. Doda was Moorosi's son. Hope's action therefore alienated Moorosi and his family from the Government. Moorosi and his people repaired to their mountain fortress— Qhobosheane ea Moorosi—and resisted the British forces who stormed the mountain. For months on end they couldn't take the mountain.

Mhlontlo couldn't hide his admiration of the Baphuthi people as he narrated the story of their bravery. In the deep of the night Moorosi's soldiers made forays down the mountain to get food supplies and to attack the colonial encampment. A number of Cape Mounted Riflemen were killed. The British were becoming increasingly frustrated by the day when they couldn't suppress what they called a rebellion. Instead they were suffering untold casualties. Even the most important person in Government, Prime Minister Gordon Sprigg, couldn't make Moorosi surrender unconditionally after travelling all the way from Cape Town to negotiate with him. After months of holding the fortress siege, the wily British finally found ways to climb the mountain.

They captured the mountain and killed Moorosi.

'It was only ten months ago that they killed him,' said Mhlontlo. 'They cut off his head and displayed it on a pole.'

That was not the end of King Moorosi's head. A lesson had to be made for all future rebels. The head was transported all of two hundred and fifty-five miles to Kingwilliamstown where it was exhibited for all to see. Later it was returned to the mountain to be buried with Moorosi's body.

'I am still grieving my friend's death,' said Mhlontlo, his tired voice nevertheless devoid of emotion.

In the meantime Mthwakazi was hiding among the boulders in the same way Gcazimbane usually hid. Malangana was getting frustrated because he couldn't locate her.

'*Heyi wena Mthwakazi, apho nd'zak'fumana khona!*' he yelled. *Mthwakazi, woe unto you when I finally find you!*

Mhlontlo and Gxumisa were startled. They stared at him. Had Hamilton Hope's cat-o'-nine-tails made the young man lose his mind?

MONDAY DECEMBER 14, 1903

He sleeps for the whole day. He feels drained and his body is like *umqwayito*—the salted sun-dried meat that the Trek-Boers call *biltong*—a result of all the water that flowed out of his eyes. Around midday a little girl brings him soured sorghum porridge to drink, but it rebels in his stomach. He stops drinking lest he retches. It would have been a disaster, messing up his hosts' freshly polished cow-dung floor.

In the late afternoon he is awakened by the night-watchman. He is going back to work.

'I'll come with you,' says Malangana.

'You're not well,' says the nightwatchman.

He assures Malangana that he should not worry; his children will look after him until he is strong enough to be on his way. Malangana is grateful. Much as he would not like to impose, he needs the rest. Only for one night though. He must make haste in the morning. He cannot afford to relax.

Mthwakazi must be found.

The song of the girls outside is grating to his ears. It is *umbhororho*, the night-time practice of songs and dance steps in preparation for a wedding. Perhaps it is the first night of practice and the voices do not yet harmonise. There is more argument about which songs to sing and how they should be adapted to mock the groom and his party than there is singing. Malangana cannot help thinking wistfully of his boyhood before he went to the school of the mountain. Weddings were the highlight of any teenager's year because of the singing and dancing at the *umbhororho*. And, of course, cavorting with the opposite sex. Weddings begot weddings.

His chest rattles with anger that no one ever held *umbhororho* for him and Mthwakazi, thanks to Hamilton Hope.

The scent of burning *umsintsi* wood and roasting maize hovers above his mat. He squints his eyes and can see in the thin light filaments of smoke creeping under the door. He wakes up, draws on his heavy khaki pants, but not before inspecting the padded bottom and feeling with a touch that whatever is hidden in a secret pouch is safe. He puts his grey 'donkey' blanket over his shoulder. He reaches for his crutches. He opens the door slowly, as if afraid it will disturb someone's sleep. He hobbles into a night illuminated only by a sliver of a moon, the stars and a bonfire a few yards from where the boys and girls are practising their wedding songs.

The nightwatchman's father is sitting by the fire even though December nights are warm. He is blind. Two young shepherds are roasting maize for him. Malangana stands there for a while and watches them pick the kernels from the roasted side of the cob with their thumbs and hand them to the old man. He chews slowly, putting a lot of effort in every crunch.

'Is that you, Malangana?' asks the old man.

They were introduced in the morning.

'Yes, it is me, *bawo*. How did you sense me?'

'Your bones. They rattle like the seashells of the diviners. Come, join us and share our roasted maize. I always prefer that they boil it first for a long time before they roast it. But I have lazy grandchildren.'

This corn of the white man is becoming more widespread even among those people who are not *amakhumsha*, Malangana observes to himself. Perhaps it will not behave like soft sorghum porridge in his stomach, perhaps it will settle. So he accepts a cob from one of the shepherds.

'My son told me you knew Mhlontlo son of Matiwane,' says the old man.

He can talk with these people; they are not the interloper amaMfengu but the vanquished amaMpondomise.

'I am of Matiwane's testicle from Iqadi House,' he says.

'Thanks to your brother we lost our kingdom. We lost everything.'

Though Malangana is taken aback a little, he does not respond. He didn't expect that there would be some amaMpondomise who'd place the blame on Mhlontlo instead of where it rightly belonged: on Hamilton Hope and the English. But those are not the things he wants to think about. They have been far from his mind since his return from exile. Only Mthwakazi occupies his thoughts.

'I was telling these boys that our people were once great heroes,' says the old man. 'They see the world as it looks today and they think things have always been like this.'

Malangana takes a close look at the old man. The face is furrowed by the ravages of weather and age, but Malangana can see traces of familiar features.

'You were once at Sulenkama, weren't you?' he asks.

'That was another age, another world,' says the old man chewing loudly.

'I knew that I saw you there,' says Malangana.

'And what were you doing there when you saw me, lest you reveal my scandals to these young people,' says the old man and breaks out laughing. 'I'm asking you a silly question. You did say you are Matiwane's son from Iqadi House.'

'I looked after King Mhlontlo's horse,' says Malangana.

The old man rubs his eyes as if willing them to see. They won't.

'You are the boy who looked after Gcazimbane? What happened to you, now that your bones rattle like the ankle-shells of a dancing diviner?'

'I fought a war and lost.'

'You are the boy who hankered after a Bushman girl.' Malangana winces and beads of sweat break out on his brow.

'You knew about that?'

He wipes his brow with the back of his hand and wonders how his body is able to produce some moisture despite the rivers that flowed from it last night.

'Everybody knew about that. I was one of the diviners who tried to heal the queen and failed. We joked about you.'

'I don't see white beads on your wrists and ankles,' says Malangana.

'The ancestors retired me. I lost my sight and my calling.' And then he bursts out laughing again. 'You were like a puppy sniffing around for a lost bone. We teased the Mthwakazi about you loitering at the Great Place pretending to be looking after Gcazimbane, and the girl giggled coyly.

Obviously she was flattered to be sought after by the king's groom. We could see she was playing for time... she wanted you too. How did you manage to lose her?'

'How do you know I lost her?'

'You're not with her now, are you?'

'You're right, I am not.'

'And you were not with her the last time I saw her.'

'I am looking for her,' says Malangana. He is trying hard to suppress the edge in his voice. 'I am here because I'm looking for Mthwakazi. The last time you saw her? Where was that?'

'In the streets of Tsolo,' says the old man.

She was a beggar-woman there.

'And you saw her? How did you see her when your eyes cannot see?'

The old man laughs and says, 'I see with the eyes of a boy, man. The boy who guides me when I go to town to beg as all blind men must do, so that I can buy my own snuff without bothering anybody for their money and pay my tax and avoid jail.'

'You spoke to her? You actually spoke to her?'

'The boy who guides me said, "There's that Bushwoman who wears golden earrings." And there she was indeed. Yes, I spoke to her. The kinship of beggars. Once in a while she's seen in the streets of Tsolo. She used to be seen in Qumbu as well, but that was many years ago.'

He had not seen her for almost a year when he met her in Tsolo recently and she told him she had just escaped from employment at some mission station fearing arrest by Government since her identity as the former nursemaid to the Queen of amaMpondomise had been exposed.

'She has no reason to be a fugitive,' says Malangana.

'I told her so. She has done nothing wrong.'

'I am going to Tsolo,' says Malangana. The old man is struck by the urgency in his voice.

'Now? At this time?'

'I will walk through the night. I must find Mthwakazi.'

The old man will not stop him. He listens to the bones as Malangana hobbles away until the rattle is swallowed by the night.

MONDAY OCTOBER 4, 1880

The night of the new moon. A prolonged drought scorched the land and Mthwakazi sat flat on the ground at *ebaleni*, the clearing in front of the Great House. With her legs stretched out and a diviner's drum between her thighs she beat it with her hands in a slow tired rhythm. This went on for hours until the ears of the people within its range became accustomed to the lamentation and could hear it no more.

She heard a loud moan from the house, and then a sharp wail. She knew immediately that what the nation dreaded had finally happened. She had been waiting for it. She hastened the tempo. One wail became two. And then three. Soon there was a wave of wails, relayed from the Great House to the Right-hand House; from the Right-hand House to the Left-hand House; from the Left-hand House to the Iqadi House. Until the whole of Mhlontlo's Great Place was drenched in wails. The animals in the kraals, in the stables, in the pounds, joined in their various voices.

By the time these sounds reached Malangana in an adobe rondavel where he slept, dreamed of Mthwakazi and played with himself to her spectre, they had swirled into a vortex of hollow howls. He knew without anyone telling him that they were announcing the death of the Queen of amaMpondomise, daughter of Sarhili, King of amaGcaleka, they who descended, together with amaRharhabe, from an ancestor called Xhosa, and were therefore also known as amaXhosa.

The howls were relayed from one household to the next, until they assumed a life of their own. They were echoed by the hills and the cliffs and the caves, across the streams to the rest of Qumbu, and across Itsitsa River to Tsolo. Those who were sleeping could not but wake up and the owls of the night stopped their labours and added to the howls with their hoots, making the vortex fatter and fatter. As it gathered volume it also gained force, sweeping the land, uprooting trees in its path and hurling emaciated cattle across the valley as if they were dry leaves.

Its sheer rudeness silenced Mthwakazi's drum. She held tightly to it nonetheless, and buried her face on its taut cowhide drum-head. She wept quietly. Even the most powerful herbs of her abaThwa people had failed to save the queen. She had given up long before the diviners had, and had whispered her opinion to those who would listen that the daughter of King Sarhili should be released so that her spirit might find its path in peace from the land of amaMpondomise to the land of her amaXhosa ancestors. It was a long way for a spirit to travel and ceremonies would be held by both nations to ease its journey and to welcome it in the dimension of the dead and the unborn. But that would be for the coming days, and none of those rituals would have anything to do with her except as a drawer of water and carrier of wood. For now she wetted the cowhide drum with her tears.

Malangana's first thought after cursing death for stealing the beloved queen was of Gcazimbane. He rose to his feet, put on his pants and a blanket over his shoulder and struggled against the momentum of the howls to the Great Place. He headed straight to the kraal where Gcazimbane was snorting and squealing in turn among bellowing bulls. He embraced the horse tightly around its neck until it gradually calmed down and began to snicker. He led it out of the kraal but once there he did not know what next to do with it.

The howls were now a distance away, leaving deathly silence in their wake. Mthwakazi resumed beating the drum. Its tempo went back to slow and tired.

'What are you doing here?' Malangana was startled by Mhlontlo. He had not heard him approach; his face had been buried in Gcazimbane's neck.

Mhlontlo's voice was shaky and he was sniffling.

'I caught a cold,' he said.

Although Malangana couldn't see his eyes in the dark he knew that a cold had nothing to do with it. He was crying. He was a man and a king, yet he was crying. The queen had been his partner, companion and adviser. Having been raised in the court of King Sarhili, regarded as the greatest of all the monarchs in the region, she had been wise in all matters of statecraft.

'Take him back to the kraal,' said Mhlontlo. 'What has happened has happened. We cannot undo it.'

Malangana led Gcazimbane back to the kraal and secured the gate of tree trunks. He hesitated when he saw that Mhlontlo was waiting. Then he joined him and they quietly walked towards the Great House.

The two men stood in front of Mthwakazi as she beat the drum. She did not look up. She continued as if they were not there. Malangana was visibly shaking, trying very hard to suppress the hyperventilation that had suddenly overtaken him. Mhlontlo placed his hand on the head of the drum, stopping her from beating it. She looked up for the first time and saw the two men distorted by a glass of tears.

'Go, child of the people of the trance. It is enough. The land has heard,' said Mhlontlo.

'It is to accompany every step she takes to the land of her ancestors,' she said.

'It is too early for that, child of the people of the eland. She will only become an ancestor after we have performed *umbuyiso* ritual. For now, go and sleep. That's what we must all do.'

Mthwakazi rose to her feet and tiptoed into the Great House to join the other mourners. Diviners and the old women of Sulenkama had swiftly congregated to prepare the queen for burial. Their songs were subdued.

Malangana took the drum. It would serve as a good excuse to see Mthwakazi again. Mhlontlo did not ask him why he was taking the drum. Perhaps he did not even notice. His mind was occupied with how he would cope with grief— for the passing away of his queen and for the drought that was killing the earth. It had been an omen, this drought. A harbinger of the greatest death his Great Place had experienced so far.

Malangana could not fall asleep after that. He sat on his *icantsi* bedding and contemplated the drum. His body began to shake when the significance of its presence in his room

hit him. This was Mthwakazi's own drum. Not just a drum;
a sacred drum. This was the drum she beat when she com-
muned with her ancestors. What if the spirits of all the dead
abaThwa lived in it? How would it be possible to sleep in
their presence?

Occasional waves of distant wails reminded him that
sleeping should not be a priority on a night like this in any
case. Perhaps he should have stayed with Mhlontlo instead
of rushing home to sleep.

The king had not been himself lately. Even as the queen
lay sick he was making extravagant promises to Hamilton
Hope. Only four days ago Malangana had accompanied him
to yet another meeting with the magistrate, after which Hope
entertained them to a dinner of lamb, peas and mealie-rice
on the veranda of The Residency. The magistrate looked
frail, and he indeed confirmed that he had been in bed with
a fever. Malangana wished in his heart that the man was
suffering from more than just fever; maybe from consumption. He had seen when he was in jail how deadly
the disease could be. It ate its victims to the bone and then
killed them. It would be wonderful if Hope was getting his
comeuppance from the protective ancestors of the
amaMpondomise people for using his whip indiscriminately
on revered elders. Malangana was smarting inside even as
he sat in the shade of the veranda chewing on the soft lamb
and doing his best to interpret for Hope, who spoke in a
mixture of English and Sesotho, sprinkling them with the
few words of isiMpondomise he had learned since being
assigned to Mhlontlo's jurisdiction two years before. He
would never forgive Hope for his *kati*. His buttocks still

twitched whenever he thought of the two occasions he had been its victim.

Sunduza—the brother of the Reverend Davis, trusted by both amaMpondomise and Hope—was not there to interpret for the magistrate that day. The only other white man present was Warren. He sat quietly throughout, only jotting down notes in an exercise book with a new-fangled fountain pen. Hope kept looking at the pen with fascination as it left a trail of blue behind its nib without needing to be dipped into an ink bottle after every word or two.

Mhlontlo was making his point to the magistrate: what the amaMpondomise people hated more than anything was judicial control. Government was taking away all the powers of the chiefs. What good was any chief without judicial control?

'I keep my promises to those who are obedient to the Government,' Hope said. 'I will return some of your power over the smaller chiefs provided you raise the army we need and lead it against Magwayi. You need to prove yourself, Umhlonhlo.'

'Haven't I proved myself?'

'Oh, you've been very good so far. But the expedition against Magwayi will be the ultimate test.'

Mhlontlo assured the magistrate once more that he would indeed be part of the expedition.

'*Nd'zak'fel'aph'ufa khona*,' he said. The king had said this before; at that meeting with the magistrates. *Where you die, I will die.*

Malangana's consternation was not lost on Hope. He gave the young man what he thought was a benevolent smile and shook his beard in his direction. He then poured his guests shots of brandy and asked how they liked the fire-water, as their fellow natives called it. Mhlontlo and Malangana mumbled their pleasure. Warren raised his glass and said 'Cheers' before swallowing the shot in one gulp.

'The Dutch are getting better at this all the time,' said Warren.

'Maybe someday one will retire in a Cape vineyard,' said Hope, and the two white men chuckled. 'Find refuge in a distillery.'

The chuckles became laughter. It must have been an inside joke because the two amaMpondomise men did not get it.

'And how do you like the new extension to The Residency?' Hope's question was directed to Warren.

'Mrs Hope showed me around,' said Warren. 'Solid construction, sir. One doesn't see this kind of workmanship in these parts.'

Hope went on about how parsimonious the Government could be. It had not been easy to get approval for these improvements.

'It reminds me of when I first came here two years ago, all the difficulties I encountered getting approval for the erection of suitable quarters for myself and my clerk,' said Hope sadly. 'I had to live in a Kafir hut.'

That, of course, was an extremely uncomfortable situation for him and his dear wife, Emmie. They had been brought here from Basutoland where he had constructed two beautiful houses at his expense, which he had to abandon at short notice. Surely the Government did not expect him to use his own meagre resources to build a house. For months on end not only did he reside in a Kafir hut, he conducted the administration of the district and presided over court cases in Kafir huts. It was demeaning to the dignity of the Government that its officers had to live and transact business in that kind of environment. He had to struggle before funds were allocated to build The Residency and the Courthouse. And now finally there were the extensions that Emmie was very pleased about; creating a drawing room that was separate from the dining room.

The two amaMpondomise men just sat there and listened and said nothing.

As they were riding back to Sulenkama Mhlontlo asked Malangana what Hope and Warren were talking about.

'It was just a lot of nonsense about how he struggled to get Government to build him a house.'

'So he doesn't always get what he wants from his masters?'

'Ultimately he did.'

'Only ultimately. He may not get the guns we have asked for. We won't fight the war against Magwayi if he doesn't supply us with guns.'

'You promised him... "Where you die, I will die."'

'You will never understand matters of statecraft,' said Mhlontlo firmly, indicating that the subject was closed.

They rode silently for a while. The sun had long set, yet the earth was breathing out heat through its fissures.

'This confounded drought!' said Malangana.

'It knells death, little son of my father,' said Mhlontlo.

Cattle were emaciated and crops were withering away. Even Mhlontlo's own fields were cracked like the heels of an old woman. His sorghum, beans and pumpkin had died prematurely, soon after peeping out of the ground. A week before he had sent Malangana and his eldest son Charles to sell some of his cattle to purchase grain. Some cattle died on the way.

But the drought did not only knell the death of cattle. The queen's life was ebbing away and the king feared the worst. What frustrated him most was that he was himself a healer, *ixhwele*, yet he was hopeless against the evil forces that were consuming his wife to the bone. amaMpondomise had a saying that a doctor could not heal himself. It was obvious that he could not heal his wife either. He became an angry and impatient man. The diviners and herbalists dreaded his visits to the Great House. He would kneel by the queen's bedding, hold her limp hand and gaze into her eyes. But her eyes did not return the gaze. They hid behind a pane of greyness instead. He would then rise to his feet and pace the floor, yelling at everyone and calling them names.

'You're all useless! If you had lived in the domain of Shaka kaSenzangakhona he would have killed you all.'

He summoned his uncle Gxumisa to the Great Place. Gxumisa suggested that abaThwa rainmakers should be called. Healing the land from the drought might also serve to heal the queen from her ailment. abaThwa were always the final resort when things were really desperate. amaMpondomise despised them as people who owned no property, especially cattle, and whose dwellings were the natural caves in the mountains. Yet they were in awe of these small-statvured people for their prowess with curative herbs and for their skill in the manufacture of rain. Both of these gifts were a result of the fact that as mountain dwellers they were close to the rain clouds and to the roots and berries that grew only on the steep slopes. They were people of the eland and the praying mantis and the snake. It was believed that many of them were *iinzalwamhlaba*—autochthons.

Gxumisa led a delegation to the mountains to look for a rain doctor of the abaThwa people. Malangana had wanted to be part of the delegation if only to observe at first hand how abaThwa lived and conducted their affairs, which might give him some guidance on how to deal with Mthwakazi and slake his unrequited love for her. He was hoping to learn a thing or two that he might use to impress her. But Mhlontlo would not allow him to go because he needed him to interpret in his meetings with Hope. And there seemed to be more and more of them lately.

The delegation walked for five days before they reached the Caves of Ngqunkrungqu. They came back with a troupe of abaThwa who danced and tranced and boiled herbs that they fed the queen. They bathed her in them and made her throw up and emptied her royal bowels with enemas. Still the heavens refused to open up and shower the earth with its blessings. And the queen refused to get better.

Hamilton Hope, on the other hand, was getting better, which was a blow to Malangana and all those who had hoped his spirit was about to float across the oceans to the land of his ancestors.

Malangana stared at the drum and thought of its owner. She had been elusive. Sometimes he even suspected she was an illusion. Until he went by the Great House and saw her outside dancing with the diviners or chanting with the shamans and *amaxhwele* herbalists. It assured him she was real. As real as the woman who had argued with him about the number of suns in the skies. Why, she appeared real even in the dreams where she hid herself among the boulders like Gcazimbane and he had to search for her. As real as the wetness of his wet dreams.

He remembered one day soon after they had returned from that meeting with the magistrates in Elliot. He was sitting by the kraal with a group of his age-mates listening to Gxumisa and other elders reciting some of the great historical events of the amaMpondomise nation. He decided to test the waters and bring in the issue of Mthwakazi. He seized the opportunity when Gxumisa served each man from his rock-rabbit-skin bag a pinch of *icuba-laBathwa*, the tobacco of the Bushmen, also known as *dagab* by the Khoikhoi or *dagga* by the Trek-Boers. As the men stuffed it in their pipes and lit them Gxumisa said, 'Though abaThwa are such puny people their tobacco has a gigantic punch.'

The men laughed as they puffed on and filled the air with the dizzying aroma.

'Talking of abaThwa,' said Malangana, 'where did this girl who nurses the queen come from? Who are her people?'

'No one knows,' said Nzuze, one of Mhlontlo's younger brothers.

'How is that possible?' asked Malangana.

'It is true,' said Gxumisa, blowing a helix of smoke. 'She is a child of the earth.'

Malangana discovered for the first time that Mthwakazi was not born of any woman nor begot of any man. She sprang from the earth like a fresh millet plant. It was like that with some of the abaThwa people. They were children of the earth—*iinzalwamhlaba*.

'So what's going to happen when someone wants to marry her? With whom are his people going to negotiate *lobolo*?'

Mahlangeni broke out laughing. Though he was older than Malangana, and was a family man the two men had established a close friendship after Mahlangeni sacrificed his buttocks that were ripped to bits by Hamilton Hope's salted cat-o'-nine-tails. Malangana once confided in him how he was being haunted by Mthwakazi. Mahlangeni, of course, had pooh-poohed the whole idea. How could a noble Mpondomise man even entertain such thoughts about a low-born woman? Or an autochthon as it had now been revealed?

Malangana glared at him.

'I didn't say anything,' said Mahlangeni, giggling like a naughty girl.

'Why, nephew, are you thinking of taking her for a bride?' asked Gxumisa.

He was quite perfunctory about the question. He thought he was just teasing his nephew.

'No, no, I am just asking,' said Malangana.

He was fidgeting, rolling the bowl of his pipe in his palms.

'Yes, yes,' said Mahlangeni, laughing.

'What's wrong with that?' asked Malangana. 'She's a person too.'

Everyone stared at Malangana. It hit them for the first time that something was serious here. Nzuze contemplated him sternly.

'You look as shocked as if I said I want to marry a clanswoman,' said Malangana.

Marrying a woman from your own clan would, of course, have been a taboo of the first order. amaMpondomise clans took wives from other clans to avoid inbreeding, even though their common ancestor dated back to the 1500s.

'You can't be serious, younger brother,' said Nzuze. 'She is of the abaThwa people.'

Gxumisa took a long drag from his pipe and ejected one long jet of smoke.

'I thought this was a joke,' he said. 'Does Mhlontlo know about this?'

'Nzuze and Mahlangeni are the ones who are making this a serious issue, *bawo*,' said Malangana. 'For me it was just a fleeting thought. The king knows nothing about it.'

'*Hayi hayi hayikhona!* His reaction tells me that this is serious,' said Nzuze. 'Listen to me, little brother. Do not even entertain such thoughts. You are the son of Matiwane. The grandson of Myeki. Look for a wife elsewhere. Although you are from Matiwane's Iqadi House, he honoured you by naming you after our founding ancestor. You cannot disgrace our nation by marrying a Bushwoman. I am going to oppose that. And I am going to make sure that my brother, the king, does not give his blessing to such a marriage. Marry well like our king. Marry from the amaGcaleka or amaRharhabe or abaThembu or amaMpondo or any other noble nation.'

'What if I like the Mthwakazi?' asked Malangana.

'If you really like the Mthwa woman you can have her as your fifth or sixth wife, something to play with when you come home tired from the fields or from battle—not the mother of your heirs,' explained Nzuze patiently. 'Make her an Iqadi, not of your Great House, not of your Right-hand House, perhaps of your Left-hand House, which would make her sixth in rank.'

Malangana and Mahlangeni broke out laughing. In a marriage of a well-off Mpondomise man there were three main wives: the senior wife belonged to the Great House, the second wife to the Right-hand house and the third to the Lefthand House. But he could still marry more wives. For instance he could marry a wife who would act as a helper to the senior wife. She would therefore belong to the Iqadi House to the Great House. The ranking became complicated when he married more and more wives and the Left and Righthand Houses had their own Iqadi Houses— wives who served as their helpers. What Nzuze was suggesting was therefore strange to the men because it was another way of suggesting the marriage should never happen at all.

'Do you think I am going to be so rich as to marry six wives?' asked Malangana. 'Even Mhlontlo doesn't have six wives.'

'By the time Malangana is able to marry the sixth one he will be an old man and Mthwakazi will be a shrivelled old woman with abaThwa great-grandchildren of her own in some distant caves somewhere.'

'Or she'll be dead,' said another man.

'We'll all be dead,' said Gxumisa.

The men burst out laughing again. *Icuba-laBathwa* was adding to their mirth, for it was known to cause grown men to giggle and guffaw ceaselessly like maidens gossiping and shrieking at the river while washing clothes and beating the leather karosses and skirts against the rocks.

Malangana shook his head sadly. To these men Mthwakazi was a joke.

Indeed, she was a joke to everyone else at Sulenkama. For one thing, Mthwakazi did not titivate herself with white and red ochre as amaMpondomise maidens did. Her hair was unbraided and, according to other maidens, looked like *iinkobe*—by which they meant it was as though black grain had been scattered sparsely on her head. She wore only a tanned oxhide skirt and anklets of shrivelled roots instead of an *isikhakha* skirt of calico and the colourful glass beads that were popular with maidens her age throughout the land. What did Malangana see in a girl like that?

'You can whisper it to me, *mfondini*,' said Mahlangeni, 'what is it that you see in this *nkazana* of abaThwa people?'

'It will not happen,' Nzuze kept repeating. 'We'll not allow it. Just let my brother hear of it.'

'How do you know it will be an issue with him?' asked Gxumisa. 'You're all hypocrites! All of you here of the Majola lineage have the blood of abaThwa flowing in your bodies, and you are not ashamed to include that fact in your praise poetry by calling each other *thole loMthwakazi*.' *The progeny of a Bushwoman.*

He pulled hard on his pipe and blew a cloud of smoke at Nzuze's face.

'But when it comes to the real world you think you are too good to share your *icantsi* mat with a Mthwa woman, *rha*!'

The young men confessed that they had never known

how they got to be called the 'calves of a Mthwakazi'. Gxumisa told them about their ancestor Ngcwina in the 1600s, who was the grandson of Mpondomise, the founder of the nation. After marrying women for his Great House, the Right-hand House and the Left-hand House and having children by those houses, and indeed after having a rightful heir called Dosini from the Great House, he decided to take another wife for his Iqadi House.

'This is how it happened,' said Gxumisa, relishing the prospect of storytelling. 'King Ngcwina had been having dreams about a strange woman in a cave. He was a famous dreamer.'

One day the men of the amaMpondomise regiments went on a hunt on the Ngele Mountains. For three days they did not come across any animal. Just when they were about to give up they heard their dogs bark and rushed in their direction. And there in a cave was this strange girl.

'This is the girl that the king has been dreaming about,' the soldiers said.

They took the Mthwa girl back to Mvenyane, which was where the kingdom of amaMpondomise had its Great Place in those days, almost two centuries before it moved to Sulenkama. There she was welcomed with much singing and dancing and feasting.

She was named Manxangashe, and she blossomed as a maiden of beauty and honour. She was the best cook of all the women at the Great Place, and King Ngcwina was partial to her exquisite dishes. She did all her cooking at the Great House, the house of Mangutyana, the king's senior wife.

Like all the maidens of amaMpondomise she was

supposed to remain pure and unsullied until someone married her. But other women noticed that something was growing in her. When Mangutyana asked what she had been doing and with whom she pointed to the heavens. Mangutyana knew immediately that she had been impregnated by the king. Nothing more could be said about it. She, as the most senior of the wives, had to insist that the king marry Manxangashe for the Iqadi House.

'A delegation was sent to the Ngele Mountains,' said Gxumisa. 'She, in fact, led the delegation.'

His audience laughed at this.

'You never know with the ways of abaThwa. Their women are headstrong and do things the way they want to do them. When they reached the foot of the Ngele Mountains Manxangashe instructed the delegation to remain there and she climbed alone right up to the highest cliffs where the caves were located. She was gone for three days. And what was the delegation doing all that time? Kindling a fire. She had instructed them to do that. If she didn't see any smoke coming out of a fire she would not return. And of course if she didn't return they would be in trouble with the king.'

On her return she said her people wanted two black oxen as *lobolo*. The king paid this. But apparently it was not enough. She demanded that the delegation should return to the Ngele Mountains and this process was repeated until eight black oxen were paid in all. Only then could she officially become King Ngcwina's wife of the Iqadi House.

This Mthwa woman must have wielded a lot of power over the king. After she gave birth to a son, Cirha, Ngcwina made him heir to the throne, though he was of Iqadi House, instead of the rightful heir, Dosini from the Great House. That, of course, caused a lot of bitterness. But his word was final.

'Mhlontlo and all of you here are direct descendants of Cirha, the son of that Bushwoman, and today we recite that with pride in our genealogy and praise poetry. Why should Malangana not marry his Mthwakazi?'

There was silence.

Malangana sat like a rock on his bedding and stared at the drum as if to outbrave it. It stared back unflinchingly. It was as stubborn as its owner—the one who had been referred to as 'his Mthwakazi' by no less a personage than his uncle Gxumisa, repository of the history and the wisdom of the ages. He would be letting posterity down if he did not make that a reality.

His stare would not hold back the twilight before the sunrise. It crept under his bamboo door and windows.

'*Yirholeni t'anci.*' *I greet you, younger father.* That was Charles at the door.

'*Kuyangenwa,*' Malangana responded. *You are allowed to enter.*

Charles Matiwane was sporting a brown jacket with matching riding breeches and a bowler hat. He was Mhlontlo's son from the Great House, and therefore the heir to the throne. He was one of the *amakhumsha* people as his father sent him to Shawbury at an early age to receive the white man's education from the missionaries so that when he took over as king he would be able to understand the thinking of Government and would therefore serve the interests of his people better. He still had a long way to go before his booklearning was done.

'You got *umbiko*, Jol'inkomo? You must have ridden through the night,' said Malangana, asking him about the death announcement that was relayed to him, and calling him by their common clan name which was usually used as an endearment.

'Father wants us to ride to Qumbu to report my mother's death to the magistrate,' said Charles.

Malangana did not waste time with ablutions. Within minutes he was with a group of men being addressed by Mhlontlo under the coast coral trees that grew in front of the Great Place.

'I am sending a delegation to tell Hamilton Hope that my uncle Gxumisa will lead the men against Magwayi,' said Mhlontlo. 'I will no longer be available to take part in any blood-spilling.'

He had to mourn his wife. He could not go into battle. The *ukuzila* custom forbade it. He would have to mourn for many moons since this was his wife of the Great House, and therefore the Queen-Mother of all the wives and children from all the Houses. As part of ukuzila he was forbidden to eat salted meat. Also, he was not allowed to touch a woman or arms of war for a number of full moons. Salt, women and war! This abstinence would continue until umbuyiso, the ritual that happened after the period of mourning and the purpose of which was to bring the spirit of the deceased back home to the land of the ancestors. Everyone looked forward to *umbuyiso* because it was a festive occasion with a lot of beer and meat to celebrate the fact that the deceased had now become a fully fledged ancestor.

'But of course we are ahead of ourselves,' said Gxumisa. 'As of now we are faced with the more urgent problems of the burial. Nations will be gathering to mourn with us. The queen was not just an ordinary queen. She was the daughter of King Sarhili.'

Long before *umbuyiso* the Great Place needed to slaughter cattle to accompany the dead on the long road to the land of the ancestors. Nothing less than a span of fatted black oxen led by a nursing cow famed for its abundant milk would be fitting homage to the queen and to the palates of the mourners. But where would fatted beasts come from when there was so much drought in the land of amaMpondomise? As the elders raised these questions everyone knew that the answers lay with the *ukuphekisa* traditions, where neighbouring kingdoms who were on a friendly footing with amaMpondomise would contribute beasts and corn for the event, in the same way that amaMpondomise families themselves would each contribute clay pots of beer and other cooked items on the day of the event.

After all these plans had been outlined Mhlontlo instructed the delegation to Hamilton Hope to repair to Qumbu forthwith.

'Only the three young bloods will comprise the delegation, Mahlangeni, Malangana and Charles,' said Mhlontlo. 'I need the rest of you here at the Great Place to perform various tasks in preparation for the burial.'

As the three men rode out of Sulenkama they saw a puny maiden in a cowhide skirt running on a footpath in their direction and yelling: 'Malangana *weee*, Malangana!'

It was Mthwakazi.

'*Hayibo!* What does this thing of yours want now?' asked Mahlangeni.

Malangana stopped. The other two men rode on. Charles, however, slacked off a bit and kept on looking back. Mahlangeni trotted on with nary a backward glance.

'I want my drum back, Malangana,' said Mthwakazi as soon as she caught up to him.

'You look very beautiful when you are angry,' said Malangana, chuckling. '*Kodwa ke isimilo siyephi? Kuyabuliswa k'qala.*' *But where have your manners gone? Custom demands that you greet first.*

'You stole my drum, Malangana,' said Mthwakazi.

He was smiling. She must be joking. She was not smiling. She stood defiantly in front of the horse, arms akimbo.

'Stole? Me steal from you?'

'I want my sacred drum.'

'I am on an important mission for our king and you stop me to accuse me of theft?'

He gave the horse a nudge with his knee and it began to move.

'I am going to report you, *wena* Malangana,' said Mthwakazi. 'I am going to lodge a case of theft at *inkundla* against you.'

Malangana laughed out loud and said, 'You're being dramatic. When I come back we'll talk about it. Meet me by the river and we'll talk about the theft of your drum under the stars.'

He galloped away. The two men were halfway to Qumbu when he caught up with them. Not a word passed among them until they reached the magistrate's office.

'The natives must learn that they cannot just see the magistrate on a whim without an appointment,' said Henman. 'He is preparing to go to court.'

'They say it's an emergency,' said Sunduza. 'It's about the war against Magwayi.'

Thanks to Sunduza's negotiations Hamilton Hope finally agreed to see Mhlontlo's emissaries, but only for ten minutes. They were ushered into his office.

'Charles, you're back with your father,' said Hope. 'I thought you'd be at school.'

'My mother left us,' said Charles.

'She did? Where did she go? Back to the kraal of Kreli?'

'She passed away, sir,' said Charles trying very hard to keep his voice firm.

'I'm sorry to hear that, old chap. What can I do for you?'

'The king cannot lead the men to war because he is mourning,' said Malangana.

'So Umhlonhlo is now reneging, is he? Using his wife's death as an excuse?'

Malangana explained that amaMpondomise were not pulling out of the war. Only Mhlontlo would not be participating because *ukuzila* customs forbade him to touch weapons of war or to spill blood. He had appointed his uncle Gxumisa, a tried-and-tested general, to lead the forces.

'I do not accept that,' said Hope. 'Umhlonhlo is a liar!'

'This man is insulting our king,' said Mahlangeni.

'Calm down,' whispered Malangana.

'This is just an excuse. After all, you people have many wives. What's the big bother? Umhlonhlo has other wives, hasn't he? Surely he can't be a crybaby about one wife.'

'It is the custom, sir,' said Charles. His speech came in gasps and his hands were shaking. That was his mother that Hope was talking about so dismissively.

'You, Charles, should know better. You're a Christian,' said Hope.

'My father and his people are not governed by the Christian doctrine, sir.'

'Now here is my final word on this,' said Hope. 'Tell Umhlonhlo that he shall lead the Pondomise against Magwayi. I will be delivering the requested arms and ammunitions and he shall lead his warriors to war. Government is determined to be obeyed. We cannot make exceptions for him. We cannot be seen to be weak. We are not governed by native customs. You are now under Government, you cannot expect Government to come down to your level and adopt your customs. If Umhlonhlo is not willing to listen to Government then he must give way to a chief who will. Umhlonhlo used to be a wise chief who obeyed Government. He must remember what happened to his friend Moorosi of the Baphuthi tribe.'

Sunduza was interpreting all this for the benefit of the increasingly seething Mahlangeni and, as far as he was concerned, Malangana as well.

As the three men were riding home Mahlangeni was yelling at his companions: 'You people don't see anything wrong with this? The man insults our king, calling him a liar and even threatening to behead him like they did to Moorosi?'

'Of course it is wrong,' said Malangana. 'But what did

you want us to do?'

He did not answer. Obviously he did not know what they should have done.

Charles was visibly shaken. This was his first encounter with Hamilton Hope, the magistrate in action. He had only seen Hamilton Hope the benevolent member of the congregation in church who often visited the school to encourage the missionaries in their good works.

'We're powerless,' said Malangana. 'They pick and choose who our kings will be. They have done it already to the abaThembu people where they removed King Ngangelizwe and placed a person of their liking. They think they can do it now to amaMpondomise.'

'Speak for yourself,' said Mahlangeni. 'You are powerless.'

He prodded his horse and it bolted away, leaving Malangana and Charles stupefied.

WEDNESDAY DECEMBER 16, 1903

He is Thunderman. That's what they think. That's why they are chanting his name in the rain: *Thunderman, Thunderman, come into the house and drink amasi fermented milk. Thunderman, come into the house and eat meat.*

Like the true Thunderman, he does not respond. He fixes his eyes steadfastly on the ground. That convinces them. They shout even louder and encircle him. They clap their hands. The summer rain falls relentlessly. The leaves of the wild pear tree under which he stands cannot protect him from the barrage. He is thoroughly drenched. The chanters are drenched too. But they are children, so they love it. Rain makes them grow.

Fat drops ripple on muddy puddles. The children splash into the water with their feet and kick it in Thunderman's direction while inviting him to come into the house and share their *amarhewu* fermented maize beverage. Of course, there is no house to come into. They are miles away from their divers homes. Their mothers are huddled on the veranda of the general dealer's store where they have taken refuge until the rain passes. They came to sell sorghum, beans or maize to the white trader in order to purchase salt, sugar, tea and dripping from his store, or to grind maize into mealie meal at his mill, only to be stranded by the drencher. But the invitation is not out of line. It's the custom when you see Thunderman under a tree. You invite him into the house for meat and milk and porridge. It doesn't matter if you have the food or not. It doesn't matter if there's a house to invite him into or not. You still invite him.

It is also the custom for him to ignore you and to fix his eyes on the ground. Old people say that in the wondrous days of yore, when the land of amaMpondomise stretched right up to Mzimkhulu River and witches and wizards still pranced free on the hills and mountain peaks exchanging bolts of lightning with impunity, Thunderman was known on occasion to utter a few words of assurance to those who were within earshot. His role was, as it continues to be, to rein in the lightning sent by evil sorcerers to destroy the community. Ever since the land of amaMpondomise was eaten by conquest and shrank into the two districts of Qumbu and Tsolo, the art of wizardry is not as ubiquitous and proficient as it used to be. Immediately the sorcerers start their nonsense of prancing about, sending lightning from one hill to another and competing as to whose lightning can cause the most damage, Thunderman stands under a stump or a bush and fixes his eyes on the ground while working out his strategy. It is at this point that when you see him you invite him to the house for food even though you know he will not respond to your invitation. He concentrates all his power on generating a tremendous storm that swirls right into the dark clouds and drives the lightning sent by sorcerers in different directions until it is absorbed back by the clouds.

Thus death and evil are neutralised by Thunderman.

A flash and a clap send the children scuttling away to the veranda to join their mothers. The women reprimand them for playing in the rain and warn them that if ever they catch a cold they shouldn't come sniffling or coughing to them expecting any pity.

Thunderman on the other hand wonders to himself how stupid children can be nowadays. Don't they know that Thunderman is a creature of spring and not summer? A time when the world is red with the blooms of the coastal coral trees, the great *umsintsi*, and white with wild pear blossoms? A season when mountains are pink from aloe blooms and the *noqandilana* bird—the fantailed cisticola—is twirling in the sky drunk from the nectar of the *garingboom* agave?

As for him being Thunderman, what a silly notion! Thunderman is a young and fresh-faced personage in a verdant costume, a true representative of spring, not a rickety shrivelled man on crutches. He has seen Thunderman once when he was a little boy at the Great Place of the Regent Mbali who held sway on behalf of Mhlontlo since his father, Matiwane, died when he was a teenager. He, Malangana, never knew his father Matiwane, for he died when he was a baby. On a rainy day he saw Thunderman standing under a pole that had been erected outside Iqadi House for the very purpose of dispelling lightning. And there he was, Thunderman, all in green. His eyes too, and his hair, and his nails were all green. They say Thunderman never talks, but he talked to him. He remembers very clearly that he talked to him. Something to the effect that it didn't matter that he could not see his father with his naked eyes, he was there all the same, looking at him, guiding him, being proud of him. He was Malangana, named after the founding ancestor, and should carry the name with pride. Since then he looked constantly for Thunderman whenever it rained but he never saw him again.

The children don't come back even when the thunder and lightning have stopped. Perhaps they have given up on the idea that he is Thunderman. Or they don't want to be ambushed by another sudden bolt and flash while engaged in their antics.

The rain tapers off and stops. It was only a cloudburst that overstayed its welcome. Suddenly there is an outburst of the rays of the sun. And the general dealer's store becomes animated with customers taking their places in the long queue and others being pushed away from reclaiming spots that were never theirs ahead of everyone else.

Malangana takes a few hobbles from under the tree to the clearing in front of the store so that the warm rays of the sun can dry him. The vengeful children will not forgive him. Three of them walk past him.

'He's no Thunderman,' says one of them.

'He lied to us,' says another.

'*Rha!*' says the third, spitting in front of him in disgust.

'*Ngunyoko ke lowo,*' says Malangana. *That is your mother.*

Just the mention of 'your mother' in that tone is a grievous insult to amaMpondomise. The children run back to their mothers shouting that the ugly old man on crutches has insulted them about their mothers. A whole gang of women start yelling at him in unison from the veranda and the steps.

'Why don't you fall down right there and die?' one of them curses, while the rest back up the suggestion.

'I refuse to die before I find Mthwakazi,' he yells back. His defiance silences them.

Boys in grey blankets lazing about among their donkeys laden with bags of grain for the mill titter and snigger. 'What did he say?'

'He is refusing to die before he finds Mthwakazi.'

'Who is Mthwakazi?'

These are not his people. His people were never rude like this. These must be the new people, those who came after the war and took over the lands of amaMpondomise. Granted, the world has changed after twenty years, it is possible that even amaMpondomise could become modern and rude. But to this extent? *Hayi!* Or perhaps it is just that amaMpondomise of Tsolo are different from amaMpondomise of Qumbu in manners and etiquette. Qumbu was King Mhlontlo's territory, where Hamilton Hope had his jurisdiction, and Tsolo was King Mditshwa's. His magistrate was A.R. Welsh, a man of a different temperament to Hope. A man of different methods too. Never whipped respected elders with cat-o'-nine-tails as if they were undisciplined adolescents.

Malangana casts his eyes on the people of Tsolo and their mangy dogs and their scraggy asses and their runty children and spits out a phlegmy curse on the ground. And defiantly stands in the sun to dry. How he despises them. He remembers that on quite a few occasions more than twenty years ago he had been determined to emigrate from Qumbu to Tsolo to seek refuge under Mditshwa when he had been disgruntled with Mhlontlo—especially when Mhlontlo seemed to be taking Hamilton Hope's side against him. And then Mthwakazi happened. Perhaps if he had moved to Tsolo with Mthwakazi at that time things would have taken a different turn. Perhaps the twenty years wouldn't have happened.

He casts his eyes among the rude people of Tsolo once again. He pans from right to left and from left to right in two sweeping movements. There is no sign of Mthwakazi among them. Perhaps standing in one place is not the best way to find her. It may not be the best way to get dry either. So he slowly hobbles away from the general dealer's store through the boys and their donkeys.

Some of the aged faces here would have been familiar if he had emigrated.

How did amaMpondomise have two rival kingdoms in the first place?

He can hear Gxumisa of old telling the story; he's all but a ghostly shadow in his memory. The years have blurred his once sharp features.

The trouble started when the land of amaMpondomise was ruled by the Regent Velelo. Myeki, the rightful heir to the throne, was still young. Myeki is the one who later begot Matiwane who then begot Mhlontlo. It was during the era of Shaka kaSenzangakhona, and he was creating havoc invading and conquering nations, causing the great migrations of iMfecane. He dared attack amaMpondomise. Malangana can hear Gxumisa's voice, albeit now distorted by the distance of time, extolling the brilliance of Velelo as a general. The amaZulu regiments crossed Mzimkhulu River into the land of amaMpondomise where a battle was fought on the mountain of Nolangeni in Kokstad. On that mountain Shaka's regiments were thoroughly defeated by Velelo's regiments.

But, of course, Velelo was only a regent. Myeki came of age and took over the kingdom. He proved to be a very weak king. He couldn't withstand persistent attacks by amaZulu, though to his credit he once defeated Shaka's much-feared Dukuza Regiment. That was the only victory he ever earned. Under his command amaMpondomise lost many a battle.

amaMpondomise began to quarrel among themselves. Some wanted Velelo back because he had been such a strong leader. But others felt that Myeki was the rightful king and the laws of succession shouldn't be trampled upon for any reason. It was 1828 and in that year Shaka was assassinated by his brothers. Myeki's supporters hoped that the wars of conquest would come to an end and amaMpondomise would live in peace with their weak king. Oh no! said Velelo's supporters. Shaka was not the only threat. There were other nations that would prey on weaker nations. amaMpondomise needed to be strong against all other nations. And who said amaZulu's ambitions for a world empire would die with Shaka?

The quarrel resulted in a civil war that split amaMpondomise into two—the amaMpondomise of Myeki and those of Velelo. It was only after this split that they were defeated by amaZulu, and then later conquered by the British. Their kingdom had shrunk from all the land between the Mzimkhulu and Mthatha rivers to what we see today. Mhlontlo, the grandson of Myeki, was confined to the district of Qumbu and Mditshwa, the grandson of Velelo, to the district of Tsolo.

'That was a curious thing to say, *bawo*; you'll not die before you find Mthwakazi.'

Malangana is startled by the voice, and right behind him is a short man dressed completely in European clothes. He is not wearing a blanket or kaross over his shoulders as ordinary men do; not a string of beads either. He is obviously one of *amakhumsha*. Malangana gives way to him on the narrow footpath but he does not pass.

'It is not for us to know the hour or the day,' he says, smiling at Malangana. 'But you, sir, have decided that you will not die until your quest has been satisfied. Those *amaqaba* women have loose tongues. Perhaps you were just responding out of anger?'

Malangana is becoming irritated with this man. Quite presumptuous of him to think that he does not know what he is talking about and just babbles things out of anger. It is true, the women are loose-tongued, but *amakhumsha* can be so arrogant, calling other people *amaqaba*—those who are backward and smear themselves with red ochre. Just because they have imbibed white man's education they think they are better than their own kinsfolk.

'You would not die either if you knew Mthwakazi,' says Malangana.

He hobbles off. He must get as far away as possible from this man. *Amakhumsha* are the eyes and the ears of Government and anything that has to do with Government is his enemy, though he is no longer a fugitive.

'Wait,' says the man, laughing patronisingly. 'I did not mean to offend you. Perhaps I can help you.'

'The only help I need from anybody is to find Mthwakazi,' he says, trying hard to hasten his pace. To the able-bodied man his attempt to escape is rather pathetic.

'I don't know any Mthwakazi. I know a place where they help people like you. Where all *amaxhoba* go.' Amaxhoba are victims. Men and women crippled by war and consumption.

The man gives Malangana directions to Ibandla-likaNtu, a congregation of rebels who have broken away from Christian denominations to re-establish the broken bond with the God of their fathers. Many *amaxhoba* gather there, not necessarily for spiritual nourishment but because some believers donate food; they believe it will bring them good fortune to feed *amaxhoba*.

'If this Mthwakazi is a beggar-woman, as you say, then someone there is bound to have seen her.'

Slowly he works his way towards Ibandla-likaNtu. The place is on the outskirts of town, in a hamlet on the banks of Goqwana River.

Mthwakazi has been here. Even as he walks on the path that leads to a compound of dilapidated thatched rondavels enclosed in a fence of reeds he can feel the *umkhondo*. He stops to catch his breath. He has not felt *umkhondo* since that day he had seen amaMfengu women in his mother's field and the preacherman had abducted him to church. He thought he had lost the ability to feel Mthwakazi's aura just as he had lost the unwanted gift to neigh like a horse, which he discovered he had attained soon after losing Gcazimbane in Lesotho. It had quietly faded away.

Malangana stands at the entrance and leans against the pole because he is shaking so much. *Amaxhoba* are sitting all over the compound, on the ground and on the rocks that serve as seats. Others lie on the sleighs that have brought them here pulled by the emaciated oxen that are grazing a short distance from the compound. Some amaxhoba have no legs or arms or are blind. Others have no particular disability that he can see. They are just indigent people displaced by war. There are men and women of varying ages, but mostly old. The blind ones are accompanied by their grandsons who act as their seeing-eyes.

A man with a long white beard, a white blanket and white beads on his head, wrists and neck sits on a chair carved from a *garingboom* trunk. He is addressing *amaxhoba*, most of whom are not paying much attention. Their focus is on the bread and milk and sundry victuals they are gormandising.

'We are now a confused people for we don't know which God to follow,' says the bearded man. 'Perhaps that is why we are like this, we the children of abaMbo. We, the amaMpondomise people have our God, uQamata, who is also the God of other nations such as amaMpondo, amaXhosa and abaThembu. The Khoikhoi people, I am talking of amaQheya as we call them here, have their own God too. His name is Tsixqua. He has a son called Heitsi Eibib, who died for the Khoikhoi people. The God of amaZulu is uMvelingqangi. You will remember that it is the praise-name of our God as well, for his origins are a mystery. The God of Basotho is Tladi, the one who speaks in the voices of thunder. The God of abaThwa is Kaang, he who married the sorceress Coti who blessed him with the two sons, Cogaz and

Gewi. Each nation pleases its own God according to its own traditions. Ours is angry with us because we have deserted him. That's why we are here as *amaxhoba*. That's why we are like this.'

'It is the same God,' says a man who is likely to be an *igqobhoka*, a Christian convert, or a former convert since IbandlalikaNtu is reputed to be populated by those who became disillusioned with the religious denominations of the white man. 'Various nations use different names to call him. But it is the same God, the one who created all humanity, and all heaven and all earth.'

'*Hayikhona,*' objects a sceptic. 'How come the God of one nation enjoys carnal pleasures when the God of the other nation doesn't? In one nation their God has children, in another their God doesn't have any. And yet you say it is the same person? The God of the Khoikhoi has one son; the God of the abaThwa has two sons. The God of the white man, who is called uYehova, has one son called uYesu, yet ours have no children at all. It is just him and the hierarchies of the ancestors who surround him.'

Like most of the *amaxhoba* Malangana is not paying much attention to the theological debates. His concentration, however, is not on the food. His eyes are scrutinising every woman in the crowd, paying particular attention to those of small stature. What if one of them is Mthwakazi? How is he going to know her after twenty years? He knows that he has changed quite a bit, but he doubts if Mthwakazi could have undergone that drastic a transformation. In any event her *mkhondo* is very much alive in these environs. It is bound to be even stronger in her presence.

As soon as the bearded man gets tired of the pointless debate and silences it with a dismissive wave of the hand a group of women pounce on Malangana.

'Come here, I have food for you,' says one.

'Oh no, I saw him first, follow me. I have very nice food for you,' says another.

He is helpless as one takes his crutches and tries to pull him one way while the other is pulling him another way. He is shaken out of his wits.

'They feed *amaxhoba* for good fortune,' explains an old woman helpfully. 'You are new here so they are all fighting for your blessings.'

'I'm not here for food,' says a breathless Malangana. 'I'm looking for Mthwakazi.'

'Look, you are scaring the poor man to death. You're going to be responsible if he has a heart attack.' That's the man with the white beard to the rescue.

They all let Malangana go at once and he falls on the ground. They apologise and try to help him up and give him back his crutches. The man with the white beard helps him to a rock where Malangana sits down. He points at one of the women who were fighting over Malangana and says, 'You, feed him.' Others mumble their disgruntlement: *Yhu! Uyakhetha. Uyamkhetha ngoba ngumolokazana wakho. Oh, you're not fair. You choose her because she is your daughter-in-law.*

As Malangana drinks amasi with sorghum bread he answers their questions about the woman he is looking for. He does not know her name. Only that she is Mthwakazi. He does not want to give them the whole history of who they once were at the Great Place of King Mhlontlo. After all, this was King Mditshwa's territory. He does not know where these people stand on old disputes. Nor does he even know if they are all amaMpondomise. The land has been overrun by all sorts of people, many of whom are here as a reward for fighting on the side of the English.

abaThwa people keep to themselves out there in the wilderness and do not mix with other people, says one man as if explaining to a child or a stranger. Except once in a while there are those who come peddling ostrich eggs or crude handiwork to ward off famine. It would be impossible for the community of Tsolo to know the whereabouts of one nameless Bushwoman. The man then breaks out laughing at the ridiculousness of it all.

'Except one,' says a woman. 'There's one who doesn't live in the wilderness; we often see her here.'

'Yes, there was a Mthwakazi here yesterday,' adds another woman. 'The one who wears golden earrings.'

The other women chuckle. They know exactly who she is talking about. There must be something funny they remember about her.

'She must be the one,' says Malangana hardly hiding his excitement. He has heard this thing about golden earrings once or twice before since he started his search.

'Oh, the one who never shuts her mouth?' says another woman. '*Akapheli apha* with her funny stories.' *She comes here quite often.*

'She left yesterday afternoon. We haven't seen her today.'

FRIDAY OCTOBER 22, 1880

Three men were sitting on the adobe stoep outside Mahlangeni's Great House enjoying gourds of sorghum beer. The host's face was beaming with pride for he was the new father of a baby boy. His two guests were Malangana and Nzuze. This was not a formal ceremony. He had invited them so early in the morning to share with them his excitement. At dawn his baby was visited by *inkwakhwa*, the brown mole snake.

The baby was very new, so new that his *inkaba*, umbilical cord, had only recently dried and fallen, and the ritual of burying it, connecting him with the land and the ancestors, was done the day before. The most important ceremony, the *imbeleko*, had not yet been performed to introduce the baby to the community, inducting him into the clan's membership by slaughtering a goat and making him wear a part of its skin on his wrists and neck. It was therefore unusual that the snake had already visited him even before he was made a fully fledged clansman. It meant that there was something very special about this child, hence Mahlangeni's beaming face.

The tradition of the snake had started with Qengebe

almost two hundred years before. After his father, Mhle, died and was buried at Lothana in the Qumbu area, he moved the Great Place of the amaMpondomise Kingdom to Mzimvubu, the area that is known as Kokstad today, and there he married a woman from one of the clans. She became pregnant. Nine months later the midwives gathered at the Great House when the queen began to feel the pains of birth. As they were assisting the process of parturition the midwives screamed and ran away. A brown mole snake was slithering out of the queen's passage of life. The queen had given birth to *inkwakhwa*. The shamans, diviners and healers declared that it was sacred and could not be killed. A few minutes later the queen gave birth to a baby boy. He was named Majola, the name he shared with the snake. The snake regularly visited the boy. When the baby prince was sick the snake came and coiled itself next to him; the next day the baby would be up and about, laughing, playing and crying for food.

Majola grew up to be a wise king of the amaMpondomise people. When he died he was buried in a lake in Mzimvubu and was succeeded by his son, Ngwanya, who was followed by Phahlo, and then by Mamani, about whom we have already spoken, the woman who married another woman. Mamani, as we have said, was succeeded by Ngcambe, and then by Myeki, and by Matiwane, and finally by the present king, Mhlontlo—not counting any of the regents between some of the royal heirs. And since King Majola, all these descendants and their relatives were often visited by Majola the snake. When that happened, it augured well. The Majola snake did not only visit babies. It might visit the king, for instance when he was facing some dire problems. Such a visit meant that there would be a positive outcome.

'You know, of course, that the good fortune brought by Majola this morning does not only belong to the baby alone,' said Nzuze.

'It had better not,' said Mahlangeni, with a broad smile.

He scooped more beer from the clay pot with a gourd and handed it to Nzuze who gulped it greedily.

'He shares it with the whole household,' added Malangana.

'The little imp cannot hoard it all to himself,' said Mahlangeni. 'It's mine too. Things will turn out well.'

Mahlangeni handed another foaming gourd to Malangana.

'We are going to war in a faraway country against the fierce Basotho and you promise us things will turn out well?'

'We are going to war only if Gxumisa leads the army,' said Nzuze. 'Magistrate Hope is stubborn. There is a stand-off, but we're not giving in on that.'

'We are going to war, but it might not be the war you think,' said Mahlangeni breaking into a wicked laugh.

Despite all the talk about war, things were looking good. Even the earth bore witness to that. Verdure was returning to the veld, to the shrubs, bushes and trees. The eyes of men no longer wept involuntarily at the sore sight of parched grass and wilted leaves in the middle of what passed for spring. For the past two days it had rained after months of drought. And the three men couldn't help but occasionally sniff into their nostrils the thrilling smell of wet soil.

The men did not believe that anything could spoil their high spirits until a messenger came from the Great Place.

Gxumisa was giving them two options: either they convince their mate Malangana to return forthwith Mthwakazi's drum which she alleged he had stolen, or if Malangana denied the theft they should all repair to the *inkundla* so that the said Malangana could answer before his peers to charges of theft laid by the aforementioned Mthwakazi.

Malangana broke out laughing.

'This is no laughing matter,' said Mahlangeni. A cloud had descended on his brow.

'I'm laughing because I didn't steal anyone's drum,' said Malangana.

'We are in the middle of a stand-off with Hamilton Hope and here you are playing games with a Bushman girl,' said Nzuze.

The messenger's eyes darted from one man to the next expectantly.

'These are the problems of socialising with a bachelor,' said Mahlangeni.

'He is playing with our time,' said Nzuze. 'Today of all days.'

'Why are you angry with me? What wrong have I done?'

The messenger said, 'So what should I tell *uTat'u*Gxumisa? He says if *uMkhuluwa uM*alangana denies any knowledge of the drum...'

'I am not denying knowledge of the drum,' said Malangana. 'I'm denying knowledge of the theft.'

In which case, the messenger explained, the men should all assemble at *inkundla* for a trial. The matter had to be disposed of immediately because the king was expecting *iindwendwe*—guests—in the afternoon. The Bushman

girl was insisting that her sacred drum had been stolen by
Malangana. She was also insisting that King Mhlontlo was
her witness because he was present when her drum was
stolen. At this Mahlangeni and Nzuze glared at Malangana,
one with widening eyes, the other only baring his teeth,
while Malangana giggled as if he was enjoying the whole
thing. The girl was obviously dragging the name of the king
into this matter in order to shame the elders into immediate
action. That was why Gxumisa wanted Malangana to deal
with it straight away, either to give back the sacred drum if
it was true it was in his possession, or to face an immediate
trial at the *inkundla*. The nation had more important things
to deal with today.

'Tell Uncle Gxumisa that there is no need for a trial,'
said Malangana. 'I have the drum in my possession. I did
not steal it, though. I was with the king when I picked it up
at *ebaleni* of his Great House where the girl had abandoned
it. I will give it back to her today before those visitors get
here. I must not be rushed though. I'm still rejoicing with
my older brother here whose family has been visited by the
snake. Uncle Gxumisa must not panic. The world shall not
be made to stand still by the tantrums of a Bushman girl.'

The three men sat quietly for some time watching the
messenger's galloping horse disappear in the distance.

'The impudence of it all,' said Mahlangeni, shaking his
head.

'They treat her as something special because she was the
queen's nursemaid. I guess they think she has strong medicine,' said Nzuze.

'If her medicine was strong the queen would be alive,'

said Mahlangeni.

'*Sukani apha*, elder brothers, you can't put that one on her head,' said Malangana. 'She was not even the main doctor of the queen. She was merely an assistant.'

'She is impudent still,' said Nzuze, shaking his head, his jaws clenched.

Perhaps it was because she was an *inzalwamhlaba*—an autochthon; a person not born of humans but emerged from the earth like a sorghum seedling. That was why she had scant respect for the authority of men. She did not know any differently. While the men—the two men, that is, for Malangana did not seem to be bothered by the bad behaviour of the Bushman girl—were muttering and moaning their outrage, Tsitwa came limping and muttering to himself. He was swishing his *itshoba*—the medicine man's staff with tassels of an oxtail.

'Why are you people still here?' he asked, staring at his son Mahlangeni.

'We thought we should start the day by celebrating the snake, father.'

'Majola is not your business,' said Tsitwa. 'He visited my grandson, not you.'

Malangana and Nzuze sniggered.

'You just want to steal my grandson's glory for yourself,' added Tsitwa for good measure, relishing the effect of his humour. 'You and I should be mixing and boiling the medicines for strengthening the soldiers. By the time iindwendwe arrive this evening our medicines should be ready for the rituals of the umguyo dances. Tomorrow we are marching to war.'

The three men looked at Tsitwa with wide eyes. They had not associated the iindwendwe with Hamilton Hope and his war machine.

'Yes, we have no choice but to give in. The stand-off is over,' said Tsitwa.

Nzuze was crushed. He stayed on the adobe stoep, his head buried in his hands. Malangana and Mahlangeni paced the ground, beads of sweat erupting on the former's brow. Both were mumbling their disgust at Mhlontlo who could not stand up to Hope and was apparently now going to lead the men to war. They had been sitting there blissfully celebrating the snake, only to discover that behind the scenes the elders were conspiring to betray the nation of amaMpondomise by allowing the king to go to war while he was in mourning.

Like all the peoples of the eastern region, amaMpondomise were known for their hospitality. But these particular iindwendwe were not the most welcome guests in the history of kwaMpondomise. Everyone had been dreading their arrival from the time spies reported that they had left Qumbu with a caravan made up of one wagon loaded with five hundred Martini-Henry rifles for the thousand men that Mhlontlo had promised Hamilton Hope, a Scotch cart loaded with ammunition comprising eighteen thousand ball cartridges, two other wagons loaded with mealies and potatoes, another Scotch cart loaded with the things of the white people, and a slew of black servants—mostly amaMpondomise and amaMpondo converts and a few amaQheya or Khoikhoi. The caravan was led by the four white men on their horses, Hope, Warren, Henman and Davis.

Qumbu was only eighteen miles from Sulenkama so they had arrived the same afternoon, and had set up camp on a hill about a mile from the village. Even before they could send a messenger to Mhlontlo's Great Place the king sent his own messenger to them, a man called Faya. The king was reiterating what he had said before; he would not lead the army to war. His army was waiting for the orders, all ready to go, and his uncle Gxumisa was ready to lead them anytime he was called upon to do so. He, Mhlontlo, King of amaMpondomise, was in mourning because his senior wife, daughter of the most revered monarch in the region, King Sarhili of amaGcaleka, also known as amaXhosa, had passed away, and according to the customs of his people he had to stay in seclusion and observe certain rituals. He could not touch weapons of war during mourning.

Of course Hamilton Hope had heard all this nonsense before. He sent Faya back to his master with a stern message: the British Empire could not be kept waiting on account of heathen customs. The war would be fought and the Pondomise warriors would be led by none other than Umhlonhlo. He, Hamilton Hope, Resident Magistrate of the District of Qumbu in the Cape Colony Government of Her Glorious Majesty Queen Victoria, was summoning the Pondomise paramount chief Umhlonhlo to come and meet him in person forthwith and take orders to march to war against the rebel Basotho chief Magwayi, failing which he would be stripped of all vestiges of chieftainship and his Pondomise tribe would be placed under chiefs of those tribes that were willing to cooperate with Her Majesty's Government.

As Faya galloped away with the dire message, Hope fired a few shots after him to illustrate that he was serious, to the laughter of his entourage. Faya hollered all the way to the Great Place that someone should save him; the men whose ears reflected the rays of the sun—*ooNdlebezikhanyilanga*—were trying to kill him.

For two days Mhlontlo kept Hamilton Hope waiting. That was the stand-off that had excited the young men. At last the elders were fighting back. Finally the king was refusing to be treated like an uncircumcised boy by a couple of white people whose own penises were undoubtedly still enveloped in foreskins. In the evening they cast their eyes on the hill and saw the fires at Hamilton Hope's camp and went on with their lives as if all was normal and the world was at peace with itself.

Of course Hope was not amused. On the second evening he sat at the camp fire with his three aides, Warren, Henman and Davis, eating bully and bread and playing cards.

'You still doubt my premonition?'

The aides merely shook their heads and continued to chew and take sips of tea from enamel mugs. Their black servants could be heard in the background singing and ribbing one another to great laughter.

Before they left Qumbu the magistrate had said to them, 'Look, fellows, I'll give you your choice. I have heard certain things which make me suspect that Umhlonhlo intends turning traitor. I am too much involved, besides I am an Englishman and can't turn back. You fellows may turn back if you choose and I will think none the worse of you.' The three men had insisted that they were Englishmen too and would not turn back.

'I will not allow Umhlonhlo to defy me,' said Hope. 'That would be the end of me. I am known by my peers and by the Chief Magistrate of East Griqualand, and you can be sure even by the Governor, for my discernment and knowledge of the native character. What will happen to that reputation if Umhlonhlo defies me and gets away with it?'

'He will get away with it unless we send a CMR column to crush him once and for all, which is what we should have done to the Basotho rebels in the first place,' said Warren.

'We are not at war with Mhlontlo,' said Davis. 'He is our ally. He is willing to supply us with a thousand men to fight. He is just not willing to lead them.'

'The two of you are two extremes that I must bring to the sensible centre,' said Hope. 'Firstly, the Cape Mounted Riflemen are spread thinly already, what with the Gun War in Basutoland. With the change of Government in England and our Governor recalled, the new Government has a strict policy that no new Imperial troops will be allowed to take part. We are on our own. We have no choice but to get the natives to fight for us, which is the normal practice as you know since they are now subjects of the Crown.'

'What we want is to crush the rebellion of Magwayi's Basotho in Matatiele,' said Davis. 'We have Mhlontlo's men. We have everything we need. His uncle Gxumisa will lead his men. I suggest we go to war.'

'Then he will have prevailed on me,' said Hope. 'No native will ever obey me after that.'

'Anyway, this Gxumisa is an old man,' said Henman. 'How's he going to survive a war with a ferocious tribe like Basotho?'

'Mhlontlo is an old man himself. He is fifty-three.'

Hope looked at Davis for a long time.

'Are you this man's advocate, Captain?'

'No, sir, I am advising you, as is my role.'

'Thank you, but I am not taking your advice on this one. I want you to get on your horse right now and go down that hill and tell Umhlonhlo that tomorrow afternoon I am moving my camp to just outside his Great Place. He should have his warriors ready. I will be addressing them. The next morning he will be leading them to war. If the chief won't ascend the hill the magistrate will descend, and you can be sure it is the last time the magistrate does that.'

That was the end of the stand-off and the beginning of the preparations for *iindwendwe* in Sulenkama, though they were of the unwelcome variety. Mahlangeni, despite himself, followed Tsitwa to grind and boil the concoctions that were going to strengthen the soldiers and Malangana dawdled to his house to get Mthwakazi's sacred drum. Nzuze left the adobe stoep and went to join his brother at the Great Place to find out what exactly was happening. The joys of the snake's visit were all forgotten as the matters of statecraft became the focus.

Malangana sat on a stool and stared at the drum. He did not know where to find Mthwakazi in order to return it. He certainly would not make himself a laughing stock carrying it all over the village and asking people where he could find her. By now he was sure gossipmongers knew that he had been sued for theft and would be making silly jokes about him. What was Mthwakazi thinking, accusing him of theft, besmirching his name like that? The right thing of course would be to take it to Gxumisa since he was the elder who had summoned the *inkundla* for the case. He would know how to get it to the silly girl. That's what he should do and get it over with. He would have liked to hand it to the girl personally though and give her a piece of his mind too.

A horse whinnied outside. Malangana went to the door and looked at Gcazimbane swooshing his tail impatiently. This was a new habit, this of trotting in from the veld and routing his groom out of his quarters when days had gone by without seeing him. Not that Malangana's attachment to him had diminished. These days his time was occupied mostly by the affairs of the Great Place. The nation was still in bereavement and Mhlontlo spent all his days in seclusion mourning his beloved queen. Malangana was therefore the one who was always around for errands. He was the trusted messenger who was sent, sometimes with Charles or with Nzuze or with any other of Mhlontlo's kin, to other chiefs in the region or to the white traders or missionaries about matters, often disputes, that had to be postponed until the period of mourning was over. Gcazimbane would be taken by the herdboys in the morning to graze with the cattle in the valleys. It was from there that he would sometimes escape to look for Malangana at his house. He would whinny outside. On most occasions Malangana would not be there and the horse would finally wander away and in the evening the herdboys would be

whipped by the men in charge of the royal herds for their care-
lessness. Malangana would only hear from neighbours that his
horse, as it was now called, was looking for him. During those
days of grieving Malangana would get to see Gcazimbane
only in the evening. He would walk to the cattle kraal where
Gcazimbane slept with the cattle, let him out, and brush his
neck and his mane, while singing the horse's praises, or
sometimes his own. Occasionally he threw glances at familiar
pathways hoping to see the puny figure of Mthwakazi. On
some errands Malangana would beg Mhlontlo to let him
ride Gcazimbane: 'You've not been riding him since you've
been mourning. He'll get lazy.' Mhlontlo would reluctantly
agree: 'But don't get used to it. Gcazimbane is my horse, not
yours.'

For most errands Mhlontlo insisted that Malangana use
one of the Basotho ponies that were a gift from his late friend
King Moorosi of the Baphuthi people. So, Gcazimbane went
grazing with the cattle and played his tricks on the herdboys and occasionally disappeared to look for his groom and
friend.

Today, unlike most other days, he found him.
Gcazimbane held his tail high and snickered and blew.
Malangana broke out laughing. The horse started prancing
around with excitement and Malangana clapped his hands,
singing its praises. A few of the neighbours who were outside
sweeping the grounds or tending to *umhlonyane* herbs in front
of the rondavels started ululating and waving the brooms and
clapping their hands and dancing around and singing along
in the chorus: '*Nanko ke, nankok'uGcazimbane; ngobuhle
bakhe bonke, nankok'uGcazimbane.*' There he is, there he is,

123

Gcazimbane in all his beauty.

Malangana ran into the house and raced out with Mthwakazi's drum. He continued to sing Gcazimbane's praises accompanied by the drum and the women's ululation. Gcazimbane neighed and stood on his hindlegs, and circled around his worshippers in a canter. Malangana jumped on him and settled bareback as the horse continued with the dance unabated. He prodded Gcazimbane with his feet and the horse took off at full gallop. Malangana controlled him only with his heels and knees as there were no reins and his hands were fully occupied with beating the drum while singing not only the horse's praises but his own as well. The neighbours were left laughing and applauding in admiration of the king's wily horse and its devoted groom.

It was as though a whirlwind was carrying them through the village pathways. And Gcazimbane was ignoring all the protocol of slowing down whenever they passed one or more adults so that Malangana could greet them and enquire after their health, and maybe exchange a few titbits of what the return of the rains after such a long and vicious drought meant to the crops in the fields and to the welfare of the nation. Some looked at the dustless whirlwind and merely shook their heads as they rearranged their izikhakha skirts and karosses disturbed by its force. Others muttered something about the recklessness of youth; it was high time Malangana got married so that his blood could be calmed by a good woman.

'Even the school of the mountain and the prison of the white man could not tame his wildness,' observed an elderly man to his elderly wife. 'That is why he is now even stealing sacred drums from *inzalwamhlaba*, those whose womb-home was the earth.'

As he said this he spat on the very ground from which the autochthon was supposed to have emerged.

These words did not bother Malangana because he heard none of them. His whirlwind raised its invisible dust-storm until it slowed down at Mhlontlo's Great Place. This was Gcazimbane's home turf, yet today there were strange sights and sounds in the place where he was often harnessed under the umsintsi trees waiting to take the king on his trips. Malangana willed him to a halt as he marvelled at the changed scene before him. Under the coast coral trees were three wagons and two Scotch carts forming a half-moon—not quite the laager of the Trek-Boers—and two tents pitched at one end. Hamilton Hope had come down from the hill and had made himself comfortable a few yards from the entrance to the Great Place. A number of villagers had gathered and were already feasting their eyes on the *iindwendwe*. The eager but shy spectators were all standing at a distance, fearful of attracting the wrath of the white man and his cohorts. It became obvious to Malangana that the crowds he denied due protocol on the pathway—not a result of any bad upbringing, but because when Gcazimbane was possessed of the rapscallion spirit he tended to trample etiquette under his hoofs—were on their way to the Great Place to see with their own eyes these men whose ears reflected the rays of the sun and to hear for themselves about this war with the Basotho into which all the menfolk of arms-bearing age were being conscripted.

Outside one of the tents Malangana could see Nzuze

talking animatedly with two white men, perhaps Davis and Henman, although he couldn't be sure about that. He prodded the horse to flee lest he be roped into the meeting or be given some chores before he disposed of the silly matter of the sacred drum.

Malangana and Gcazimbane stole away in the direction of Gxumisa's homestead.

Nzuze trudged into the Great Place as if his feet were weighed down with granite rocks. He was becoming increasingly exercised as this was his third trip between Mhlontlo's quarters and Hamilton Hope's tent, and the magistrate was immovable. So was Mhlontlo. The king was insisting he shouldn't be appearing in public because he was in mourning, and now Hope had sent Nzuze with a final warning: if Umhlonhlo did not come out, Hope would march in with his officers and rout him out. Nzuze had warned the magistrate that if he did that he would be creating bad blood between the Government and amaMpondomise people. Hope said his patience had run out and therefore bad blood was the least of his worries.

'Basotho chiefs out there are shedding real rather than figurative blood,' he had said blowing smoke into Nzuze's face. 'I'm talking of Lehana of Batlokwa and Lebenya of Bakwena.'

Nzuze stared at him blankly. Hope had explained to him slowly, as if to a child, for he wanted him to make the urgency of this matter clear to Mhlontlo that those two Basotho chiefs had joined Magwayi's rebellion and were causing problems for Government forces.

'"Problems" is an understatement,' Hope had added and Davis had translated as he had been doing throughout Hope's tirade. 'They have unleashed untold savagery, killing white people and our allies, the Fingoes, in Mooiterie's Kop in Matatiele. They are killing traders and looting their stores. And I am sitting here begging a native chief to be man enough to come out of his bedroom.'

There was a buzz among the crowd that had gathered. The king would be coming out. A number of armed men formed into a guard of honour and soon Mhlontlo, Nzuze, the doctor Tsitwa and three other elders walked out of the Great Place led by the royal *imbongi*, the bard, reciting the king's panegyrics, focusing on his genealogy and the heroic deeds of his ancestors, and how their greatness was flowing in his blood, and reminding the audience that this was the king who, when still a young *umkhwetha* initiate, led amaMpondomise forces against ferocious amaBhaca, who had invaded the land, and swiftly routed them.

Hamilton Hope, Warren, Henman and Davis stood next to the wagon loaded with arms to meet him.

'You see,' said Hope as he extended his hand to greet him, 'these are the guns you asked for.'

Mhlontlo did not return the gesture but glared at him.

'*Ndi-zi-li-le*,' said Mhlontlo, emphasising each syllable. *I am in mourning.*

Davis did not interpret it that way though. He gave it a very polite spin that came out as *the chief begs to be allowed to mourn.* Hope was no fool; he saw the man's expression and responded with similar belligerence.

'The British Empire will not grind to a halt because of

one man's mourning. Surely you understand that?'

Mhlontlo listened to Davis' translation. Instead of responding to Hope's question he broke into a smile and asked him about his family. How was his brother the missionary doing? Both the Davis sons had taken after their father and had turned out to be fine upstanding men.

'Tell your brother next time you meet him that my son Charles has told me he is well looked after at the mission school,' said Mhlontlo. 'I am ever grateful for that.'

Davis did not want to leave Hope out of the conversation; he explained what the 'chief' was saying. This broke the tension as all the white men joined to praise the great work that the mission station at Shawbury was doing to educate young Christian converts into teachers and nurse aids and domestic science practitioners and carpenters who would build a strong, healthy God-fearing native nation.

Hope suggested that they should sit down under the wagon and share a meal and a few drinks while they thrashed out their differences. They had to leave early the next morning for Matatiele. There was no time to waste.

'Where is Malangana?' asked Mhlontlo as he took his place under the wagon. Davis was a good man, but he needed his own man to interpret into his ear as well. *Bangamhlebi kaloku.*

'I was with him this morning,' said Nzuze. He then turned to the crowd and yelled, 'Has anyone of you seen Malangana?'

The crowd yelled back with various answers: He was spotted galloping around irresponsibly on Gcazimbane. He was last seen singing and dancing with the king's horse to the singing and clapping of idle women. Some pointed him in the direction of old Gxumisa's compound where the wind blew him like the leaves of a tree in autumn, holding high as if in triumph a stolen sacred drum with a horse snorting at his heels.

The message was relayed to Mhlontlo with relish and further ornamentation. He could only shake his head and say, 'Send someone to search for him. He seems to think that my horse is his plaything.'

'That is always the problem when you have to depend on a bachelor for serious matters of state,' muttered Nzuze. He was quite fed up with his brother from the junior-most Iqadi House.

'It is true,' said Mhlontlo. 'A man does need at least one woman in the house to wean him of immaturity.'

The men were seated on rocks and stools and all seemed to be relaxed. The spectators were at ease. But Hope stood up again and invited Mhlontlo and his entourage to follow him to the wagons. The other white men followed as well. Hope took pride in showing Mhlontlo the guns. Henman and Warren were quite eager to demonstrate with some of them, aiming at the spectators to their screeching discomfort and urging Mhlontlo to touch them and aim as well. But the king shook his head; he would not touch arms of war at that time.

And then they uncovered the ammunition.

'You see,' said Hope smiling at Mhlontlo as he led everybody back to their seats, 'I kept my side of the bargain. You must keep yours.'

Mhlontlo sent out for Gxumisa and the rest of the

elders of amaMpondomise, the commanders of the various *amabutho* regiments and the herdboys who had to round up fourteen cattle to be slaughtered for feasting. Women who had any beer in their homestead were asked to donate some in the *ukuphekisa* tradition. There was no time or inclination to brew any beer at the Great Place since it was a homestead of mourning.

That evening Hope and Mhlontlo sat under the wagon and broke bread together, though Mhlontlo refused to partake of the white man's *umkhupha*, not because he was snubbing it, but for the reason that he knew it was most likely salted. As a royal man in mourning he had to avoid salt. Even the meat that he ate was specially roasted for him by his own men on an open fire. They made certain that it was not seasoned with salt or with anything else as there was no guarantee that the seasoning would have no traces of salt. Hope and his men watched all this with interest.

'You are quite serious about this mourning business,' observed Henman.

'We said no one is going to mention that word again,' Hope admonished. 'From now on it is business as usual. We are talking of nothing but our war plans.'

Davis did not translate any of this and everyone continued to chew in silence for a while. Mhlontlo shifted on his seat uncomfortably. He did not want anything that was said in his presence to pass him by. He turned to Gxumisa, who had now joined his king, and asked him what had happened to Malangana because he was reported to be the last person to see him that evening.

'I settled his case with Mthwakazi. It was just a

misunderstanding really,' said Gxumisa. 'He brought back the sacred drum. Apparently the young woman was so over-whelmed by the death of our queen she forgot her drum at *ebaleni* of your Great House. He was on his way from grooming Gcazimbane when he picked it up.'

'I am not interested in a silly case, Uncle Gxumisa,' said Mhlontlo. 'Where is Malangana now?'

'I don't know. I left him talking with the girl at ebaleni of my homestead.'

Nzuze decided to send not just an ordinary messenger but a group of elders from the House of Matiwane to search for Malangana so that when found he would understand the seriousness and urgency of the king's summons.

There was a festive atmosphere that evening and men were singing and dancing. Hope's servants kept themselves entertained on their own close to the wagons. A number of fires were burning, with men roasting meat. When a few men arrived with a message that King Mditshwa of the amaMpondomise of Tsolo would give his word the next day about supplying more men, Hope was satisfied that his plan was coming together well. The next day the march northwards would undoubtedly begin.

Mhlontlo would be supplying the bulk of the army, Hope said.

'It looks as if this is my war now,' Mhlontlo said to Davis.

'That's what it means to be the paramount chief,' said Davis, without taking the question to Hope first. 'It comes with responsibilities.'

As they enjoyed the victuals and the brandy Hope outlined the strategy that would outwit the Basotho. Both

Davis and Warren were military men, Captains in the newly established Cape Mounted Riflemen, formerly officers of the Frontier Armed and Mounted Police. Hamilton Hope would lead the force with their assistance. Henman would continue his usual role as his clerk. Mhlontlo would lead his Pondomise warriors, and by implication all native warriors who would be under their own chiefs would be answerable to him as the paramount chief. This force led by Hope would approach from the southern side of the region. A force of European volunteers led by Thompson, the magistrate of Maclear, would approach from the direction of Maclear and meet Hope and his regiments at Chevy Chase.

From there the forces would proceed to Matatiele to slaughter Magwayi's rebels.

Mhlontlo listened to all these plans in silence. His opinion was not sought. It was a done deal. He was to lead the amaMpondomise regiments. The white men raised their mugs and cheered Hope for a great plan and wished him Godspeed.

'I'm only a Government servant and must do the work of the Government,' said Hope, nevertheless acknowledging the praise.

Mhlontlo laughed mockingly and, pointing at Hope, said to his people, 'There is your God. I am only a dog.'

Hope, Mhlontlo and their respective entourages spent the night sleeping under the Scotch cart full of ammunition and in tents in wonderful camaraderie.

SATURDAY DECEMBER 19, 1903

It is a nightmare that he thought would never return. It used to haunt his nights quite often during his Lesotho exile. He even went to *lingaka* traditional healers to exorcise himself of it. It was quite stubborn. It would leave him for a number of nights and when it thought he had forgotten it would attack him again. But as he made his way back to the land of his fathers, gradually it faded away from his nights, until the nights were so peaceful that the only thing that woke him up was the bladder that needed occasional emptying.

Now it is back.

It takes him by surprise as he sleeps rolled into a bony bundle under an old donkey blanket on an adobe stoep at the Ibandla-likaNtu compound. First he hears the sound of the water. He is not sure if he is awake or asleep; he hopes it is not rain. Summer rains have a tendency of falling without any provocation. As they did three days ago, forcing him to seek protection under a tree among the Tsolo crowds who were so vulgar their children didn't know the distinction between Thunderman and a lovelorn mortal caught in a cloudburst.

Soon it becomes clear that it is not rain. It is a river. *The* river.

Each river has its own sound determined not only by the amount of water running in it but by the grains of sand and the shape and size of pebbles and rocks on its bed. This is the river of his boyhood, the Sulenkama River. Not the western or the eastern branches, but the southern branch, on the exact spot Sulenkama River meets Gqukunqa River on the particular night he sat under a bush with Mthwakazi with their feet in the water and watching the stars after doing the unspeakable.

He is sitting under the same bush, his feet splashing impatiently in the water. Further into the water, a figure completely covered in green algae is swimming. He cannot see the face but he reckons it is Mthwakazi. He must have been sitting here waiting for her for ages. He looks at his fingers and his knees and legs. They have become bony. He looks at himself in the sluggishly flowing water. The skin barely sticks to his smiling skull. An occasional dead fish floats by. More dead fish fly into the sky and splash back into the river as the swimmer attacks the water with a flurry of backstrokes. But they are short-lived. Soon everything is languid again. A lone fly whines its way around his head and he swats it away with both hands.

He looks towards the northeast; there are the mountains. The mountains of his youth. Now that he has been to Lesotho and has seen real mountains these are only hills. They still touch the sky, though they look malnourished and skeletal.

'Come on, Mthwakazi, let's go,' he says.

His voice is echoed by the hills. He wonders how they

can do that when they are nothing but bare bones of hills.

'I'm not done yet,' the swimmer responds. Her voice is tinny and hollow and sounds as if it comes from a long way off.

The rays of the sun as it moves towards the top of the hills reflect prismatic tints on the river, and on the surrounding bushes and cliffs.

'Please, Mthwakazi, let's go.'

The river laughs. It has never laughed before. Malangana raises his head and rubs his eyes with the back of his hands.

The laughter is not from the river. It is from the aged man with the white beard and the white blanket who was pronouncing on the Gods of nations on Wednesday. He has walked out of his rondavel to meditate to the colours of dawn and has perched himself next to the bundle that is Malangana.

'You found her in your dreams, then, did you? In the flesh she's not been seen here yet. It is as though she smells you and stays away, for she was a daily occurrence here for many days before you came.'

Malangana unbundles himself. After staring at the sky and at the aged one, and after taking in his surroundings, he reassures himself that he is not at the confluence of the Sulenkama and Gqukunqa rivers but at the compound of Ibandla-likaNtu. He is a bit embarrassed that the aged one was present during his nightmare. How much he heard of it he does not know. What if he is one of those who can spy into people's dreams? He just might as well open up to him.

'I was young when this recurring nightmare started years ago,' says Malangana. 'Always me sitting on the bank waiting for her to finish swimming.'

In the early years everything was beautiful. There were flowers and the water was fresh. There were birds. There were fireflies and butterflies. Both the swimmer and the waiter were young and fresh. The nightmare became a mirror to the metamorphosis of ageing on his body, and he hated it every night it decided to haunt him.

'Why do you call it a nightmare when it is such a beautiful dream?' the aged one wants to know.

'Any dream you hate to dream, however beautiful it may be to someone else, is a nightmare to you.'

'You are right but for different reasons,' says the aged one. 'There is nothing like a beautiful dream. All dreams carry anxieties with them. It may begin as beautiful, but somewhere it will carry some fear. *Amaphupha kukunya nje qha.*' *Dreams are shit.*

They sit silently and watch the skies unfold. Outlines of mountains and trees begin to distinguish themselves on the horizon above the low wall of the compound. The aged one is lost in the theological musings of the day. Malangana is digesting the morning's interruption of his nightmare.

'Did you mean it?' he asks.

There is no response from the aged one. He is startled when Malangana shakes his arms.

'*Yintoni ke ngoku mfo kaMajola? What is the matter, son of the Majola clan?* 'When I said *amaphupha kukunya nje qha?*'

'Not about dreams. When you said maybe Mthwakazi can smell my presence and she is staying away?'

'Did I say that?'

136

'You know you said it. Did you mean it?'

'I was just talking nonsense. People come and go. They are here today, gone tomorrow. We never know when they will be here again, if ever.'

'But how did a thought like that come into your head? They say you are a prophet. Could it perhaps be that the ancestors want you to tell me that?'

The aged one stands up and paces the ground in front of Malangana.

'Listen, if you want to give up your search, don't use me as an excuse,' he says. 'I said one stupid thing when I thought you were asleep and you want to use that as a crutch, ascribe it to the ancestors? You're welcome to that if deep down in your heart you feel your search is futile. But don't blame me. Don't you know that old men like me are apt to say stupid things? That's what we do. We are old.'

'I'm old too, but I don't say stupid things,' Malangana says.

'Well, people age differently. You want to take me to *inkundla* for that?'

The aged one walks away. Malangana shakes his head and laughs. He marvels at himself that, yes indeed, laughter has returned in him, however weak. He might be on the road to wholeness.

'I don't have time to waste suing you,' says Malangana.

The aged one stops and says, wagging his finger at him, 'If I were you I'd go to the source.'

'What source?'

'To stop the nightmares once and for all. I'd go to the river where they are happening. Face the real river and tell it to leave you alone. See how different and how fresh it continues to flow in its real self. It should stop lying to you who are atrophied and decayed.'

Malangana just stares at him as he disappears into one of the rondavels. He will do no such thing. His time is precious. He will spend every minute of it looking for Mthwakazi instead of wandering in the wilderness communing with a lifeless river. The aged one was correct in one thing; foolishness comes with old age. It hasn't happened to him because he is not really old. He only looks old because the world has battered him and beaten him to a pulp and then ground him to powder. In the past few days he has learned to pass for an old man when it is to his advantage instead of taking offence when he is mistaken for one.

The compound is coming to life. Fires can already be seen outside some of the houses. *Amaxhoba* are beginning to arrive. Most of the blind are led by little boys or by young women. The crippled brought by sleighs pulled by emaciated oxen are carried into the compound by friends and relatives, men and women, and are placed on the ground. Logs are placed under their heads as pillows, while others prefer to use their own elbows for the purpose. Some of the *amaxhoba* are able to walk on their own. They may have a limp here or an arm missing there, or they may not indicate impairment of any limb but even as they walk Malangana can see that they are just as broken as those who are physically wrecked. He feels fortunate that at least he can walk and can wander the countryside in search of his heart's desire without anyone's assistance.

He needs to stretch his legs; he hobbles out of the

compound. At the entrance women are coming in pushing wooden wheelbarrows with pots of steaming food. He can identify one of them as the woman who was assigned to feed him that first day. He has tried to avoid her in the past three days because she nearly killed him with food. She kept on piling and piling even when he told her he was full beyond bursting point. She shamed him into sweeping the plate clean because the world out there was starving.

'You're still here? Your Mthwakazi hasn't come then?' the woman asks.

'Your eyes are not deceiving you. I am here.'

'You've been avoiding my food? It's not good enough for you even though the prophet said I should feed you? You think the blessings are good only for other women and not for me?'

It's not only food that she piles up but questions too. Malangana does not know which one to answer first so he just stands there looking confused. She opens a pot of steaming sorghum hard porridge.

'That's what you're eating today,' she says with a beaming smile. 'With pumpkin and pumpkin leaves. That's what I have in the other pot. As long as you're here we're going to feed you until your bones fill up.'

This sounds quite ominous to Malangana. Sorghum hard porridge with pumpkin leaves and pumpkin flesh is the best meal any human being can wish for. It is the kind of food that is nourishing; that even mothers throughout the land tell children to eat and finish because it will make them big and strong. It is also the kind of food he would like to avoid, especially when it is given to him in abundance. He is salivating already. He hates the woman for this.

'I only want food that holds the breath together, not food that fattens,' he says weakly.

That is why if he had any choice at all he would opt for the white man's corn, maize, which just tastes like paper and is likely to leave him the way he is. How will Mthwakazi believe that he suffered for her if when they finally meet he's plump and all filled up with nary a rattling bone?

Before the woman can dismiss his wishes as those of a silly old man who does not know what's good for him she is taken aback by a sound that she is certain comes from his mouth. It is the neighing of a horse. Other people can hear it too for they all turn their heads in his direction, but they conclude that there must be a horse on the other side of the wall and carry on with their business. The woman is standing close to him and hears the neighing again. He is frantically trying to stop it by closing his mouth with both hands while balancing against the wall as his crutches fall.

'How did you do that?' she wants to know.

'I don't know,' he says. He is embarrassed. 'Please don't ask me that. It just happens sometimes. Or it used to happen a long time ago. It had stopped. Get me my crutches.'

'Trying to escape?'

'Just going to the dongas. Are you here to police the bowels of men?'

She helps him with his crutches. He hobbles away.

'When you come back this food will be waiting for you,' she says. 'You don't get away with those blessings that easily. What a trick! Neighing like a horse just to get away from eating my food.'

This thing of neighing like a horse, it used to attack him quite frequently in Lesotho. It started soon after the demise of Gcazimbane. He does not want to think about it. How Gcazimbane ended living inside him. He thought he had exorcised him and since coming back from exile he has not neighed like a horse, not until now. Not for a single day. And today he is being attacked by his Lesotho terrors: the neighing and the nightmare. On the same day too. He is back from exile, back in the land of his ancestors. They must leave him alone.

He hobbles down to the Goqwana River. He hopes to find a secluded spot for private ablutions. He debates whether he will return to the compound of Ibandla-likaNtu at all after these embarrassments. Especially after the threat of nourishing food.

He can hear the voice of the aged one, the prophet as others call him, booming in the distance and knows that the theological discussions have started. The devotees will argue with him, which is what he enjoys most, but the rest of *amaxhoba* will languidly carry on with dozing and swatting flies and chewing cud and scratching the itches of fleas and crushing lice with their fingernails. The women who feed them will carry on their business, indifferent to the theology.

'When we started Ibandla-likaNtu we had a big war of words,' says the aged one. 'Some of us left the churches of the white man—whether the Methodists or the Romans or the Anglicans or even the French for those of you who are Basotho—to return to our God, uQamata. We wanted to leave everything behind. Others said let us bring the Book along with us for it says some beautiful things that we will find comforting and liberating. Others said no, it is a bad book, a book of lies and slavery. They said it is a book of hellfire, a book that is against *amasiko nezithethe*—customs and traditions—of our ancestors. I have been thinking and thinking and thinking about this. Now that our anger has dissipated I think we should talk about this again. I think there is no contradiction between the Bible and our amasiko. The Bible is a good book for it says what you want it to say.'

Malangana can no longer hear what others are saying. But from what he has seen in the past few days there will be vigorous debates. He is surprised that no physical fights have ensued as some devotees do seem to take matters personally.

He will return after his ablutions. He has to. He can still feel Mthwakazi's *mkhondo*, although he is now confused about what it all means. Does it, for instance, merely mean she has been here? Then can you really call it *umkhondo* in that case? Of what good would it really serve him? What kind of *mkhondo* is this that only tells you she has been here but is silent on whither she went?

He would never forget this. And he was ashamed. She seemed to enjoy his shame and looked him straight in the eye and giggled. It was like that with abaThwa. They came from a different world and their ways were different. She thought Malangana's ways were strange and foolish. He thought Mthwakazi's ways were forward and shameless, yet much more enjoyable than the ways of amaMpondomise maidens. This tryst in the bushes by the river, for instance; it was something his body had never experienced before. Even the intercrural business he used to do with other herdboys could not match this by any measure known to man. He wanted to take the whole thing with him, the whole organ, the whole person, the whole experience, and hide it in his *egumbini*— his sleeping quarters.

They sat on the bank at the confluence of the Sulenkama and Gqukunqa rivers. Gcazimbane let them be and grazed a short distance from the river. They just sat like that, silently listening to their bodies.

The only thought that was running through Malangana's head was that they had broken the law. He therefore had to take her to his home and place her behind the door. And then send his people to inform her people she was behind his door. When a young man did that he was admitting that he had broken the law by taking the maiden without first asking for her hand in marriage, but he was willing to pay a fine for that crime and then to proceed with proper negotiations for the marriage. But how did one do that with Mthwakazi, *inzalwamhlaba*, when one did not know who her parents were or where they were located? She was a child of the earth—an autochthon.

They were still sitting like that when the night fell. They forgot about Gcazimbane as he wandered away back to the village to his regular place of sleep among the cattle at the Great Place.

'I want to marry you,' he said finally, cued by a shooting star.

'Why?' The question seemed to be disinterested.

He did not expect that kind of question. He ignored it.

'If I place you behind my door how do I find your people to pay the fine?'

She found this very funny and she giggled.

'I would not agree to be placed behind the door,' she said.

'Why not? I thought we have an understanding. We did adult things already because we are looking forward to a future together. Is that not why you allowed me into yourself?'

'No one places anyone behind the door among my people,' she said. 'People would think I am mad if they found me sitting—or do I stand?—behind the door.'

The abaThwa were not just one people, she explained to

him. Depending from what branch of the people-tree they came—be it the /Xam branch or !Kung branch or something else—they all had different customs. She herself did not know this when she was growing up. She only learned of it during the wanderings of her group of people when they met other groups that spoke different languages and prayed to different spirits and espoused different values.

Malangana thought she was telling him this as a way of turning down his proposal; she was saying they were from different worlds and therefore could not marry. He was becoming desperate.

'What does it matter if we are different?' he said. 'Listen, you don't have to sit behind my door. If you want me to woo you first, to court you, and then to send *uduli* delegations to your homestead to ask for your hand in marriage, as I would do with even a royal maiden of amaMpondo or abaThembu or amaGcaleka or any nation in the world, I can do that. I want to marry you. Don't ask me silly questions about why I want to marry you. It is what I want to do because the heart tells me so. It is not because I have eaten the food that you carry with you. I have wanted to do so even before. I even spoke to my uncles about it.'

'Among my people we marry first and woo later,' she said.

This was not as preposterous as it sounded, she explained to an astounded Malangana. What would happen was that they would marry and then continue to live in their separate homes, she with her own parents and he with his. Every day Malangana would go out to hunt and would bring the quarry to his in-laws, particularly the mother-in-law. She would look at it and thank the son-in-law and tell him that it was good, but not enough. The husband and wife would meet during the day and the courtship and the wooing would happen at that time, but when evening came each one would return to his or her respective home. The following day Malangana would go to hunt again and bring the quarry to the mother-in-law, and then spend some time with his wife, and the courtship continued like the day before. Every day things would happen like that until the in-laws decided that they were now satisfied with the quarry, which of course is the *lobolo*, and the couple would now be allowed to live together. Their courtship was over and they could consummate the marriage.

Malangana was fascinated by this and he said, 'Yes, that's how we should do it. I want to marry you the way of the abaThwa people.'

'The problem is how to find my people,' said Mthwakazi.

They sat silently, the water washing their feet as it rushed on its long journey down the Gqukunqa River to join Itsitsa which would meander through valleys and mountains until it joined Tina, which then connected to the great Mzimvubu which roared for miles and miles to spew their invisible foot moults into the Great Ocean. They looked up towards the northeast, to the distant mountains. Hills, perhaps in the daytime, but at night just a blotch of black mountains. They looked at the stars that touched the top of the mountain and then spread to the rest of the heavens.

'We can reach the stars,' said Mthwakazi.

'We can reach the stars?'

'If we walk that way. If we walk and walk and walk and walk and walk right up to the top of that mountain.'

'Yes, we can touch the stars on top of that mountain,' said Malangana. 'Some are practically sitting on it.'

'We can climb from star to star. We can live in the stars together. There you can do all the marrying and the courting and the hunting. I must have a star-mother there who will accept the animals you have hunted.'

This sounded like a fascinating idea to Malangana only because he would be with Mthwakazi there. Nothing else mattered.

'Yes, let us go now before the sun rises and sweeps the stars away,' he said.

'It does not matter if it's daylight. We'll walk in the same direction and wait for the night under that mountain. And then climb to the stars.'

Malangana jumped up. He was eager to start.

'And when we are up there I will prove to you that there are many suns,' he said triumphantly.

'When we are up there you will see there is only one sun,' said Mthwakazi, also getting to her feet.

They were both laughing as they fell into each other's arms. They were startled from the embrace by the neighing of horses. There was Gcazimbane leading four horsemen. As they got closer Malangana knew that something serious had happened when he identified them as the elders from Matiwane's various Houses, ranging from the Right-hand to the Left-hand and one from Iqadi. There was Sititi, Ndukumfa, Hamza and Cesane. Gcazimbane obviously led them to him. What a traitor!

'The king has been looking for you everywhere,' said Sititi.

'The king is in mourning. Why should he be looking for me?'

Hamza did not have the time for his games. He dismounted his horse with a whip ready to attack Mthwakazi. Fortunately Cesane, the youngest of the brothers, was fast to manoeuvre his horse between him and the girl.

'You are sitting here for the whole night doing *amanyala* with this Bushman girl while the nation is on fire?' said Hamza. 'And you call yourself a son of Matiwane?'

'Wait, Hamza,' said Cesane. 'Do not take it out on the girl. She is only a girl. You know how easily they can be led astray. The one who deserves a thorough beating is Malangana.'

'Not when they have been properly brought up like our amaMpondomise maidens,' said Hamza, nevertheless turning his wrath towards Malangana.

Ndukumfa agreed with his brothers. 'Malangana behaves like a boy who has not even gone to the initiation school.'

'Who was his principal *ikhankatha*? He must be held to account,' said Sititi.

Malangana shook his head at his conservative kin. Now they were placing the responsibility for his behaviour on his principal tutor at the initiation school. They instructed him to mount Gcazimbane forthwith and ride with them back to Sulenkama where Mhlontlo needed him urgently.

'I can't leave her here,' said Malangana.

'Mhlontlo asked us to come with you,' said Hamza. 'He didn't ask us to come with anyone else.'

'Then I am not going without her.'

Mthwakazi begged him to go with the elders. She would find her way back to the village. But Malangana insisted that he would not leave without her. The elders of the House of Matiwane relented and agreed that she should ride with Malangana on Gcazimbane back to the village, although she would have to get off before they entered the public spaces of Sulenkama lest they be accused of condoning *amanyala* and *amasikizi*—shameful and scandalous behaviour.

Various *amabutho*—regiments—had gathered already when Malangana and the elders arrived outside the Great Place and their songs could be heard from a distance. He walked around trying to locate the king and his council. He found them sitting with Hamilton Hope and Davis outside a tent near one of the wagons. Gxumisa was among the councillors. A Khoikhoi servant was offering Mhlontlo bread, coffee and eggs. He shook his head.

'Come on, you must have breakfast,' said Hope. And then turning to Malangana, he continued, 'We shared a tent and he was restless the whole night. Didn't sleep at all. He has to eat something. You can't fight a war on an empty stomach.'

Mhlontlo raised his head and immediately as his eyes fell on Malangana his face quivered. Before he could even utter a word Malangana begged for forgiveness. He did not know that he would be needed, he said. No one told him the esteemed visitors would be here today. The last thing he had heard was that there was a stand-off.

Gxumisa mumbled to the king to calm down and Malangana was relieved to see the tension leaving his face.

'Is it a foregone conclusion we are going to war?' he

asked.

'It's always been a foregone conclusion that we are going to war,' said Hope after Davis translated Malangana's question to his king.

'Actually, I was asking the king,' said Malangana. 'As far as I know he is in mourning and is not supposed to touch weapons of war.'

'We dealt with all that yesterday already,' said Davis. 'I don't think Mr Hope wants to go over that again today.'

'The king should not be appearing in public,' said Malangana in English. 'He is in mourning.'

'Where does this man come from?' asked Hope impatiently. 'We are done with that, man. If you try to put a spanner in our works now you will taste more of my *kati*. Davis, remind Umhlonhlo about the loot. The war has its own rewards. When he agreed to lead his people in this war I consented, subject to Government approval of course, that all the loot he captures will be his to distribute as he chooses. You're going to be very rich after this war, my friend.'

He patted the king on his back as he said this; Mhlontlo coughed. Both Davis and Malangana interpreted this, the latter with a sneer for they had spoken about this promise before. Mhlontlo was indeed tempted by the booty, as any war commander would be when there was a strong prospect of victory. Booty was the main thing that was motivating the petty Basotho chiefs who had fallen in line with Hope, namely Joel, Lelingoana and Lehana. It would have been a strong incentive for Mhlontlo too. But mourning took precedence over all the greed in the world.

Hope poured himself brandy in a mug and asked if

Mhlontlo would have some.

'Yes, I'll have some of that,' said the king.

The song of the *amabutho* was gathering momentum as more men arrived. Hope was getting excited. He told Mhlontlo the plan was surely working out well.

'Magwayi will not withstand your forces,' he said.

'amaMpondomise alone? What about amaMfengu and Lehana's people and all the others who promised to join the war?' asked Mhlontlo. 'amaMfengu are Government people. You cannot drag us into this war and leave them out of it.'

'That's not what I meant. We trust the Fingoes. They have a long history of loyalty to the Cape Colony and they'll be in this war. So will all the allies who attended the meeting. What I meant was that your forces are so strong under your command that even on their own they can beat Magwayi. Not that they are going to be on their own, old chap.'

It was becoming clear to Malangana that the night he spent with Mthwakazi by the river had wrought changes in the lives of his people that could not be reversed. Decisions were made under those wagons which in his view were to the detriment of his people. And all because of a woman he had not been part of those decisions. He felt a deep anger towards Mthwakazi for capturing his spirit so mercilessly that he became derelict in his duty to his king and to his people. His brother the king had already shown himself quite weak by uttering such statements to the white magistrate as 'where you die, I will die'. And here he was listening to revelations about the king having spent the night with this white man, in the same tent, and now they were sharing breakfast and brandy. He should have known better than to leave him to his own devices without his wise counsel to guide him.

Although the king was not alone. He was with Gxumisa and other councillors. How could Gxumisa agree that the king should lead *amabutho* to war while he was in mourning? How could the other elders? How could Sititi and Ndukumfa and Cesane and Gatyeni and Hamza? Of course they were old and conservative and tended to follow the king's word, however foolish, instead of guiding him on to the correct path. These elders of the House of Matiwane had been searching for him through the night instead of counselling their king to do the right thing and stop being clay in the hands of the white man. Where were the like-minded and hot-blooded young men like Nzuze and Mahlangeni when this decision was taken to go to war under Mhlontlo's command?

What convinced Malangana that Mhlontlo had decided to lead the men to war was that he was armed, though as a man in mourning he was not supposed even to touch arms of war. He had with him an assegai and a double breech-loading gun, both of which were weapons that he took out only on very special occasions.

Malangana walked away in disgust, but Gxumisa called him back.

'Where do you think you are going? The king needs you here to interpret.'

'*Nank'uSunduza; akaxakwa ngulomsebenzi,*' said Malangana. *Here is Davis; he does not find that job difficult.*

'*Uyay'qond'intok'ba uJola ufuna nincedisane,*' said Gxumisa, holding him back by his blanket. *You know that Majola—the king's clan name—wants you to help each other.*

Davis stayed out of the argument. He was well aware that Mhlontlo always wanted his own interpreter present to ensure that the white people were not saying things behind his back. He and the other white people had often joked about it, and the shortcomings of the said interpreter in mastering the intricacies and inconsistencies of the English language.

The festive mood of the people belied the sombre mood of the elders surrounding the king and the four white men with them. There was plenty of laughter and song and eating and drinking. Then Tsitwa, the chief army doctor, and two soldiers came rushing to the elders and the white men and announced that the men were ready to be enrolled for the military and to be given their marching orders. He, Tsitwa, had performed his duties of doctoring them in readiness for the war.

Hope was a bit startled when one of the soldiers caught his beard and playfully caressed it, saying, 'You'll see what we're going to do to the enemy today.'

'They can be like children sometimes,' said Hope, chuckling and brushing the soldier's hand off.

Mhlontlo and Gxumisa gave the soldier an admonishing stare while Warren, Davis and Henman tried to hide their embarrassment with uneasy smiles.

'Where is Mahlangeni?' Malangana asked Tsitwa about his son.

'He was with me when I doctored the troops. He must be somewhere here.'

Hope turned to the other white men and said, chortling, 'Let's go, fellows. Carry your revolvers and carbines. I believe our throats are going to be slit today.'

The three white men laughed nervously at his joke. Davis did not interpret it to Mhlontlo and his entourage. Nor did Malangana. Perhaps he had not heard it. His mind was too preoccupied with the betrayals that were gnawing at him.

Mhlontlo and Gxumisa led the way, followed by Malangana. Hope limped behind on his uneven legs, followed immediately by Davis, Henman and Warren. And then the rest of the amaMpondomise elders walked gravely after them. The crowd gave way and ululated as Mhlontlo's praise poet came forward in his regalia of jackal and leopard skins reciting genealogies of his family and the landmark deeds of some of the characters in that line.

Malangana's eyes were darting all over the crowd looking for the men he considered like-minded, who would hope-fully put him at ease about the events of the day. And there among the maidens carrying clay pots of beer on their heads was the puny figure of Mthwakazi. His body was suddenly seized by spirits that could not be anything but evil for they transported him back to the bushes by the river and to that moment of lawlessness. He had to battle very hard to return to the present. He had to turn his gaze away from the maidens and focus on the soldiers who were dancing in their various formations. This was the beginning of the *umguyo* dance.

He told himself he had no business being angry with Mthwakazi. Mthwakazi could only be Mthwakazi. And who could say if he had been there for the night he would have changed the path of history, would have dissuaded the hard-headed and cowardly elders from going along with the plans of the white man? No, it could not be Mthwakazi's fault.

Mthwakazi could continue to weave whatever magic she was weaving around him for it was gratifying. He should be strong enough to look at the maidens and be transported to the bushes by the river and bask in the pleasurable memory. But when he did look again the maidens were gone. The soldiers had danced themselves into a semicircle and there were hundreds of them. Perhaps up to a thousand or more. They were all armed with spears and shields. A few also had guns and rifles.

A groom brought Saraband, Hope's horse, for the magistrate was required to sit on it as he addressed the troops so as to have a view of all of them—both the inner and the outer circle—and be seen by all. Davis would stand next to him to interpret, and Warren and Henman would be seated behind.

Hamilton Hope sat on his trusty horse and surveyed the troops swaying like waves in front of his eyes. He lit his pipe and said to Davis, 'I may as well have another smoke before my throat is cut.'

Davis was beginning to get worried. This was the third time the magistrate had made this silly joke. He hoped one man's wit would not turn out to be another man's premonition.

The *umguyo* continued in earnest as the men sang their war songs and danced their war dances, closing the circle with the king and his *iindwendwe* inside. The whistles and the drums and the screams sent shivers down Malangana's spine. The ululations of the women could be heard in the distance. They were now far away, for *umguyo* was the business of men. The time for the feasting was over. Shields thundered as they struck against each other in time with the dance steps and spears sent flashes of lightning as they also clashed in the air. Legs flew high in the air and a thousand cowhide drums boomed as feet hit the wet ground all together at the same time. The earth shook and the white men's eyes seemed about to pop out of their sockets. The tiny figure of Hamilton Hope looked very forlorn on Saraband.

'If these warriors create so much fear simply by dancing can you imagine them fighting?' Warren said to Henman. But he couldn't hear what he was saying. He kept on saying 'What? What?' Warren said, 'Never mind' and watched the dance.

Suddenly there was a piercing whistle that went on for a few beats. It was followed by a sudden silence. Everyone stood still. Mhlontlo's praise poet jumped into the centre and said the king will utter a few words before the big white man on a horse, who is nevertheless very tiny, gives his orders of war. The men chuckled but immediately fell silent when Mhlontlo stepped forward.

'*Mampondomise amahle, amazwi am aphelile,*' said Mhlontlo. *Beautiful amaMpondomise, my words are finished.* 'This is your king whose orders you are now to take.' He pointed at Hope as he said this, and then he continued, 'He is the one who has closed the door against amaBhaca and amaMpondo, so that you are now fat and don't have to sleep in the veld in fear of your enemies. You all know I'm still in mourning. I am mourning for my wife, the daughter of King Sarhili, and I had asked that Gxumisa, a general tested in many wars, should lead you. Yet Hope insists that I must go to war *ngenkani*. I did not know that I could be forced to go to war while mourning. But Hope has forced me to go. I am now going, but be careful of your new king, Dilikintaba, the white man. We must now obey the white king. He is the king and I am no longer one. I am nothing.'

Davis was interpreting to Hope what Mhlontlo was saying. *Dilikintaba* was the praise-name that amaMpondomise were giving Hope, as all kings should be greeted with one. It meant 'the-one-who-demolishes-mountains', not quite accurately translating the name. That would have been Dilizintaba.

The soldiers all shouted in unison: 'A! Dilikintaba!' in the manner that kings were saluted. It sounded like thunder.

'I am only a Government servant doing Government work,' said Hope. 'I am glad you are going to lead your men to war. They are a formidable force under your leadership. Indeed, we would not go without you.'

Mhlontlo pointed at Hope and shouted, 'There is your God; I am only a dog.'

Once again the soldiers shouted: 'A! Dilikintaba!' and bowed before Hope.

The white men, including Hope himself, shifted uneasily. But Mhlontlo smiled amicably and looked at each one of them as if to reassure them that he meant well.

'We are Government people in the true sense of the word,' he said. 'The Government is our rock and our shade.'

Mhlontlo turned to Davis and said, 'This child has no fault. He grew up among us. He is one of our blood.'

He then pulled Davis by the shirt sleeve.

'Come here, Sunduza,' he said. 'I want to talk to you privately. I have a secret message that I want you to convey to the magistrate.'

Mhlontlo led Davis out of the circle. Malangana hesitated at first because he was not sure whether or not he was supposed to follow. He decided to stay in the circle in case Hope was going to make a speech and his interpretation would be needed. But Hope was not making a speech. He was just sitting on his horse looking lost. There was some commotion at the far end of the assembled men.

Hope looked at his pocket watch. It was 1:05 p.m. Time had been wasted already. He began to make his speech, just when Malangana was pushing his way out of the circle wondering whether to follow Mhlontlo and Davis.

'Men of the Pondomise,' Hope began, 'you are today men of the British Government.'

Before he could go any further a man had jumped on his horse and grabbed him by the beard. Others threw him off the horse. Mahlangeni, the leader of the assassins, stabbed him with his assegai. Warren and Henman tried to defend themselves but were not given the opportunity to fire their pistols. Mahlangeni's men fell on them with their assegais and stabbed them over and over.

Malangana saw Mhlontlo holding Davis in a tight grip, trying to stop him from returning to the circle. He did not go up to them but returned instead to the circle to see what the commotion was all about. He was too late. The white men were already dead and Mahlangeni was standing over Hope's body, his assegai dripping blood.

Malangana's chest expanded to bursting point as he wailed, 'Why did you leave me out of this? Why? Why? Why?'

'Where were you?' asked Mahlangeni. 'On top of a Bushman girl?'

Malangana lifted his assegai and stabbed Hope over and over again. He was going to kill him again even though he was already dead. He aimed for the heart. No one was going to deny him the opportunity to kill Hamilton Hope.

The assassins began to strip the white men naked. Mahlangeni took Hope's coat and wore it, though it was too small a size and was bloody. The rest of the white men's clothes were too tattered to be of any use to anyone. But their body parts would be useful as war medicine. Mahlangeni hollered for his father Tsitwa, the head of the war doctors. In no time three war doctors were there, and later Tsitwa joined them. They were particularly keen on Hamilton Hope's testicles which would make strong war medicine.

Malangana went back to join Mhlontlo and Davis, brandishing his bloody assegai and singing his own praises. Davis was sitting flat on the ground, weeping with his head buried between his knees. Between the sobs he accused Mhlontlo of provoking the Government which was a dangerous thing for amaMpondomise. This made Malangana very angry.

'He must shut up, or does he want us to kill him too?' he said.

'He's just sad because he has lost his friends,' said Mhlontlo. 'We must protect Sunduza. We'll hand him over to the school people who'll take him to his mother.'

In the commotion that followed the white men's servants tried to escape. However they did not want to leave empty-handed; they first went to the wagons to rescue whatever they could. That was where some of them met their fate. amaMpondomise soldiers were waiting there. This was their booty and they meant to protect it. Malangana got a shirt from an escaping policeman's back. He also came out of Henman's tent with a pile of blankets. Three of Hope's servants were frogmarched to Mhlontlo at assegai-point and gun-point. They asked Davis to plead for their lives to Mhlontlo, but he was too busy crying for his fallen comrades.

'I am not killing you,' said Mhlontlo to the policemen. 'I am only killing this little lame man and the white men from Mthatha who were forcing me to go to war against my will. Davis is our child. We would be sinning if we killed him.'

He ordered that the servants be released.

There was the matter of Saraband, Hope's horse.

'He is your horse now that you have defeated his master,' said Malangana. 'It is part of the loot.'

'No,' said Mhlontlo. 'I cannot in good conscience ride this horse. It must be returned to the man's wife in Qumbu.'

Davis wept even more at the mention of Emma Hope, widow of the late Hamilton Hope, who did not yet know of her new marital status.

'Don't worry, Sunduza,' said Mhlontlo. 'We have already summoned *amakhumsha*. They will be here soon to accompany you to your mother.'

Hamilton Hope had finally been vanquished, Malangana thought. amaMpondomise had finally learned the lesson. If any white man came to subjugate them again, they would fight and defend their land. Now he could go and look for Mthwakazi. The journey to the top of the mountain could begin.

MONDAY DECEMBER 28, 1903

Malangana is a descendant of dreamers. The first among the dreamers was Ngcwina who was famous for killing a rhinoceros with his bare hands when others could only trap the beast and kill it with spears in hunting parties. Ngcwina was the fourth king of amaMpondomise after Sibiside, the first known leader of the abaMbo from whom such peoples as amaSwati, amaMpondo, amaMpondomise and aboMkhize descended.

He is thinking of Ngcwina today as he sits in the ruins of the Tsolo Jail. He discovered this nook where he can have some privacy among the sandstones once shaped by masons. For many years this place was abandoned. But now it looks more like a construction site. There is a pile of sand and a load of bricks. Some stones are being dug out from the mound that had buried them for twenty years. They are bringing the jail back to life. Perhaps they are no longer haunted by the memory of the white women and children who locked themselves in here, hoping they would be safer in jail than in their houses, while the natives rampaged and set Tsolo on fire and Mditshwa's forces besieged the magistrate during the War of Hope.

He takes off his pants and spreads them on the floor.
He looks around to make sure there is no one watching.
It is quiet outside although it is a Monday morning.
Amagqobhoka—the Christian converts—are trying to recover
from the festive weekend which started on Friday when they
celebrated Christmas. They went to church in the morning
to worship and eat bread and drink wine. And then they
came back in the afternoon to drink and feast and went from
house to house asking for Christmas Box. This meant you
had to give them more food. On Saturday the feasting continued because they said it was Boxing Day. And then again
on Sunday they went to worship and eat bread and drink
wine in the church. When they came back the feasting continued. No wonder they are winning more people into their
ranks, not just *amakhumsha*. Many people who can't even
read or write their names or say 'good morning, mistress'
have become churchgoers.

As for Malangana, he hates this season with all his heart.
He is grateful that he discovered this refuge—the old ruins
of the jail. He hates all enforced merriment. Gaiety by decree
of the white man's book.

Having assured himself that no one is spying on him,
Malangana unbuttons a secret pouch sewn inside the bottom
of the pants, takes out a number of banknotes and counts
them. They are in hundreds, his hoardings from his early
years in exile when he used to sell the *mokhele* ostrich feathers
with which Basotho soldiers dressed their shields. He is satisfied it is all in order. He never bothers this stash. But once
in a while he wants to satisfy himself. He separates one note
which will take care of his meagre needs for months to come

and puts it in his normal pocket. He puts his pants on again.

Now he can return to Ibandla-likaNtu, though the place is getting on his nerves. He has been there now for twelve days; he has counted as each one of them dawned and dusked without any appearance of Mthwakazi. Perhaps he is getting on people's nerves too. There is a lot of irritation in the air.

Christmas was the worst, with every preacher outdoing himself about the birth of the baby Jesus who came to save the world. Many of these preachers were *amaxhoba* themselves. Why didn't the baby Jesus save them? Anyway, didn't these people say they left the white man's churches in order to worship their own God? How did this baby Jesus follow them all the way to the compound on the banks of the Goqwana River?

Malangana decides that he won't return to the compound yet. He will sit here for a while and listen to himself and to his longing. The Gcazimbane in him has been silent since that one surprise attack at the compound and he is grateful for that. He is still puzzled why it happened then when he thought he had been cured of him. A *lethuela*—diviner—in Lesotho once told him he would be cured only if he erased his memory of Gcazimbane and of the meat that he ate. But how do you forget a horse like Gcazimbane?

His mind darts back to Ngcwina, the wonderful dreamer. He dreams like Ngcwina. But Ngcwina was a king and a powerful one at that. He had the power to make his dreams a reality. He is the one who once dreamed a hunting party of his amaMpondomise people came back from a hunt in the Ulundi Mountains with a strange animal that had no fur on its body. He knew immediately that the dream had a meaning. He then sent a hunting party to the same mountains which on the third day at Ngele—today's Mount Ayliff—found a Mthwa woman in a cave. They knew immediately it was the fulfilment of their king's dream and brought her down. That was the woman who became Manxangashe, Ngcwina's wife of the Iqadi House whose son became heir to the amaMpondomise kingdom.

As Malangana sits on the heap that was the jail of Tsolo, and that will rise to be the jail again, he tastes the bitterness in his mouth that, unlike Ngcwina who did have his Mthwakazi, he still cannot have his own Mthwakazi after all these years. It is all because of one man: Hamilton Hope. amaMpondomise knew right from the beginning when this man was planted among them that he was not bringing them any good. They did not want him. They had heard of him from King Moorosi. Even after he had been posted they demanded he be expelled. But the Government was deaf to their pleas. Now see what had happened?

Malangana takes his crutches and slowly works his way towards Ibandla-likaNtu. He has disturbed the banknotes; they cause some discomfort. Soon they will settle and his bottom will be at home with them again.

At sunrise a party of more than three hundred armed horsemen departed from Sulenkama. They were led by Mhlontlo and the elders of the House of Matiwane. Mhlontlo's uncle Gxumisa was not one of them. He remained with the rest of *amabutho* at Sulenkama who had to be prepared for war under his command in case of an attack by the Red Coats of the Cape Mounted Riflemen. Before Davis was taken away to his mother by *amakhumsha* the night before, he assured Mhlontlo that the killing of Hope, which he variously called murder and assassination, would not be the end of the story. The CMR would not rest until they avenged his death. amaMpondomise should therefore prepare for war.

'We'll fight them,' said Mhlontlo.

'If they couldn't raise an army big enough to fight Magwayi how will they defeat us?' asked Gxumisa. 'Yes, we'll fight them.'

Malangana was finally proud of his king. He had never seen him so resolute. The elders of the House of Matiwane and all the other councillors were just as determined. For once the so-called agitators of Mahlangeni and Malangana's generation were in one voice with these usually conservative elders who were believed to have succumbed to English rule.

Malangana was not in the party of horsemen pacing their horses in pairs in a long line of rhythmic gait, with women ululating all along the way. Mhlontlo ordered him to take Saraband to Hope's house and then join the rest of the men in front of the courthouse, known as the House of Trials by amaMpondomise, where he would hold a meeting with the white people of Qumbu.

Malangana, now dressed in the policeman's shirt, first went to Mahlangeni's homestead. He knew that he was not among the horsemen riding to Qumbu because he had to be with his father to doctor the troops for any impending war. And indeed there he was under a *umsintsi* tree conferring with a group of men whom Malangana had not seen before, drinking beer so early in the morning and eating roasted meat spread on the fresh skin of a goat. Malangana dismounted Saraband when Mahlangeni beckoned him to join them. Mahlangeni was still wearing Hamilton Hope's coat, now cleaned of the soil and blood.

'It's a good thing you inherited the magistrate's coat,' said Malangana. 'It suits you. They should make you our next magistrate.'

'You inherited his horse,' said Mahlangeni. 'It should be mine. I did the real killing. You killed him when he was already dead.'

Malangana tied the horse to a nearby tree stump.

'I wish I was inheriting it,' said Malangana. 'I am taking it back to his wife. The king's orders. He says we can't keep it.'

'Your brother is still soft. Nothing will change him.'

Mahlangeni introduced Malangana to the men. They were from Tsolo, from the Great Place of King Mditshwa. When one Mpondomise was hurt all amaMpondomise were hurt. It did not matter if they owed their loyalty to Mhlontlo or to Mditshwa. If a war with the English broke out, the people of Mditshwa would make common cause with the people of Mhlontlo. This was the message of these men. A rebellion against white people had already started in Tsolo. Shops had been looted and a mission station attacked. A group of white families had locked themselves in the Tsolo Jail where they thought they would be safer than outside. These men came directly from Mditshwa who was much more prepared to go all the way than Mhlontlo who was still talking in terms of appeasement.

'Tell your brother that he has an ally already in Mditshwa,' said Mahlangeni.

When Malangana left Mahlangeni's homestead he was more inspired than ever before. The English would be stupid to start a fight with amaMpondomise. If they came they would meet their match.

It was time for him to get married immediately and be a man. Then he would not be sidelined in some of these important war plans. Like Ngcwina, the ancestor who was a dreamer, he who married a Bushwoman, he would marry his Mthwakazi today. There was no time to waste. Since Mthwakazi did not want to be placed behind the door—where women who had been taken by force without permission of their kin in the *tsikiza* tradition were compelled to sit until their parents were informed of the abduction—but wanted to walk hand in hand with the man to the top of the mountain and then to the stars, they would have to start the long walk that night. When the war came, if it came, all the essential rituals must be complete and they must be man and wife. She must be accepted by the elders of the House of Matiwane as Matiwane's daughter-in-law and he must be granted his due respect as a family man who is consulted in the affairs of state and is not a mere groom of the king's horse whose sole role is that of a messenger.

He galloped to the Great Place. The wagons and Scotch carts were still there, but now stripped of everything, including the canvas canopies. He dismounted at these skeletons of what used to be majestic vehicles and sent a girl among a group that was playing the *ingedo* game to call Mthwakazi from *entangeni* where the maidens who were helping with the feast spent the night. After some time the girl came back; Mthwakazi said she would not come out.

'Tell her that if she doesn't come out I will go in there and fetch her by force, which will shame her in front of everyone,' said Malangana. 'I am not playing with her.'

The girl skipped back into the Great Place. In no time she returned with Mthwakazi.

'What do you think you are doing, embarrassing me here at the Great Place?' she asked, arms akimbo.

He could not help but chuckle to himself because Mthwakazi had covered her whole body in red ochre, the fashionable body decoration that the amaMpondomise girls—who were not red-ochre people normally—had copied from abaThembu maidens. It did not suit her at all, thought Malangana, but of course he dared not utter that thought. abaThwa women usually used white clay sparingly on their faces or bodies or no make-up at all. She stood there defiantly in her tanned-hide front-and-back beaded apron, the only thing that covered her nakedness.

'You are coming with me,' said Malangana. 'I am marrying you today.'

He did not give her the chance to protest. He grabbed her and flung her on to the horse. Then he mounted and they galloped away.

'I told you, Malangana, you cannot *tsikiza* me. I am not one of your amaMpondomise girls. If you marry me it will be like a decent girl of the earth people, the people of the eland and of the praying mantis. You will do what I told you: walk with me, marry me, and then woo me, in that order.'

Malangana did not respond. Instead he pressed his heels firmly into Saraband's flanks to make him gallop even faster.

'What will people say, *wena* Malangana?' screamed Mthwakazi.

'Since when do you care what people say?'

Actually he did not know what to do with Mthwakazi at that point, especially when he remembered that he was on a mission to return Hamilton Hope's horse to his wife, and then to join Mhlontlo and his troops at the House of Trials for an important performance and for a meeting with the white people of Qumbu. The performance depended very much on his presence for he was the director. The meeting with the white people needed him too, for he was the interpreter. Mhlontlo was in Qumbu already by then waiting for him, and he was not there. He had let him down again, thanks to Mthwakazi.

'If you think you're going to take me by force and put me

behind the door, Malangana, you're playing with fire, I tell you. I'll walk out of that door and shame you.' Mthwakazi was not letting up.

Malangana snapped, 'Shut up, Mthwakazi. I have let down my people for the second time, and it's all because of you. Shut up.'

So Mthwakazi just kept quiet as Saraband galloped into Qumbu.

The troubles had reached this town already. Malangana could see some sporadic damage that had happened in some places, mostly houses set on fire. When they passed the general dealer's store looting was in progress. Though Malangana knew he was already late there was no way he could pass without taking part. While most people were focusing on the store itself and were taking groceries and blankets from the shelves, Malangana went to the back of the building, to the residential house where the servants were cowering in the kitchen, begging not to be killed. The trader and his wife were at that moment attending Mhlontlo's meeting at the courthouse, the maid said. They had been routed out in the morning by armed horsemen who frogmarched them to the courthouse.

While Mthwakazi remained outside holding Saraband's reins Malangana went to the bedroom to look for something interesting as a gift for Mthwakazi. He found a purple satin dressing gown which he liked for himself; he did not know it was meant for a woman. For Mthwakazi he found gold earrings and a silk red-and-white floral dress.

Mthwakazi giggled as she dressed up in the silk dress on top of the red ochre that covered her body. She also wore the gold earrings. The dress was too big for her so it formed a train behind her, which occasionally she had to lift up and put over her shoulder and then hold the hem with both her hands.

Malangana wore the dressing gown, which was too tight for him.

'At least they won't know who we are. It is a good disguise,' he said as they got back on their way. Saraband knew the road home and galloped straight there without much egging on. He stopped right in front of The Residency. The place was still intact though it didn't look as though there was anyone around. Malangana dismounted and helped Mthwakazi down. They tied the horse to a tree trunk and were about to leave it there when a man appeared at the door.

'I am Mr Mqikela. What do you want?' he said.

A black Mister was bound to be one of *amakhumsha* who were teachers or clerks.

'We brought Saraband,' said Malangana.

'I don't know what to do with this horse. You take it, you murderers of the magistrate,' he said, his voice shaking with emotion.

'Mhlontlo said we should bring it back,' said Malangana. 'It's up to his wife what you do with it.'

'Mhlontlo's word means nothing,' said the servant. 'We are just waiting for him to come here and kill us all. He had promised all our white masters would be safe, but just this morning he has captured the whole of Qumbu and your people are burning and destroying. Yes, you can come and kill us. You call us amaMfengu. Come and kill us and be done with it.'

Malangana spat in his face and said, 'You're too old to waste my assegai on.'

He then grabbed Mthwakazi by the arm and led her away. He walked towards the courthouse with Mthwakazi following him, dragging her big silk dress.

'You don't say things like that to an old person,' said Mthwakazi. 'And you don't spit at people.'

'You say them and you spit too if you have been whipped by Hamilton Hope with his *kati* on two occasions and thrown into prison and abused by amaMfengu guards,' said Malangana.

Mthwakazi found this rather funny and sniggered.

'I am told that *kati* really ripped your buttocks to shreds. That story made you famous. I knew you long before I met you.'

More people were walking in the same direction. They said they were all going to see the white people of Qumbu who had been arrested by Mhlontlo. It seemed that's what all those horsemen were doing the whole morning; rounding up white people from their houses and their general dealers' stores and even right up to Shawbury Mission Station where Mhlontlo's own son Charles was a student. They were all gathered outside the courthouse and people were going to see the spectacle of white people as Mhlontlo's prisoners.

Malangana became excited. No wonder people were looting and burning down the general dealer's store. Mhlontlo had finally done the right thing and had taken the white people prisoner. The best thing to do would be to kill them before any rescue attempt by the Red Coats. He wanted to increase his pace in order to feast his eyes on the prisoners, but his companion was burdened by a dress.

'As soon as I am done with what Mhlontlo wants me to do we'll walk back to the river and do what you want us to do,' he said to Mthwakazi who was still giggling.

'But I left my drum at Sulenkama. I cannot go without my drum.'

'Yesterday the problem was *tsikiza*, now it is the drum. What will it be next?'

'It is not my fault that you want to marry a diviner.'

'You're not yet a diviner from what I hear. You're an acolyte,' Malangana said in a belittling or even mocking manner.

She sat down on the ground and refused to move.

'I am not going without my drum.'

He walked on without her. She did not follow. He stopped and looked back.

'It is fine, we'll go to Sulenkama first and pick it up, and then proceed to the river,' he yelled.

Only then did she stand up, put the train of her dress on her shoulder and skip after him. They proceeded to the courthouse.

Malangana pushed his way through the excited crowd. And there in the centre were the white people, about fifteen of them. Most of them were from Shawbury, although two or three were traders from Qumbu. They were surrounded by a circle of Mhlontlo's soldiers, fully armed with assegais, guns and rifles. Mhlontlo was sitting on Gcazimbane as Hope had been sitting on Saraband the day he was killed. Next to him was Alfred Davis—the Sunduza of amaMpondomise—interpreting for him in a shaky voice.

Among the white people was his brother, the Reverend William Davis, on whose account Sunduza's life was spared.

Mhlontlo was in the middle of his speech: 'I assure all of you that amaMpondomise mean no harm to the white people. You can carry on with your lives in peace among us. Traders can carry on with their trade and missionaries can carry on with their work. Our quarrel is not with you but with the Government and the magistrates.'

Malangana was crestfallen. These people were guests, not prisoners.

A white woman spotted Mthwakazi in the crowd trying to push her way to the front in order to get a better view of the so-called white prisoners.

'Mr Umhlonhlo! Mr Umhlonhlo!' the white woman started screaming and pointing at Mthwakazi. 'That girl is wearing my dress! And my gold earrings too!'

All heads, including Mthwakazi's, turned in the direction in which she was pointing.

'You promised we would be safe and our property would be protected. Our house must have been looted.'

At that moment a white man spotted Malangana.

'And that man is wearing your nightgown, dear,' he said.

'Malangana!' shouted Mhlontlo.

'*Botha, Nkosi!*' responded Malangana. *Your Majesty!*

'Why are you only arriving now? A simple thing like taking the magistrate's horse to his house takes you the whole day? We delayed our proceedings waiting for you. You know I always want you to help Sunduza with interpreting for me.'

The white couple was getting frantic for it was obvious to them that their home had been looted. The other white people were trying to calm them down lest the armed natives became agitated and changed their minds about peaceful coexistence and started mowing them down.

'I will deal with you when I finish with these men and women whose ears reflect the rays of the sun,' said Mhlontlo. 'What I am saying is it is Government that we are fighting, not the missionaries, not the traders. Government has treated us very harshly. We came under Government in order to gain peace and quietude. Instead we have been in a state of unending unrest because of the harsh treatment we have received. The magistrates have broken faith with us. Our cattle are being branded and now our arms are being taken away. And our children are to be taken away by Government across the great waters to the land of the white man. We can only take so much. Now we have decided to fight back. We know they are going to send their Red Coats here. We are going to stand our ground and defend our land and our people. I shall not be taken alive. A man can die only once.'

These last words moved Malangana and he vowed that he would be with Mhlontlo wherever he died. Still, he did not agree with sparing the lives of these white people. If only like-minded people like Mahlangeni were here. The elders were too accommodating.

The meeting was over. Mhlontlo asked the white people to return to their homes, and those who were afraid would be given guards to accompany them. The biggest group was going to Shawbury and would be accompanied by a troop of horsemen.

The Davis brothers wanted to confer with Mhlontlo before leaving. Malangana had to be part of that. But first

Mhlontlo called him aside to admonish him about his lack of responsibility which was the result of his bachelorhood. It surely was high time he settled down so that he could focus more on national issues.

'I don't understand why you say white people must not be harmed,' said Malangana instead of addressing the issue of his indiscipline. 'Not after what Government has done to us.'

'They are not Government,' said Mhlontlo.

'Government will return through them,' argued Malangana. 'We should be killing everyone whilst we have the chance. They will call other white people who will make war on us. There is a machine there in that building that they use to talk to other white people far away in other countries. The telegraph, it's called. That's where we should have started.'

'Let's destroy the machine and not the people,' said Mhlontlo. 'I was assured the wires were cut last night. I was told that machine works through wires. I instructed that their poles should also be set on fire. First let's hear what Sunduza and his brother want.'

The Reverend Davis was making a request that he and his Methodist Church be allowed to bury the mutilated bodies of Hope, Warren and Henman, which were still lying out in the veld in Sulenkama. '*Siyacela Nkosi-e-Nkulu yaMampondomise*, it is an unChristian thing for their bodies to be lying there unburied,' said William Davis. *We beg you, Paramount Chief of amaMpondomise.*

'You are a man of compassion, William Davis,' said Mhlontlo, 'as was your father before you. Both you and your father worked well with our people. And of course your brother Sunduza here who is a person of Government is a good man too. Even my son Charles stays with you at your school. I would like to show you similar compassion on this matter. But I can't. The customs and practices of my people do not allow me. Those are bodies of fallen enemies and must remain in the veld and be carrion for the birds and scavenging animals of the wild. Their bones must scatter in the winds; otherwise the medicines made from their parts will have no potency.'

The Davis brothers left downhearted. As they were walking away, heads bowed, to join the wagon ferrying families to the mission station, their hopes were raised a bit when Mhlontlo called Sunduza's name. But all he was saying was: 'I have just been told there has been some looting and burning of some houses and stores. I am very sorry about it. It was not meant to be.'

As the horses and Scotch carts and wagons of the white people and Mhlontlo's soldiers accompanying them back to Shawbury disappeared on the winding path, the praise poet performed a clownish dance in front of the king and then shouted: *'Diliiikaaa weee ntaaba! Idilikil'intaba namhlanje!* *The mountain has fallen today.* Dilikintaba, Hamilton Hope's praise-name, means 'falling or demolished mountain'.

This was the glorious moment Malangana had been waiting for. He was the leader here. Even the king was going to follow his direction. About two hundred soldiers took their guns and their shields and spears and fell into line. And into song. The kind of song that men sang when they came back from a successful hunt with a sizeable kill.

A buffalo, perhaps. Or a rhinoceros. Malangana's ancestors were reputed to kill rhinoceros with their bare hands.

While the praise poet led the king into the House of Trials Malangana led a few men to the Telegraph Office to make sure the machine was destroyed. The machine was not there, the poles destroyed and wires cut. But they found a lot of guns that were stockpiled in the room. These had come from Butterworth and had arrived in Qumbu after Hamilton Hope had already left for Sulenkama. The papers indicated that there were 265 Snider rifles and 15,750 rounds of Snider ball cartridges. Mhlontlo's army would be well armed. Malangana selected one of the rifles as his own and took it with him. He left the men to guard the loot and proceeded to the House of Trials for the glorious moment.

Inside the courtroom Mhlontlo was sitting at the bench. He was Hamilton Hope the magistrate. Malangana was the interpreter, sitting at the interpreter's table next to the witness box. Various amaMpondomise soldiers had taken roles as officials of the court, ranging from prosecutors to lawyers to clerks of the court and sundry mandarins whose roles were undetermined. They were quite a sight in a Western courtroom in their isiMpondomise military regalia of animal skins and shields and ostrich feathers, with guns and assegais on their shoulders.

Mhlontlo opened the big book on the magistrate's bench that recorded the names of accused persons, their crimes, the verdicts and the sentences—the Great Book of Causes, as Mhlontlo called it—and read from it words that no one could understand in the nasal accent of the English, while paging the big leaves of the book. Malangana translated the words into isiMpondomise.

A soldier was hurled into the witness stand by other soldiers who played the role of policemen. Mhlontlo read from the Great Book of Causes. Malangana interpreted: 'You, Gatyeni, son of Ndlebendlovu, you are charged with the crime of owing Government tax for each one of your five huts for four years. Are you guilty or not guilty?'

'I am not guilty, Dilikintaba! Why should I pay Government taxes for my houses in the land of amaMpondomise?'

Mhlontlo pronounced the sentence in his invented nasal language.

Malangana interpreted: 'I sentence you to two years in prison without fine.'

All the soldiers in the House of Trials rose and with chants and laughter and screams of 'Death to the Book of Causes! Death to the rule of Dilikintaba!' they stabbed the book with their spears right there on the bench in front of the king.

The audience that had by now filled the courtroom and was crowding at the back cheered and ululated. Malangana could see Mthwakazi in her red floral dress, eyes agog in the crowd. He felt proud that she was witnessing him playing such a crucial role in the ritual of mocking Hope's judicial power and rendering it impotent and ineffectual once and for all, and thus consigning it to the ashes of history.

'Silence in the court,' said Malangana, as the soldiers went back to take their positions. A new accused was ushered into the witness stand.

'I am Mzazela, son of Hamza,' said the accused.

Mhlontlo pronounced the sentence and Malangana interpreted, 'I find you guilty of stealing your neighbour's chicken. I sentence you to six months in jail.'

Once more the soldiers attacked the Great Book of Causes with their spears and stabbed it repeatedly. Mhlontlo helped them too by adding a few stabs of his own. So did Malangana before he returned to his interpreter's seat and called the court back to order.

Mhlontlo tried to turn the pages of the Great Book of Causes but by now it was too tattered. He lifted it up and uttered some pained words. Malangana translated: 'Oh, now that the Great Book of Causes has decided to leave us, how will I know what crimes you have committed?'

This was greeted with much laughter and cheering.

'Silence in the court!' shouted Malangana. 'You will not get away with your crimes. I will still know them in my head. Even without the Great Book of Causes I can see just by looking into your eyes that you are criminals. The trials will continue.'

And indeed the trials continued in similar vein. Even some of the villagers, those who were not shy to volunteer to be the accused and be found guilty of witchcraft or allowing cattle to graze in other people's fields, got the opportunity to stand in the witness box and be laughed at by the rest of the audience. This went on until the king became tired of the game, though Malangana was still possessed by the spirit of performance.

Night had fallen when the crowds left the House of Trials in song and unabated euphoria. The soldiers set the building on fire with the tattered Great Book of Causes on the magistrate's bench. The fire caught quickly and in no time turned into a blaze. Tongues of flames were the crowning glory of their victory.

The brown shadows of the horsemen looked tall and thin as they trotted away from the black, brown, red and yellow flames. After a while the silhouettes of Malangana and Mthwakazi walked away against the flames and the brown smoke. He had to look for her first among the singing and dancing and sneezing crowds.

The walk had begun. It was eighteen miles to Sulenkama. They would walk it slowly, savouring each other's company. The dress was a hindrance. It was a European dress nonetheless, made of rich smooth material, and it looked splendid on her especially with the red ochre that covered her body.

At Sulenkama she would go to her wards, the king's diviners, and get her sacred drum and anything else that she needed, and go to the confluence where Sulenkama River joined Gqukunqa River. She would wait for him there. He would go to his house and do whatever he had to do. He would quickly confide in Gxumisa so that at least one person would know that he had gone to marry his Mthwakazi and then he would go and meet her by the river.

They would walk to the top of the mountain.

SATURDAY FEBRUARY 27, 1904

Mthwakazi's people invented the sun. These white women can bask in it and enjoy it as if they own it, but they owe it all to Mthwakazi's people. It is quite early in the morning yet they are already sitting on garden benches on the sprawling lawn of what used to be The Residency. They are all wearing white dresses, white stockings, white shoes and white hats. Malangana could have sworn they were nuns, like those he saw at Holy Cross in Lesotho. Perhaps The Residency has become a convent. It's been rebuilt into a beautiful white-washed building with big windows. But the women's hats are different from the nun's veils. They are like the panama hats that Sunduza liked to wear when he was smartly dressed. Malangana had thought such hats were worn only by men.

He stands at the knee-high fence and watches one woman roll a big black ball on the grass with two other women standing next to her. There are many other big black balls on the grass. The women on the garden bench are talking animatedly and looking quite amused. They notice him and shoo him away. He smiles at them and waves.

'He thinks we're waving at him,' says one of the women and giggles.

They all break into giggles and shoo him away even more vigorously, uttering such words as: '*Hamba*, go away, *voetsek*!' This last one amuses them no end because it is the language of the crude Trek-Boers and doesn't quite roll off their polished English tongues. So they keep on repeating it and laughing at their attempts: '*Foot-sack! Foot-sack!*'

He waves back and smiles even more broadly, playing the monkey.

A younger woman stands up, takes a biscuit from a saucer and walks to Malangana. The other women give a collective gasp and squeal, one even hiding her face in her hands. Another one says, 'Oh, Margaret, always the bleeding heart.'

'You want a biscuit?' says Margaret to Malangana.

Malangana shakes his head shyly.

'Come on,' says Margaret. 'It won't bite you. It tastes good.'

'I used to work here,' says Malangana, as he reaches for the biscuit.

'You speak English?' This seems to be an exciting discovery for Margaret. She turns to the other women and announces: 'He speaks English.'

'This used to be the magistrate's residence and it was called The Residency. I looked after his garden. I was what you would call a houseboy,' he says. He does not find it necessary to tell her he was a prisoner.

She is impressed.

'Then what happened?' She seems concerned. She looks him over from head to toe.

'Actually, I came here looking for an old friend. Do you know a man called Sunduza? That's who I am looking for.'

Then he suddenly remembers that a white woman would not know Sunduza. She would know Davis instead. 'I mean Mr Davis,' he corrects himself.

The woman calls to the others: 'He is looking for a Mr Davis!'

They relay the message, but don't seem to know any Davis, until it gets to the woman who is bowling. She says, 'Oh, that was a long time ago. The Reverend Davis of Shawbury passed on years ago.'

'I am looking for his brother, Alfred Davis,' shouts Malangana.

'He passed on too... years ago,' says the bowler.

'What about the Reverend Davis' wife?' asks Malangana.

'She sailed back to England soon after her husband's death,' responds the bowler, and her hands fly to her chest as she gasps. She has had a conversation in an unguarded moment with a dilapidated native about white people; particularly the whereabouts of a white woman.

She yells, 'Margaret, come back here right away!'

Margaret stands there, puzzled; she's not aware that she has done anything wrong.

'Tell the vagabond to go away, Margaret,' yells the bowler. 'You encourage these natives, they start stealing.'

'He speaks English,' says Margaret, nevertheless walking back to the garden bench.

Malangana stands there for a while, his body tensing and his nostrils flaring at being called names by the white woman. He and his people had destroyed all this with flames but in twenty years it has risen with a vengeance in greater splendour with even more arrogant people occupying it while he has been reduced to bones.

'In case you are wondering who I am,' he shouts. 'I am the man who killed Hamilton Hope.'

They all turn their heads in unison and look at him wide-eyed.

'Hamilton Hope?' he repeats. 'The magistrate? The one who used to stay here at The Residency before I burned it? Don't you remember?'

They all burst out laughing.

'Umhlonhlo murdered Hamilton Hope and we know where he is. You are not he,' says the bowler, and then rolls her black ball.

A heavy sigh and then Malangana hobbles away. He hates thick-skinned white people who refuse to be provoked into anger. They are all the same; in Sterkspruit and in Kingwilliamstown they refused to give him his due respect there as well. He must have the last word. He stops and glares at the white women, now at some distance.

'I don't care what you say, my spear tasted his heart even though he was already dead,' he yells, though feebly.

They ignore him. He decides to leave them with their arrogance. He didn't come for them here in Qumbu anyway. He came on the advice of the blind man, the father of the nightwatchman at whose house he once slept many months ago; the man who had seen Mthwakazi begging in Tsolo. After Malangana had waited at the compound of IbandlalikaNtu for two months because every day the aura of Mthwakazi lingered in the air, the blind former diviner came as one of *amaxhoba* who occasionally visit and was surprised to find that he was still there waiting for Mthwakazi. He said to him,

'How do you know if you are not waiting for *ukuza kukaNxele?*' *The coming of Nxele*. Nxele was the nickname of Makhanda, the left-handed Prophet. He was the military adviser of King Ndlambe of the amaXhosa when they were in a civil war with King Ngqika who was in alliance with the British. He was incarcerated on Robben Island where he died in December 1819 trying to swim to freedom. His followers did not believe that he was dead and were still waiting for his return. Malangana, of course, had no way of knowing if he was waiting for something that would not happen.

'*Umkhondo* tells me I am on the right track,' Malangana told the blind man.

'What if *umkhondo* merely tells you she has been here but is not giving you a guarantee she will be back? Yes, we do return to places we've been, but not always.'

'What else can I do?' asked Malangana. He was helpless.

'I don't know. But waiting is not doing anything. As a diviner myself, I would go and see other diviners to smell her out for me. Obviously she is no longer a diviner. At least when I saw her she was not. She was only an acolyte when we worked together. Maybe she never became a diviner at all. You may be lucky and find that some of the diviners who worked with her are still alive and are still diviners. They may still remember her and may still have something that may help them smell her out. This may or may not succeed but it's worth trying.'

He grabbed the blind man and kissed him all over the face and head. People thought he was mad. So did the blind man. He screamed that Malangana should leave him alone. Malangana immediately grabbed his crutches and left

IbandlalikaNtu.

That is why he is in Qumbu today. Sunduza was his biggest hope. He was the only white man he knew in Government. White people keep names of everybody in their books these days so that they can chase them for taxes. They know who is dead and who is alive. Sunduza would have helped him locate those diviners who nursed the Queen of amaMpondomise when Mthwakazi was an acolyte just before Hope was killed. Sunduza's books would know those who are still alive and what their names are.

Now he will have to do it the hard way. Walk to Sulenkama, try to find the old inhabitants and ask questions. It will not be easy. He has been there before, the time he found his family fields being hoed by strangers. People have been dispersed, their homes taken over by strangers. People don't want to talk about the past.

As Malangana hobbles back to Sulenkama he remembers the walk he took on this very path with Mthwakazi more than twenty years before—he, robust and youthful, resplendent in a purple satin gown, and she petite in an overly voluminous red-and-white silk dress, the bulk of which she had to carry over her shoulders in order to manage to walk.

He remembers the laughter. It was the only time they ever spent together. Besides the time they did adult things in the bushes by the river. Which he was embarrassed about. Which she was not. This was the only time, and it lasted for eighteen miles, and it was full of laughter. And of stories.

She told the story of the sun: that the sun was invented by her people, even though his people have named him Malangana, Little Suns, as if there were many suns when in reality there was only one—the one that wouldn't have been there if it were not for her /Xam branch of people.

Then she told the story in a singsong manner: 'Two women of the first race; one an old woman without children of her own; one a young woman, the mother of sons; two women of the first race ask boys to creep up on an old man who was hiding the sun under his armpit, hoarding its light all to himself.

'"Do not laugh while you do it," the old woman warned them. "Do not laugh."

'The boys crept up on the old man while he slept and held him by the leg. And tickled the soles of his feet. He couldn't resist laughing, and while he laughed and laughed, they kept their own laughter in their mouths, for they had been warned not to laugh. They spun him around and tossed him into the sky, where he remained spinning around and around and around with the sun forever peeking out of his armpit. The first people all sat outside awaiting the first dawn. The day broke, the sun shone, the world was covered in warmth. Everybody congratulated the boys for banishing the darkness. Only then could the laughter burst out of their mouths.'

He stands and laughs and dances in his shaky manner as he remembers her 'try and better that one' little dance after telling that part of the story. It is as vivid in his mind as if it was only an hour ago.

Mthwakazi continued her story: 'But that's not the end of it. Not everyone was happy. The sun found that she was not alone in the sky. The moon was there and was jealous that someone was trespassing on her territory. She attacked the sun, but the sun fought back. The sun cut the moon with a knife, leaving only the moon's backbone for the sake of her children. Every time the moon grows the sun cuts her with a knife again.'

And then Mthwakazi giggled and tried to cut Malangana with an imaginary knife; Malangana jumped out of the way causing Mthwakazi to trip on her dress. She rolled on the ground which he found utterly hilarious. He let her roll down a slope for a while before running after her. She was stopped by a boulder and he was worried that she could be hurt. But she was tough and boasted that she was not moulded from the soft Mpondomise clay.

Malangana takes this road very slowly. He has no choice in his condition. But the past keeps him company. He savours the memory for that is all he has for now, until he finds Mthwakazi. His hope has been reignited. It had ebbed in the two months at Tsolo. Thanks to the blind former diviner the *umkhondo* on this road is stronger and fresher as he relives the stories of that walk.

People meet him on the road and look at him curiously. He does not seem to see them. He is too self-absorbed. Some think he is mad for occasionally he talks to himself. He responds quickly and absent-mindedly to those who care to greet him, for they have interrupted something compelling into which his mind has been transported.

When it was his turn to tell a story he remembers that he was still proud of the flames they had just left behind in Qumbu. Mhlontlo had shown his mettle. Many people, including Malangana himself, had forgotten just how much of a hero he had been in the past. As a king he had become mild and accommodating of the white man. So when he became resolute and led the war so bravely they said: '*Ewe, nguye kanye uMhlontlo esimaziyo esakhula ke lo.*' *Yes, this is the Mhlontlo we remember as a youth!*

Malangana remembers how he told Mthwakazi Mhlontlo's story of heroism when he was still an *umkhwetha*, a pupil in an initiation and circumcision school. It was during the rule of the regent Mbali after the death of Mhlontlo's father Matiwane. Mbali was reputed to be a weak ruler and during his time amaMpondomise were always in danger of being conquered by other nations. His rule was reminiscent of Mhlontlo's grandfather, Myeki, who was remembered for being weak and cowardly.

The story is always told of how the land of amaMpondomise was invaded by amaBhaca when Mhlontlo was in the school of the mountain being initiated into manhood. He was actually going through the circumcision ritual when amaBhaca soldiers attacked the initiates at the school and killed some. amaBhaca were led by Makhawula, the son of Ncayaphi—the very Ncayaphi whose wife, MamJuxu, had been given refuge by the regent Mbali in the land of amaMpondomise and granted the whole of what is Mount Frere District today for her and her people to settle after Ncayaphi was killed by Faku of amaMpondo. Now his son had turned against the hand that fed him and his mother and was attacking his erstwhile benefactors at the moment of their weakness.

Malangana remembers how Mthwakazi's eyes were all agog at this saga. He also remembers how impressed he was with her because most amaMpondomise girls of her age in those days were not interested in stories of war and statecraft.

He recalls how he acted out some of these events, which prolonged their walk to Sulenkama. Sometimes Mthwakazi became a prop of war to her shrieking pleasure or dismay depending on whether victory or defeat was the outcome.

The amaBhaca had reinforcements from many other smaller wandering groups including stray Basotho clans under Serunyana and Lipina. When they besieged the land of amaMpondomise the regent Mbali said, 'We cannot fight such a formidable force. Let us surrender. Let us take out all our cattle and parade them in the open so that they can capture them. Then they will leave us alone and not kill us.'

But Mhlontlo would have none of that. He and his fellow *abakhwetha* rallied the men to fight against amaBhaca. Mbali thought he was mad. He ordered that he be tied up with rope and that the cattle should be released at once. But Mhlontlo's fellow initiates untied him. Using smoke and forest fires in a strategic manner Mhlontlo led amaMpondomise in a number of battles in Qumbu and Makhawula's forces were decimated. 'Kill them all,' he said. 'Do not come back here until they are all dead.'

'Mhlontlo said that?' Malangana remembers Mthwakazi asking incredulously.

'Yes,' he remembers answering. 'He was merciless in those days. Not like today when he says we should let the white people go free. He was only a boy, an initiate, and yet he saved his people and their cattle. But, you know, even then when Makhawula conceded defeat and submitted himself to him Mhlontlo stopped the slaughter and accepted him as a vassal chief.'

After that war Mhlontlo returned to the initiation school to complete the ritual and came out as king. People honoured him as a hero king who was not afraid of war, unlike his grandfather, Myeki, who allowed amaZulu to devastate amaMpondomise because of his weakness.

It is dusk when he arrives on the outskirts of Sulenkama. He is exhausted from reliving the stories and the walk of the past and also from the walk of the present.

From the hill where Hamilton Hope had camped during the two-day stand-off Malangana can see Sulenkama. The smoke billows from the evening fires. Vaguely he can see trees in the vicinity of what used to be his house. A single tear drops from his eye, like the one that dropped on that day when he thought of Gcazimbane.

MONDAY MAY 2, 1881

It was the month of Canopus; the brightest of all the stars of the southern skies. The amaMpondomise people called it Canzibe. The month was named EyeCanzibe after the star. It was the month of harvest, and therefore of brewing and of feasting. It was the month of plenty in most years, save for those cruel years of drought and famine. This was not one of those years though. For most people this was a good year.

Not for Mhlontlo. It had nothing to do with the capriciousness of the weather. He was missing Gcazimbane. He sat alone on a fallen trunk in a clearing deep in a forest in the Ntabankulu District in the land of amaMpondo. He wept. And broke into a song:

uGcazimbane
uZwe lezilingane
Ndingumntu nje
Intwehlal'ihlal'ifuduke
Ndingumntu nje
Intwemxhel'unge njenganstimbi
Ndakubonga ndihlel'iphi na
Gcazimbane

Zwe lezilingane

Gcazimbane/Land of equals/As an ordinary human being/ I'll have occasion to migrate/I am only human/I am not made of iron/From whose land will I sing your praises/Gcazimbane/ Land of equals?

And then he wept again. He was all alone. It was safe not only to weep but to wail. He wailed for a long time, and then the wail became a whimper, a snivel and a sniffle. He felt much better after that.

His eyelids were heavy even though it was early morning. He and his men had walked the whole night without taking a rest. He lay on the dew-covered ground and placed his head on a mossy tree trunk. He slept. Not quite. He had to sleep like the proverbial hare, with one eye open. If the dogs of amaBhaca or of amaHlubi or amaMpondo sniffed him out he should be able to escape. Many nations of the world were after him.

He could not leave that spot until his men returned from a hunt. And they'd better not find him bawling like a baby.

For a few hours he would be safe here, he thought. Even if the CMR and their allies were coming in this direction they would be a day away. He had a good headstart.

Yesterday he attended their meeting in disguise in the village of Chief Mqhikela more than a day's journey away. His men tried to stop him for fear that he would be recognised and arrested.

'You are playing with your life and ours going to a white man's meeting even while they are looking for you,'

Malangana had said.

But his king was stubborn as usual. He wore a knitted woollen cap and covered himself tightly with an old blanket. He took his spear and went to the *imbhizo*, of which the specific agenda was the hunt for Mhlontlo, at the chief's *inkundla*. He joined the rest of the community members and listened to the Red Coats address them through an interpreter.

'The white man says Mhlontlo is here, hiding in the land of amaMpondo,' the interpreter was saying. 'So you, *Inkosi* Mqhikela, should open up every part of your jurisdiction so that the Government can search for him.'

Mqhikela said, 'Oh, no, Mhlontlo is not here. He can't come here. He knows that amaMpondo are the allies of Government. I can't let the Red Coats search all over my villages because they will disturb our children.'

Mhlontlo knew that Government was just following protocol asking the chief's permission to search his villages so as not to alienate an ally. At the end of the day Government would do exactly what Government came to do.

'We must search for him ourselves because if he is here there is nothing you yourself can do,' said the officer. 'You can't arrest him.'

Mhlontlo stepped forward and, pretending to be one of Chief Mqhikela's subjects, addressed the chief.

'Allow the white men to search, my Nkosi, because if you don't they will continue to bother you. Let them see for themselves that you are a man of your word.'

The chief considered this for a moment and consulted

two of his councillors sitting next to him. He told the Red Coats to go ahead and search for Mhlontlo.

That gave Mhlontlo and his men a headstart. It would take the whole day for the Red Coats to search Mqhikela's entire jurisdiction, by which time he and his men would have made it to a new hiding place.

Now, though his body was exhausted, his spirit refused to rest. The thought of Gcazimbane nagged him. He must be dead by now. No doubt, he must be dead. Once more tears rolled down his face on to the mossy trunk.

His ears were very sharp, particularly the one on the trunk lying on the ground. He heard footsteps at a distance and determined they were of men and not animals. Two men, to be exact. That was how skilful he had become in the art of survival as a fugitive in the forests, mountains and caves since losing the war.

He jumped to his feet, his spear at the ready, just in case these were not his men returning. He took cover behind a tree and waited. After a while Malangana and Feyiya approached, each carrying on his shoulder half a carcass of a sable bull, its majestic horns dragging on the ground behind Malangana.

Feyiya was another from a junior House of Matiwane, although much older than Malangana in years. His great affinity for Malangana on this road as escapees was because they were both lovelorn. Their hearts were in Sulenkama where their loved ones were waiting: Malangana's by the river to take a walk with him to the top of the mountain; Feyiya's at his homestead where she had just given birth to their first child, named Charles after Mhlontlo's heir to the throne, on October 31, 1880, when the war started in earnest and the men had to leave and fight. As lovelorn men they could share sentiments that other men thought were foolish and womanish and soft and maudlin and not worthy of soldiers hardened by war and fleeing for their lives.

But softness came in other ways too, as Feyiya could immediately see on Mhlontlo's face when he stepped on to the path to meet them.

'Ah, you've been crying again,' said Feyiya. 'Please stop that.'

'Gcazimbane was a very special horse,' said Mhlontlo in a hoarse voice.

As Malangana was hanging the sable bull in a tree and cutting some of the meat into pieces for roasting he offered to go and search for Gcazimbane. He did not believe the horse was dead. He had survived two months being ridden by Mhlontlo in the heat of many battles and then more weeks of hide-and-seek in all kinds of terrain. He was bound to survive this latest capture as well.

He was captured only a few days ago; which was why Malangana believed he could still be retrieved. Fortunately Gcazimbane was not in his hands when he was captured, but in Mhlontlo's; otherwise he would never have heard the end of it.

It had been evening when Mhlontlo and a bodyguard took what they thought would be a short horse ride from their hideout just to get a little bit of fresh air in the valley. They had not been aware that some amaBhaca men had been spying on the camp with the view of capturing Mhlontlo for the bounty that Government had placed on his head. Two men approached them and shouted 'Sinika!'. Mhlontlo and his bodyguard relaxed, for that was the password of the amaMpondomise military intelligence. They responded '*Sinika!*' and stopped to chat to the men who they thought would have news of the new positions of the enemy. The amaBhaca men pounced on them and stabbed the body-guard to death. Mhlontlo rolled on the ground with the first Bhaca man and stabbed him repeatedly with his assegai. When he sprang to his feet to face the second Bhaca man, the latter had already mounted Gcazimbane and was riding away on him.

Mhlontlo and his men had to vacate that camp immedi-ately because they knew that within minutes the Red Coats and their amaBhaca allies would be on to them. It had been like that these few months since the decisive defeat at the Battle of Tsita Gorge. Playing the hide-and-seek game with the enemy. And it would be like that until they reached Lesotho where King Letsie had sent a response through their messenger that they were welcome to take refuge in his country.

The three men sat at the fire and ate the meat. They were silent and listened only to the rhythm of their munching teeth. The sable was an old bull and therefore the meat was rather tough. But of course their teeth were made for just that kind of meat. In any event later in the evening when the other elders arrived they would roast the liver and the kidneys and the lungs, the softer and gentler kinds of meats, before they proceeded on their long journey to Lesotho.

Mthwakazi filled almost every space of silence. The rest was filled by the war that took him away from her. Malangana's chest filled with anger at the thought of how the war was lost. It had been going well and every day he had hoped it was the end and he would go back and resume his interrupted walk to the mountain with his Mthwakazi. In his mind the walk had already started. It had started when they walked from the flames in their beautiful clothes: her floral silk frock and his purple gown. The eighteen-mile walk where they savoured each other as a precursor to the savouring that would happen on the journey to the mountain and then to the stars, and on the longer journey to the rest of life until each reached the setting of the sun. The detour to Sulenkama to collect the sacred drum was a small interruption. Mthwakazi retrieved the drum and went to wait by the river. But before he could leave for the river a bigger interruption happened. The war generals took him. They gave him arms. The war had started. The CMR was in Qumbu already. He had to go to war. No time to go to the river. No time to warn Mthwakazi. Every man to war. She waited and the war raged.

By October 29th Mhlontlo's forces had routed the British forces out of Qumbu and Mditshwa's forces had taken over Tsolo without any resistance. In Qumbu Government offices and the jail were set on fire. In Tsolo members of the white community locked themselves in the jail where they thought they would be safe and of course no one could set it on fire with all the people inside.

The CMR was indeed thinly spread in many parts of the Colony as there were what the Government characterised as 'rebellions', which were in fact a series of battles lasting at least two wars. The incitement from Lesotho had also reached Basotho clans in Herschel, Barkly East and Griqualand

East—the very fire that Hamilton Hope was trying to douse was spreading. While the Imperial troops were occupied with fighting the Gun War inside Lesotho they found it impossible to contain the Basotho clans south of the Drakensberg. These Basotho clans, on the other hand, took vengeance on those nations that were loyal to the British and were fighting in alliance with colonial forces, the amaHlubi and amaBhaca, and drove them further south.

For the rest of November Mhlontlo and Mditshwa had a free hand, winning every battle. Malangana was always by Mhlontlo's side and watched in admiration how he commanded his forces. For the first time he saw how strict and how much of a disciplinarian he was. His word was law and no one dared disobey. He was not the Mhlontlo who, according to him and his mates back home, was pliable in the hands of Hamilton Hope. He led his section of the army at various theatres: at Qunu, and Mahlungulu, at Caba and at Qanqu—territories that covered a great part of the Colony. And in all these places he was victorious. Mditshwa also led his section of the army at various theatres. Sometimes he and Mhlontlo disagreed on strategy and quarrelled. Once they quarrelled so violently they almost came to blows. But after that they went forward to fight and returned victorious.

After a series of these victories Malangana slipped away and went to look for Mthwakazi. He stole a horse in a village and rode for two days to his home. It was strange to walk in Sulenkama and find that it was a village of women and children and young shepherds and very old men who could no longer lift a spear and a shield. Every man was out fighting what had now been dubbed the War of Hope. He walked around the village asking if anyone had seen Mthwakazi. No one had seen her for months, not since the war started. He even walked to the confluence of the two rivers and sat there for many hours and dipped his feet in the water and looked at the hills that grew into mountains at night. And then he rode his horse back to war.

His comrades believed he had been captured by the enemy. To save himself from Mhlontlo's wrath he confirmed that indeed he had been in the hands of amaBhaca but was able to escape with one of their horses. He named the horse Xokindini, which meant 'You Liar'.

Malangana returned when preparations were being made to invade Kohlombeni, as Tsita Gorge was known. It was at this stage that Mhlontlo learned that amaMpondo had decided to throw in their lot with the British. He had banked on their alliance.

'We, the children of Sibiside, though we both come from the loins of Njanya, how can they turn against us and stand with those whose ears reflect the rays of the sun?' asked Mhlontlo.

'We have gone thus far without them,' said Gxumisa. 'We shall defeat the white man without them.'

'We shall defeat them and their white masters,' said Mahlangeni. He was still wearing Hamilton Hope's coat. He never took it off. Perhaps he even slept in it.

Malangana stood in awe of these generals. He knew that he would never be one of them. None of them thought of anything but war strategies and tactics. One could see that they relished what they were doing. It was like a game, even though people were falling and dying. Once in a while a horse would fall and a man would weep for it. Yet he, Malangana, was thinking of nothing but his desire for a woman. Even as he fought each battle his ferocity was fuelled by his yearning for her. She made him slay the enemy with so much vengeance for it was the enemy that took him away from her. Each morning he woke up hoping to hear Mhlontlo's voice announce: 'The war is over, let's all go home.'

Yet Tsita Gorge was the turning point. The West Pondoland Chief Nqwiliso sent amaMpondo forces to Chief Magistrate Elliot for the relief of the Tsomo magistracy. The amaHlubi and amaBhaca who were running away from the Basotho also joined the English, as did the *amakhumsha* of amaMfengu who had always been with the English anyway. What broke Mhlontlo most was the discovery that even King Ngangelizwe of the abaThembu had come out in support of the Imperial Forces against amaMpondomise.

Mhlontlo was all alone with all the peoples of British Kaffraria against him. He and his fellow Mpondomise King Mditshwa of Tsolo. By early December the Imperial Forces and their allies were already gaining the upper hand in the land of abaThembu and in Griqualand East. At the Battle of Tsita Gorge the storm of amaHlubi and amaBhaca and abaThembu and amaMfengu and a few Red Coats was too powerful. Mhlontlo's forces suffered a decisive defeat. More than three hundred amaMpondomise soldiers were killed.

One of the casualties was Gxumisa.

It was this particular death that brought Mhlontlo to his knees. He ordered his forces to retreat.

'Mampondomise, Government has defeated us,' he said. 'Those of us who can lose themselves in the mountains let them do so, and those of us who can lose themselves in the waters let them do so.'

'How do we retreat? We are being killed in every direction,' some men demanded. 'And if we do manage to escape at all, where do we go?'

Mhlontlo suggested the mountains of Lesotho, to exile.

Mditshwa said it was against the ethos and values of amaMpondomise to be a Mfengu, meaning a refugee. He would rather surrender. If they killed him, so be it; he would rather die than be a fugitive.

'I said I shall not be taken alive,' said Mhlontlo. 'Those of you who want to follow me to exile will do so.'

Mahlangeni said he would go to no exile, nor would he surrender. He was a Mpondomise man and would die fighting. He rode his horse back into the thick of the battle.

Mditshwa sent his son with a white flag to the enemy camp to say he was surrendering, while Mhlontlo and his followers, among them Malangana, Ndukumfa, Feyiya, Gatyeni, Hamza, Cesane and Sititi, his relatives from the House of Matiwane, escaped into the forest with a number of soldiers.

The eighteenth of December 1880 was the date they were to remember, since those whose sons and daughters became literate wrote it down for posterity.

Even as they were escaping from camp to camp in the forests and mountains, working their way towards Lesotho, they heard that Mditshwa had been put in chains and sent to Robben Island to serve a three-year sentence for sedition.

But their fighting spirit was not yet dead. In January Mhlontlo and a small band of his followers attacked

Commandant Usher at Fort Usher. They were unable to take the fort and lost more men.

Malangana should have listened to the sage Cesane. Don't look back so soon, he said. Look forward. Looking back flooded his mind with bitterness which in turn made the meat taste bitter.

'Bile must have spilled on this meat,' he said throwing the piece to the ground and stepping on it. 'I am not eating any more.'

'It is your own bile; it is boiling. Calm down, *mfondini*,' said Mhlontlo.

'It was not easy to kill this sable bull. You will not waste it,' said Feyiya.

'I did all the chasing, old man,' said Malangana. 'Anyway there is enough meat for most of those who are coming. They are taking their time. They should be here by now. I thought we would find them here already.'

He walked away, kicking at everything in front of him to the detriment of his bare feet. The two men didn't even look at him but put more meat on the fire.

'It is the longing that is killing him,' said Feyiya.

'For the Bushman girl?' said Mhlontlo, chuckling.

'You know about her?'

'I have eyes, *mninawe*,' said Mhlontlo, addressing him as *younger-brother*. 'I have ears too. And of course Gxumisa was encouraging him. It would not have been a catastrophe. We are descendants of a Mthwakazi. Not only was our ancestor Cirha from Iqadi House, his mother was a Mthwakazi. Who are we to stop one of us from marrying a Bushman girl?'

'Perhaps you should have told him that,' said Feyiya.

'He didn't ask me,' said Mhlontlo.

'His heart is breaking.'

'We all have our longings.'

Malangana came running back looking as excited as if he had been struck by a new idea. The two men looked at him expectantly. It was not a new idea after all. He was leaving immediately to look for Gcazimbane. Mhlontlo tried to stop him: it might take days to find Gcazimbane, if at all he did so, and by that time the party would have left that hideout. Before sunset today the rest of the refugees would arrive: Cesane, Ndukumfa, Gatyeni, Sititi, Hamza, and the soldiers who were protecting them and the animals they were driving.

'As soon as they get here we'll move on,' said Mhlontlo.

'Yes, move on,' said Malangana. 'I will follow. I will find you on the way. I am faster. Perhaps even before you cross the border I will be there. It will not be difficult to trace you.'

'Why are you doing this?' asked Mhlontlo.

'You think your longing is yours alone?' asked Malangana. 'Anyway, we can't afford your tears any longer. The tears of the King of amaMpondomise are very expensive.'

Feyiya laughed and said, 'It is for his selfish reasons. He misses Gcazimbane too. His heart has two holes. One for Mthwakazi and the other for Gcazimbane.'

This rather infuriated Mhlontlo.

'Gcazimbane is mine,' he said. 'He's only a groom. His horse is Xokindini.'

'Look after Xokindini when he arrives,' said Malangana, and left them arguing about the existence or not of his sanity. They did not understand why he would travel all those distances by foot, looking for a horse without any idea where it might be, while he had his own horse grazing right there in the forest.

Later that afternoon after walking for a few hours Malangana saw a few cattle, horses and donkeys grazing on the outskirts of a village. Their herdboys were nowhere to be seen, perhaps they were shaping clay cattle on the banks of a stream or hunting for rodents between harvested fields. He mounted one of the horses and, without reins, he galloped away bareback.

TUESDAY MARCH 29, 1904

They don't know his name. They call him *madala*, *khehla* or *xhego*, all of which mean 'old man', which suits him fine. Only three months ago when he had just arrived from his Lesotho exile he hated to be called that. He has since learned to live with it and take its benefits with grace—even those that come with superciliousness.

They are a well-meaning lot, these young men, and they have given him a place to sleep at their camp. During the day they go to work planting trees for Government on the escarpment to stop the dongas and to create a forest. Now that the natives have finally been pacified and the Boers have been defeated and subdued in the second and hopefully final Anglo-Boer War, the British Kaffraria administration can focus on taming the landscape and making it more civilised by planting pine, gum, and poplar trees imported from the mother country.

Malangana walks in the village looking for familiar faces. Occasionally he comes across them but they don't recognise him. Most of them are people who were much younger before the war, who are now the family men of Sulenkama. They mix with a lot of strangers from other nations who were rewarded with tracts of Mpondomise lands for their loyalty to the English. amaMpondomise men his age either died fighting or were dispersed as refugees in other people's countries. They are the ones who would ultimately have recognised him despite all the changes that have happened to his now convoluted constitution. The people he meets on the village pathways don't associate him with anyone who was born and grew up there. Many of the original families, even those who did not become refugees, scattered after the war. Among those that still remain, those who had known of Malangana, heard that he died in the war. Various narratives of war confuse Malangana with Mahlangeni and merge them into one. The only Malangana that people know for sure is the original Malangana, the patriarch of abaMbo who was also known as Sibiside from whom many nations were born. But that was more than twenty-five generations ago.

There is now a general dealer's store at Sulenkama and people don't have to go all the way to Qumbu to sell their hides and skins and buy sugar and tea. The habit of drinking tea has spread even among people who are not *amakhumsha*.

Malangana spends a lot of time at the general dealer's store and every time he sees someone wearing *intsimbi-ezimhlohle*, the diviner's white beads, on the wrists and on the ankles he enquires about the nature of divination they are engaged in and if they are open to consultation. When he hears that they have practised in Sulenkama for less than twenty years, or they are themselves younger than that age or come from other nations or regions, then he apologises and says they are not what his ancestors are looking for—or they are just not appropriate for his needs.

He has been doing this for the past few days, so he is not surprised when a diviner in full regalia approaches him, greets him politely and sits down next to him on the cement stoep of the store and says: *Ndingabuza tata? May I ask a question, sir?* He nods, yes.

'You are the old man who's looking for an old local diviner?'

'Yes, but you're too young to be the kind of healer I am looking for.'

'We have *intlombe* tonight. There will be all kinds of healers and diviners. You will get the healer you want. You'll be healed.'

This is very exciting for Malangana. *Intlombe* is a spiritual gathering of traditional healers and diviners where they sing, dance and perform healing and shamanistic rituals. The diviner gives him directions and he promises he will definitely be there.

In the afternoon he returns to the camp of the tree planters because they always insist every morning: 'Come back, *xhego*, come back! Don't be swallowed by the nice times of Sulenkama. We hear the love potions of the women are very strong there.' They just like his company and the stories he tells, though they think he invents them. They don't believe a decrepit old man like this can have had all those experiences. Perhaps they can't imagine him being anything but what he is now.

He fell in with the company of these young men on the very night he arrived at Sulenkama. As he descended the hill into the village and caught the first whiff of smoke he felt his lungs opening. And then all of a sudden without any warning at all the Gcazimbane in him came out in a long, full-bodied neigh. Four boys appeared from the bushes and ran towards him and stood in front of him open-mouthed. The neighing did not stop. It had never done this before. It had never gone on so long. The boys were getting scared. Was this a man or a ghost? Then all of a sudden it stopped.

'How did you do that?' one boy asked.

'I ate a horse once,' said Malangana. 'My favourite horse. Now that I am back at its home, in the land of its fathers, it was galloping out. It's gone now. It will never haunt me again.'

That must be it. This explanation was just rolling out of his mouth—he had not thought about it. But it made sense. That was why he was feeling light, as if some burden had just been lifted. To the boys it was nonsense. But it was funny. They laughed and said variously: 'The others must hear this. Come and join us at our camp. We've never heard anyone neigh like a horse before, actually even better and louder than the strongest horse. Come on, come on, we have room enough.'

He followed them and found that the camp was a yard of corrugated-iron structures where young Government workers recruited from all over the eastern Colony stayed to plant trees in earmarked areas. These camps, they told him, were temporary. When they finished planting the gum trees at Sulenkama they were going to move to some place else and set up camp and plant another forest of trees imported from England.

When Malangana returns from the general dealer's store

his four friends are already back from work. They are sitting on wooden boxes outside their corrugated-iron shack boiling water in a kettle on a *drie-voet* stand on an open fire. They are eating wheat bread with tea.

'Your horse is not back yet?' asks one of the young men. 'I told you it's gone,' says Malangana.

'Now people think we're liars when we say you know how to neigh like a horse,' says another.

They give him a mug of tea and a chunk of bread.

'You people can even afford *umkhupha*,' says Malangana. 'You eat like white people.'

They are more interested in his stories.

'Tell us about this horse that you say you ate.'

'I don't believe this eating part,' says another young man. 'How does one eat a horse?'

'My people do eat it,' says one who is a Mosotho from Herschel District. 'We learned it from the French missionaries who were the first to go to Lesotho.'

'I am not interested in the eating of the horse,' says the original questioner. 'I want to know how this *khehla* rescued the horse. He told us how the horse of his king was captured and he was going to tell us today how he rescued it.'

Malangana clears his throat; the young men chuckle in expectation of a good yarn. He can see that some of them are taking his story with a pinch of salt but he tells it nonetheless. Perhaps they think it is *intsomi*, a folk tale.

After stealing a horse from a village he rode to the nearest town, Lusikisiki, where he spent a few days with amaMpondo military people. He was pretending he was an employee of a white man who traded in horses. His master was looking for cheap impounded horses that he could buy and resell in the Boer republics of the Orange Free State and the Transvaal.

One day he was nearly caught out when someone who knew the differences between the languages of the various peoples of the Colony suspected he was a Mpondomise spy just from the words he used. He was caught out when he said he wanted to buy *ihatjhi*, which was what amaMpondomise called a horse. The rest of the black peoples of the region called a horse *ihashe*. He had to find a very fast exit from that tavern before any attention could be drawn to the possibility of his being from the enemy camp.

Malangana tells the young men that his investigations did pay off. He found Gcazimbane in Kokstad in an English army stall. The horse raised its tail high and snickered the moment it saw him. When he got into the stall and brushed its mane it nuzzled and blew. It cooperated and allowed itself to be stolen. He didn't leave Gcazimbane's stall empty, though. He left in it the nag he had stolen from the village.

He doesn't tell the young men that after finding Gcazimbane he battled with his conscience for a long time. He was tempted to ride southwards back to the land of amaMpondomise to look for Mthwakazi. He actually rode for some miles in the Maclear direction. Then he remembered the war and the devastation they had left behind. He decided he would be betraying Mhlontlo. He turned back and rode towards Maluti. He would make another plan about Mthwakazi.

The young men do not know anything about his search for Mthwakazi.

He takes up the story from where he catches up with

Mhlontlo and some of his party in Herschel and they cross the Lesotho border at Telle River. Mhlontlo was overjoyed to be reunited with Gcazimbane.

Malangana discovered that most of Mhlontlo's party which took the Matatiele route had a confrontation with a small Boer force at the border of Qacha's Nek. They were able to overpower it and crossed into Lesotho safely without any casualties.

'Now let me tell you, my friend, there is no truth in your story,' says one of the young men who might be a Mpondomise from his claim of a superior knowledge of this history. 'You should have given the horse in your story a different name, not Gcazimbane.'

The other young men laugh and encourage their mate: 'Yes, tell him, my friend. From now on, *madala*, we must call you *ihatjhi*.'

He roars with laughter. His peers think this is brilliant and join him.

'Our elders tell us that a man called Mahlangeni, the killer of Hope and a war hero during those olden days you're talking about, was shot in the back by a white man called Larry in the dust of that War of Hope. They say he was riding on... Gcazimbane. He fell with Gcazimbane and they died together right there.'

'*Uyayibona ke lonto?*' says another young man, enjoying the exposure of an old man's fibs. *You see that?* 'And yet you tell us innocent boys that you rescued Gcazimbane from the English and then ate him.'

'He even knew Mhlontlo! Did you hear that? This *xhego* was Mhlontlo's mate.'

Another round of laughter and applause. Malangana only smiles.

'Next time he will tell us he ate Hope,' another clown comes with the rejoinder.

Malangana does not take offence. He lets them have fun at his expense. It is not their fault he does not look like a war hero. They would not believe him if he told them he was in that war and that his friend Mahlangeni did not die on Gcazimbane. He was shot in the back all right, in the War of Hope, wearing Hope's coat and Hope's trousers, riding a horse, yes, but it was not Gcazimbane.

After the bread and tea Malangana tells his friends he has other engagements that night and leaves. They are worried that maybe they were too hard on him, ribbing him about his lies. He assures them that he took their jokes in the good spirit in which they were meant.

The *intlombe* is held in a big rondavel. A number of diviners are already dancing and their acolytes are beating the drums. He has been in the room for only a few minutes when he is struck by a vaguely familiar sound. One of the drums here has a sound he has heard before. He squints in the dimness of paraffin lamps and candles to examine each acolyte and then his or her drum. And there is the drum that he knows so well being beaten by one of the acolytes. Mthwakazi's drum. What is amazing about it is that it looks exactly as it did twenty years ago. He hobbles towards the dancing diviners and stands right in front of them. Some of them recognise the old man from the general dealer's store. The drummers are lined up behind the dancing diviners. Malangana holds his crutches under his armpits and half-raises his hands.

'*Camagu! Camagwini zinyanya zam!*' He is addressing the diviners in their language of the spirits. 'I am appealing to you. I want to talk to that drum. My spirits instruct me to talk to that drum. I need that drum.'

The diviners give permission to the acolyte to talk to him. She walks reluctantly to the side next to the small audience while the diviners resume their dance.

'Where did you get this drum?' asks Malangana.

'*Yho lo tata!* What do you want with this drum?' asks the acolyte.

'I know this drum. I am looking for the owner of this drum.'

For some reason the acolyte is becoming scared. 'What do you want with the owner of this drum?'

'Listen; take me to the owner of this drum. I will give you any money you want.' Malangana is trying hard not to sound desperate.

'Any money I want? Do you have money *wena*?' Obviously he does not look like someone who would have money. 'Do you want to buy this drum?'

'Yes, I will even buy it if you first take me to the owner. I will buy it for the price of a cow because my ancestors want it.'

'Two cows,' says the acolyte. 'But show me the money first.'

'Just wait, I'll be back.'

Malangana goes outside. He takes a walk. He is looking for a private spot. He walks to the kraal. The cattle are sleeping and chewing cud. He unbuttons his pants and drops them to his ankles. He visits his secret stash and with-draws a few banknotes. He dresses quickly and hobbles back to the *intlombe*. The acolyte has resumed her drumming. Malangana attracts her attention and surreptitiously shows her the money. Her eyes open so wide they threaten to pop out of their sockets—so much money!

She immediately says, 'I will give you the drum now for the price of two cows because I can see your spirits really want it for your healing.'

Malangana says, 'Actually, it is the owner of the drum I want even more than the drum itself. Give me the drum and take me to the owner for the price of two cows.'

The acolyte seems to have a problem.

'Take the drum without the owner for the price of one cow.'

'The drum without the owner is useless to me,' insists Malangana.

'*Yho lo tata!* Don't be difficult *torho*! I will tell you the truth; the owner of this drum does not know that I borrowed it without her permission for the *intlombe* tonight.'

And yet she wanted to sell it to him? What kind of a doctor is she going to be? But Malangana does not pose this question to her. He does not want to alienate her.

'Take me to the owner tomorrow. I will pay you secretly for it. We won't reveal that you stole her drum for the *intlombe*.'

She agrees. They will meet at the general dealer's store.

SATURDAY APRIL 5, 1890

Since it was something that happened only once a month, or if you were lucky twice, that the moon was completely round and so huge and so close to the earth as if you could touch it, and it made the world so bright as if it was daytime, the villagers felt it would be a crime to waste such a night. The girls were out in the village playground singing *lipina-tsa-mokopu*—the songs of the pumpkin—though it was out of season. It was all of five months before harvest time. Boys were sitting by the kraal pretending to be men, telling one another tall tales. Men were standing in groups under trees debating as to whether the diamond mine in Kimberley offered a better deal than the new gold mine in Johannesburg at the native recruiting office in Cutting Camp. Old men had invaded the silos for old dry corn and were roasting it on one side, and then battling to chew it before roasting the other side, as the women cooked food on outdoor hearths in three-legged cast iron pots.

Malangana sat on the adobe stoep of his grass thatched hut and watched the moon and listened to the dogs and the wild animals that he presumed were jackals barking at it. He laughed as some silly mongrels jumped at it with their tongues hanging out, hoping to lick it. His body began to rattle with laughter. He knew what was happening. Even when he walked it happened and he had long accepted it as his lot. And when he coughed it was worse.

He had stopped walking unless it was absolutely essential. In his early years in Lesotho he used to walk for miles each day. He was the man who linked the amaMpondomise refugees in the different parts of Lesotho where they had settled. Even after they had spread over the years and established homes in different parts of southern Lesotho they knew that Malangana could be relied upon to keep the links strong.

He used to ride Gcazimbane or Xokindini and visit Mhlontlo at Phiring near Phamong in the district of Mohale's Hoek where he was nursing his depression at the homestead the sons of Moshoeshoe had given him as a place of refuge. Or he would surreptitiously cross the Telle River at its most mountainous part to see his brother Feyiya who had established his homestead at eKra in an area that was no longer Lesotho but the Cape Colony. Indeed a number of the members of the House of Matiwane under the leadership of Cesane had recrossed the Telle River into the area of the Herschel District, part of the territory conquered from Lesotho and falling under the Cape Colony, and had established their homesteads on the mountains that used to be *Qhobosheaneea-Moorosi*—the Fort of Moorosi—where their vanquished ally, King Moorosi, had defended his Baphuthi people against the Boers, the British and the Basotho.

This branch of the House of Matiwane under Cesane on the border of Lesotho became known as *amaCesane oMda*, which meant the 'People of Cesane of the Border' (referring to the border of Lesotho and the Cape Colony) and their village was called Qoboshane after the original fort.

It was only after ten years or so of exile that Feyiya and the others gathered the courage to cross the Telle River and settle at Qoboshane. They believed that after so many years the Cape Colony Government had forgotten all about them. In any event they were never wanted men as individuals as there was never a list compiled of participants in the rebellion. The wanted people were the leaders Mhlontlo and Mditshwa, who were known by name, not the general amaMpondomise men who fought in the war and could get lost in the crowd. In a war every man was a soldier and Government could not arrest the whole adult male population of amaMpondomise. However, for Malangana things were different. He was very close to Mhlontlo. Not only was he his horse's groom, he was his interpreter and adviser. Even in the field of battle he fought next to him. He believed he was known to the white man. He would be a wanted man as an individual. He did not join those who settled at Qoboshane lest Government came knocking. He stayed with those who remained in Lesotho, and built himself a bachelor's hut in the village of Qomoqomong. That was why his visits to his brother Feyiya at eKra were made only under the cover of darkness.

When the moon was full like this and the dogs were howling and everybody was full of the joys of life his body always reminded him of its complaints against the world. The more the girls sang and the children laughed the more the aches attacked his joints and his muscles and even his bones right to the marrow.

Over the years he had watched his once strong and

muscular body shrivel and squirm. It was not the withering of age. In the early years of his exile in Lesotho he was quite active. So was Mhlontlo.

For instance, he rode Xokindini and Mhlontlo rode Gcazimbane and they visited Basotho chiefs to lobby them to make common cause with amaMpondomise. He went as far as Matsieng to the headquarters of the Paramount Chief of Basutoland, as the king of the Basotho people was now officially called by the colonial Government. Mhlontlo had thought since Basotho had not been defeated in their Gun War and the British were forced to negotiate for peace, instead of their initial plan of forcing an unconditional surrender, he would find their King Letsie still holding sway as in the old days. He thought the Basotho would still be the formidable force he had heard about from his friend Moorosi, for they used to give the latter sleepless nights. He was disappointed to find that Letsie would not make common cause with amaMpondomise.

The Basotho were now a subdued people and had sworn loyalty to the Crown. Letsie was quite happy to give 'Mamalo, the praise-name that he gave Mhlontlo, succour at Phiring near Phamong where his brother was principal chief, as long as he did not start any trouble against the English within the borders of Lesotho. They were going to give him and his followers fields to farm, and they could even marry wives if they were so inclined, and pay taxes.

'We know that the Red Coats are looking high and low for you,' said Letsie. 'They won't touch you while you are here under our protection as long as you keep the peace.'

That was the beginning of Mhlontlo's depression.

He confined himself to Phiring, comforting himself with sorghum beer and local women. Occasionally he rode Gcazimbane to visit his kin in the various parts of the Quthing and Mohale's Hoek District, or surreptitiously across the Telle River. But gradually these visits became fewer as his mood became darker.

Malangana, on the other hand, became very actively engaged in his new community. He learned from the sons of Moorosi how to make *mokhele*, the ostrich-feather gear for dressing shields that was fashionable with Basotho soldiers. They had learned the art of *mokhele*-making from their grandfather, the late Mokuoane, who was a famous hunter. The story was always told of how he befriended Barwa, as Basotho called the Bushmen, and bought ostrich feathers from them in exchange for dagga. He would then make mokhele, which were so highly prized those days that soldiers would pay for one with an ox. That's how Mokuoane became rich with many cattle.

In Malangana's day *mokhele* was no longer selling for an ox. But still he was accumulating a lot of wealth in the form of sheep and goats and actual pounds, shillings and pence. He rode Xokindini to many parts of southern Lesotho selling the headgear. Feyiya lent him his son Charles for a while to look after his sheep and goats. But all the time his kith and kin kept nagging him about getting married and having his own children. He was getting on in years, they said, for whom was he accumulating the wealth if he was not getting married and creating heirs?

Even the elder Ndukumfa lamented on his deathbed before he emitted his last breath, '*Wena*, Malangana, what do you think I am going to tell the ancestors when I meet them now that I am leaving without seeing what that penis of yours can do? *Okanye awunayo? Or don't you have it?*

Everybody laughed. And Ndukumfa died. It was just like him, leaving everyone with a smile.

They did not know that it was not for lack of trying that Malangana was not yet married. In his travels he met many beautiful maidens. Who did not know the beauty of the Baphuthi maidens? Malangana was not blind to this beauty. His heart was not made of stone. The maidens were not blind to his eligibility. In many instances he thought he had fallen in love. But something somewhere would happen, always on his side, which brought the relationship to a halt.

It would start with a dream. Actually a nightmare. The familiar sound that told him immediately that he was at the confluence of Sulenkama and Gqukunqa. The supple-bodied woman swimming in the fresh water. The birds and the butterflies and little silver and golden fishes jumping out of the water. And there would be himself sitting naked on the bank with his feet playing in the water and smiling at his stiff manhood, its one-eye staring at him. There would be the sun, but there would be stars also. It would be neither day nor night. There would be the mountain with stars on top of it rising like a series of stairs waiting to be climbed. He would be impatient for the mountain would be beckoning. But the girl, oh the girl, would like to take her time in the water.

The next day he would know that there was a woman waiting for him hundreds of miles away in the land of amaMpondomise. He would break the heart of a Mophuthi maiden.

There was a time when the elders of the House of Matiwane thought they had arranged a good marriage for him with a daughter of Doda, one of Moorosi's sons. Just when everyone thought he was going along with the idea that *uduli*—a marriage delegation—should be sent to Doda's family, Malangana announced he had changed his mind. He said his conscience would not allow him to marry a Mophuthi maiden because Baphuthi people were related to amaMpondomise. It would be incest.

'We all know that Baphuthi under the leadership of Langa branched off from amaSwati people during the great migrations,' said Malangana. 'And amaSwati are the children of Dlamini who was the son of our own forebear Sibiside.'

The elders of the House of Matiwane looked at him, stunned for a while, and then broke out laughing.

'If you don't want to marry Doda's daughter just say so, man; don't make stupid excuses,' said Mhlontlo. He was not amused that the rest of the elders had ridden all the way to Phiring, more than twenty miles for some of them, to settle Malangana's issues and he was playing games with them.

Cesane took his blanket and his stick and made to go, but at the door he stopped and said, 'It is true that Sibiside begot Njanya, Dlamini and Mkhize, and Dlamini founded the nation of amaSwati, while Njanya begot the twins Mpondo and Mpondomise who founded the nations of amaMpondo and amaMpondomise. But that was twenty generations ago. We marry amaMpondo women and it is not incest. You are just making an excuse, son of Matiwane.'

Cesane then shook his head and left. Since then

Malangana's kin stopped bothering him about marriage.

One day when Malangana returned to his hut from one of his business expeditions he found Gcazimbane grazing outside his house. He thought Mhlontlo had paid him a surprise visit, which really did surprise him because Mhlontlo never visited anyone. There was no Mhlontlo. Gcazimbane had come by himself all the way from Phiring, a distance of about twenty miles. He returned the horse two days later, against his better judgement. He could see that Gcazimbane was neglected. Mhlontlo was not feeding him well or grooming him or even riding him. The horse was running loose while Mhlontlo just sat there repeating to anyone who would care to listen over and over again that his quarrel was with Hamilton Hope and not with Government.

'I am taking this horse with me,' said Malangana. 'You don't deserve Gcazimbane. He looked after you in the war but you don't look after him.'

'Take him,' said Mhlontlo. 'But have you ever asked yourself why all those nations became loyal to Government and we stood all alone? Have you?'

Malangana was impatient with this talk and wanted to go back to Qomoqomong. He had to manage two horses for all that distance.

'That's all over and done with,' he said.

'We can understand about amaMfengu,' said Mhlontlo urgently. 'They were refugees. Everyone despised them. All the black nations looked down upon them. So they had to place their lot with the white man. They benefited from his crumbs and became *amakhumsha* from his education. Now they have inherited our land. I am told they are our masters even in the land of amaMpondomise. What about these other nations—the great and established kingdoms? Why did they become loyal to Government? Why did amaMpondo and abaThembu? How did the white man tame even the descendants of the great King Xhosa, the formidable amaGcaleka who are my in-laws and amaRharhabe?'

Malangana did not answer. Instead he went outside where Gcazimbane was already snickering at the door with his tail held high. 'Mhlontlo forgets that we are also amaMfengu now because we are refugees,' Malangana said to Gcazimbane as he saddled him. He mounted his favourite horse which now would be in his possession all the time, pulled Xokindini with his reins and rode back to Qomoqomong.

He gave Xokindini as a gift to young Charles who took the horse back with him to eKra when his father finally demanded he should return home to look after his own animals and start school like his uncle and namesake who went to Shawbury in the land of amaMpondomise.

'*Hela Malakane, Hela Malakane!*' the girls who were singing *lipina-tsa-mokopu* changed their tune when they passed Malangana's house and saw him sitting on the stoep. They were now bored with the big round moon and were going to their various homes to perform whatever chores were still undone and then to sleep. But before that they were giving Malangana a taste of their mischief.

It was the habit of the village children to make fun of the twisted man. It got worse when they discovered he neighed like a horse when he got agitated.

'*Malakane nnka Malakane, Malakane khali khali*

Malakane! At this the girls lifted their *thethana* grass and beaded skirts and exposed their bare bottoms. *Malakane* was the Sesotho corruption of his name, and they were inviting him to take what his heart desired.

He just sat there with a distant look in his eyes. He had mastered the art of ignoring all those who teased and insulted him. They moved on with disappointed giggles because they couldn't provoke one of his famous neighs. He was proud that he had not neighed. He had no control over the neighs. They just came unexpectedly.

Just as he thought he had got away with it one long and melancholic neigh came as if from the hollow of his body. The girls who were now few in number, for most of them had gradually branched off to their homes, heard it, stood and listened, and then clapped their hands and cheered.

Malangana sighed and cursed his lot.

His lot had started gradually with a sore heart and the longing for Mthwakazi. The *mokhele* also became less fashionable as fewer military people were buying them. In any event he had become less enthusiastic about travelling long distances. His wealth in the form of animals was gradually becoming depleted, though he continued to hoard hundreds of pound notes since his needs were few.

Gcazimbane was ageing as the years went by. It was in their fifteenth or sixteenth year in Lesotho—he couldn't remember—when he woke up one morning, went to the stable and found Gcazimbane dead.

He wailed as if a human being had passed on. The horse had changed drastically since participating in the War of Hope from the carefree spirit that used to enjoy playing hide-and-seek with his groom to a brooding beast that carried out orders without joy, and that even once allowed itself to be abducted by amaBhaca enemies. But Malangana remembered only the wonderful times. Why, he was with Gcazimbane when he first spoke with Mthwakazi and argued about the sun. Gcazimbane was even present when he and Mthwakazi did adult things by the river. More than any human being, Gcazimbane was the keeper of his deepest secret.

At this thought he wailed once more.

People came to console him for they thought he had lost a relative. When they found that it was only a horse they offered to get rid of the carcass for him. He was grateful for he did not know who was going to assist him in burying Gcazimbane with all his kin so far away at Qoboshane or on the mountains of Mants'onyane, for they had even spread that far away herding their sheep and goats.

The next day he was grateful for the kindness of the neighbours as they brought him meat. Some of it was cooked tripe and it was very good to eat with sorghum bread. There were chunks of raw meat that he roasted on the open fire. Neighbours became generous like that when they had slaughtered an ox or when one of their animals was dead, so he did not ask questions. When he still had lots of goats and one was injured he would take it out of its misery. He would share most of the meat with the neighbours or else it would rot. There would have been no point in hoarding meat for oneself. Two weeks later another neighbour had brought him sun-dried meat known as lihoapa. This was particularly good and he kept some for when he would go to visit

Mhlontlo.

It happened one day that in casual conversation a neighbour mentioned that Gcazimbane was not only a beautiful horse but he was very delicious despite his age. Delicious? Did these people eat his horse? He remembered vaguely that Basotho people used to be teased as horse-eaters but he had thought it was only a joke. He screamed to the heavens when he learned that not only did his neighbour eat his horse but he himself partook in gormandising chunks of prime portions of the beast.

He imagined the horse living in his stomach, gnawing his intestines. He tried to vomit it out. He felt it kicking in him. He thought he somehow needed to exorcise the cannibal in him but he did not know how. He came to believe that Gcazimbane was really living inside him. That's when he started to neigh like a horse, uncontrollably, at any moment.

Everyone had gone but Malangana sat on the stoep and watched the moon. He would sit until it set. No one could believe this was the same Malangana who had the sheep and the goats and who used to ride fat horses selling *mokhele* ostrich feathers and fraternising with princes and being the envy of everyone. Over the years he had become almost skeletal with knees and elbows jutting out like knobkerries. It was not because of ageing. It was because of the longing of the heart. It had taken its toll on him. These were its physical manifestations. When the heart was longing it ate the body bit by bit. It started with the fatty areas, and then chewed the muscles and even gnawed parts of the bones, making them brittle. Longing made his body convoluted, twisted and grotesque.

He had not been to see Mhlontlo for more than a year now. Two months before Cesane came with the news that shocked him and he felt that it was Mhlontlo's final betrayal. First, Mhlontlo had tried to commit suicide. Secondly, he had now become *igqobhoka*—a convert—of the Roman Catholic Church.

The way Cesane put it was like this: Mhlontlo, or 'Mamalo as the Basotho liked to call him, had gone to white Catholic priests at Holy Cross Mission, and had told them that he was so depressed that he went to the mountain and covered his eyes with a *qhiya* headscarf. Then he ran with all his strength towards a cliff with the intention of killing himself. But he heard a voice saying, 'Hey, you stop that right now!' That stopped him in his tracks right at the edge of the cliff. He took off the blindfold and looked around but there was nobody there. Then he blindfolded himself again for a second attempt at suicide. But he felt someone grabbing his arm and heard a voice saying, 'Go and find a church service and offer yourself to God.' That was how 'Mamalo went to the Catholic Fathers and became a man of the Church.

'Today he prays and he goes to Holy Mass every Sunday,' said Cesane. 'He carries a rosary with him all the time.'

Malangana was happy about only one thing: Mhlontlo was not alone. Charles, his son, was there at Phiring with him, although he travelled back and forth to Qumbu.

The moon sat on the mountain. The silly mongrel thought now for sure it was going to lick the moon. It jumped up with its tongue hanging and licked the air. It fell to the ground and rolled once. A jackal howled. Malangana laughed. His body rattled.

WEDNESDAY APRIL 27, 1904

iPaseka, which included Good Friday and Easter Monday, had intervened and the acolyte said she could not introduce Malangana to the owner of the drum. She did come to the general dealer the next day, but without the drum and without the owner. She refused to say who the owner was. She could only say the owner of the drum was also her owner, and as *igqobhoka* she was not available during *iPaseka* because Jesus Christ, the one who was a baby on Christmas, died and was nailed on a cross and *amagqobhoka* mourn his death on Friday, even though they know that he will wake up again on Sunday and walk to heaven after some forty days. It was not the first time Malangana had heard this tale. These were the kinds of stories the tree-planting young men should be making fun of, not his war stories.

For a number of days after that the acolyte kept coming with excuses: her owner was sick or her owner had travelled. Malangana on the other hand kept showing her the money which she would be paid only after introducing him to the owner of the drum. The acolyte had finally to confess she could take Malangana to the owner only when both the man of the house and his wife were away at the same time, which didn't happen often because the owner of the drum, who happened to be the man's aged mother, lived a secret life that involved the drums.

Throughout April, the month amaMpondomise call *uTshaz'iimpuzi*, the month of the withering pumpkin, Malangana went to the general dealer's store and sat on the stoep waiting for the acolyte. She came quite faithfully, for money has a powerful magnetic pull when the eyes have seen it. Sometimes she brought some victuals, which he nibbled just a little bit. She thought he was fussy for an emaciated man. She did not know he was wary of looking too well-fed. His body had to be a true reflection of his years of anguish.

The tree planters have long dismantled their camp and left to civilise other landscapes. On that slope on the site of their camp Malangana has constructed his own shelter with grass and leaves and branches of bushes without even asking permission from the headman who he is certain is some interloper imposed by Government. The headman and the village council, on the other hand, just let him be because they think he is mad.

Today the acolyte comes. She is excited. Today is the day. The man of the house will be away for the whole week. He has gone to Umtata to consult with Government. He is a very important person of Government. His wife has gone to Qumbu for the day to visit her own relatives and to buy a few things at the shops. The acolyte knows that she may even return the next day since the husband is away.

Malangana is taken aback when he realises that the path leads to the site formerly occupied by Mhlontlo's Great Place. He can hardly recognise it though, with all the tall pine trees instead of the *umsintsi* that used to surround the place.

It is an expansive homestead of whitewashed rondavels and four-walled *ixande* houses. The acolyte tells him it is the homestead of Rhudulu who is the only Mpondomise of substance remaining in Sulenkama. Malangana remembers him. Like him, he was an ordinary soldier in Mhlontlo's army. But he does not remember him in the War of Hope. He wonders how he became so wealthy.

The acolyte takes Malangana to one of the houses where an old woman is lying on a mattress eating roasted pumpkin seeds from a bowl. Even though she has greatly shrunk and years have furrowed her face he can recognise her. She was one of the diviners who nursed the queen when she was sick. She was robust and matronly then but *nguye lo. She is the one.*

'I have a visitor for you, *makhulu*,' says the acolyte, addressing her as grandmother.

'Who are you, my child? Even though my eyes are weak you look like you need some healing and a lot of feeding too. You bring me visitors, you know that Rhudulu does not allow me the work of the ancestors any more, you silly girl,' says the old woman.

'I am Malangana, *makhulu*. You will not know me. But I remember you.'

'I don't divine any more, my child. Ever since my son found Christ he separated me from heathen things even though the spirits of my ancestors still move me.'

The acolyte is eager to conduct business and get it over with. This opportunity may not avail itself again.

'He wants to buy one of your drums, *makhulu*,' says the acolyte.

'How does he know about my drums?'

'I told him about them. He is a good man, he won't talk about them. His ancestors led him to one of your drums in his dreams and he told me about it when I met him at the *intlombe*.'

The old woman gets panicky. No one must know about the drums. When the spirits of the ancestors possess her the acolyte and a few friends assemble secretly in her room and beat the drums and *bavumise bacamagwise*—perform the sacred rituals of diviners—until the spirits calm down. This means that whether her son likes it or not she is still a diviner; the spirits of her ancestors are refusing to leave her alone and hand her over to her son's religion. She can don the red-and-white uniforms of the Methodists on Sundays and struggle on with her *dondolo* walking stick to church, but when the spirits call the drums must sound.

'Bring the drum,' says Malangana.

The acolyte dashes out.

'I remember you from the days of Mhlontlo.'

The old woman becomes agitated. 'Don't even mention that name. It's a good thing he is where he is now. I hope he rots there. I hope they kill him dead.'

Malangana is shocked to hear this from an elderly woman of the amaMpondomise people who used to be a traditional doctor at the king's court.

'My child, *azange abenobuntu laMhlontlo*,' adds the old woman. *That Mhlontlo never had any humanity.* 'After killing poor Hope he left his body to be eaten by wild animals. It was my son, Rhudulu, who broke ranks with his army and rode all the way to Maclear to warn Government of Mhlontlo's treachery. It was too late. Poor Hope was killed. After the war it was also my son who helped that white man—I think his name was Leary—find the skeletons of the poor white men and bury them right here at Sulenkama.'

She keeps on talking, which is what old folks who are usually starved of company do once they have an audience. Her son was rewarded with five hundred morgen of land and a pension of five pounds a year, which he still enjoys to this day because Government never turns against its word and never forgets its people. And now her son has introduced geese at Sulenkama. He has many geese and has employed many people to look after them.

'Were it not for Rhudulu, Hope and his clerks wouldn't have had a decent Christian funeral,' adds the old woman with much emphasis, while impatiently beckoning the acolyte to come in and not just stand at the door.

The acolyte comes in with three drums; Malangana wonders whether she no longer remembers which drum she had stolen for the *intlombe* or whether this is just a ruse to confuse the old lady. He points at the drum he wants, and immediately beats it. At first slowly, and then in a faster rhythm.

'I have heard that sound. There is no sound like that anywhere. It reminds me of the death of the Queen of amaMpondomise,' says the old woman.

'It was played by a Mthwakazi who was your acolyte,' says Malangana.

'There was a Mthwakazi,' says the old woman vaguely.

'Where is she? I am looking for her.'

'I don't know. It was many years ago.'

'But you have her drum. How did you get her drum?'
'How would I know? All these drums and *imbhiza zethu* were in the divination house during the war.'

When the Red Coats besieged the village various doctors and diviners took whatever they could of the sacred drums and medicinal paraphernalia—*imbhiza zethu*—to save them. She had taken the drums that are presently in her possession and had kept them safe for all these years. Most of them just stay there in the room; no one ever plays them for no one knows what spirits are embedded in them.

'This drum belongs to Mthwakazi,' says Malangana. 'I am taking it. You can't stop me because your turncoat son doesn't even know that it's here.'

As he walks out he hears the old woman say to the acolyte: 'Look what you brought to my house. He calls my Rhudulu a turncoat.'

The acolyte comes running after him. He gives her a one pound note. It is a lot of money for a drum. The price of a cow. But it is a very special drum, and he wouldn't have found it without her and her thievery.

As he hobbles under the pine trees he can hear honking and screeching sounds. It must be the geese. He beats the drum.

WEDNESDAY DECEMBER 2, 1903

They refused him permission to see Mhlontlo. He pleaded and begged and threatened. They, in turn, threatened to lock him up as a nuisance. He welcomed that, he told them. He had been demanding that he be locked up with his king right from the beginning in every town he had been tracing Mhlontlo, and in every town they cursed him away. Or just laughed at him. Now here in Kingwilliamstown they were threatening, nay promising, to fulfil his wish. He begged them to go ahead and lock him up. That's where he belonged: in jail with his brother and king. When they saw that he was earnest and truly would love to be imprisoned they easily bundled him up and carried him to the railway station and dumped him there. They told him if he ever went back to the office of the chief magistrate or the chief prosecutor or the jailer or the superintendent of police or any of the officials he had been pestering they would not hesitate to shoot him dead once and for all and no one would remember he ever lived.

He gave up on Mhlontlo. Gcazimbane would forgive him; he had tried his best. He would find his way to Qumbu. In his youth this used to be a journey of three days on foot.

Two days or a day and a half on horseback. But he was now a different Malangana; the one who had been eaten by the longing of the heart. The one who must now go and fulfil that longing of the heart. The journey would be slower. Unless he got a ride on a wagon. Or maybe he could catch a train to Umtata and then walk from there. Fortunately the bottoms of his heavy khaki pants were lined with pound notes that he hoarded for years in his hovel at Qomoqomong from the heydays of *mokhele* ostrich feathers. He would pay his way in whatever form of transportation he managed to get as long as he was careful no one became wise to the fact that this bundle of bones was sitting pretty.

Now that he had made up his mind to give up on Mhlontlo he felt free. He was eager to return to the land of amaMpondomise to search for Mthwakazi. There was nothing more he could do for Mhlontlo. In any event he was still angry about how he foolishly let himself get caught.

It happened a month ago. One month, two days to be exact. October 31, 1903. But Malangana only learned of it three weeks after it had happened. He was sitting on his adobe stoep at his Qomoqomong house—which in fact had become a hovel since he did not keep up with maintaining its grass thatch and adobe walls. He was staring at the faraway hills listening to the longing that was eating his heart when a group of horsemen in Basotho blankets stopped in his *ebaleni*. He recognised them immediately as *amaCesane oMda*, his kin from across the Telle River.

'*Yirholeni, Jol'inkomo!*' their leader greeted him, using the clan name of his ancestors. He knew at once that something was seriously wrong. He suspected that there was a death in the family. A death of someone very important; a senior member of the clan. He responded in the name of one of their ancestors as well: '*Qengebe!*' And then added for good measure: '*Nina mathole oMthwakazi! I return your greeting, calves of a Bushwoman!*

They dismounted. Malangana apologised that he had no chairs so they would just have to sit on the stoep or stand if they were afraid of making their beautiful blankets dirty. He further apologised that he could not offer the *amarhewu*—fermented porridge—to drink since they knew that he was all alone in the world, racked by illness that even some of the great *lingaka* of Baphuthi could not cure. It was an illness that could only be cured once he stopped *ukumfenguza nokubhaca*—being a refugee and a wanderer—and returned to the land of his amaMpondomise people.

'We hear you, son of Matiwane,' said the leader of *amaCesane oMda*. They no longer saw themselves as refugees. They had all established themselves on both sides of the border and paid homage to local chiefs. Exile was now home. The land of amaMpondomise was now a distant memory. Only for the likes of Malangana was it still eating the heart and they felt sorry for him. But it was not the reason they were here. They had come to let him know about Mhlontlo. He was arrested on the Saturday morning of October 31, 1903. The date was repeated again and again for it had to register in the memory of all, to be transmitted to future generations as a date *yokuzila*—a date of mourning.

'That's almost three weeks ago,' said Malangana. 'Why didn't I know of this? The man lives here in Lesotho and I get to hear of his arrest from people across the border?'

'He was arrested across the border. We only heard when he was already in the hands of the police in Palmietfontein. And when we got there they told us they had taken him to Sterkspruit.'

What they heard was that Mr Cretchley, the white man who owned the general dealer's store at Palmietfontein at the border of Lesotho but on the Herschel District side, met Mhlontlo in church at Holy Cross in Lesotho and enticed him with new blankets. He told him he would be safe if he came to his store in Palmietfontein and he would be spoilt for choice of beautiful colourful blankets. On the appointed day, which was the fateful Saturday, Mhlontlo clandestinely crossed the border and visited one or two of the *amaCesane oMda* before proceeding to Palmietfontein.

'Why didn't you who were visited by him stop him?' asked Malangana.

There was some bitterness in him. He had been Mhlontlo's kin and faithful servant. Yet he never set foot at his place. Qomoqomong would have been a minor detour on his way to the Telle River and the border people and Palmietfontein and places like that. Yet he never thought of coming to greet him and ask after his health.

'He didn't tell us he was going to Palmietfontein,' said one of the men. 'We thought he was returning to Lesotho. He knew how dangerous it was for him to be seen in the Cape Colony. He knew he was a wanted man.'

Well, Mhlontlo was not returning to Lesotho. At the store Inspector Charles David Dovey and his policemen were hiding behind stacks of sisal bags of corn and maize meal. Mhlontlo was warmly welcomed by Mr Cretchley. As he was admiring the blankets Dovey pounced on him and handcuffed him. Only then did it dawn on him that he had walked into a trap.

'You see this church of his? *Ebebungene ngantoni ubugqobhoka?*" screamed Malangana. *What did he want with Christianity?*

He was furious at his king and brother for being so gullible. And he felt betrayed because ever since Mhlontlo became a Catholic he had changed altogether and no longer associated with him, and would even hide things from him. He knew nothing about his life. Where was Charles when these things were happening? He was supposed to look after his father. It was clear to him now that the white man's God tended to make these people do foolish things. He would have to go to Palmietfontein and be with his king. That's what a loyal groom of his horse would do. Even if the man had been made stupid by the Church, in memory of Gcazimbane who still lived in him and occasionally neighed from the depths of his belly—though thankfully not as often as it used to be for a year or two after he had eaten his meat—he would go and see what he could do for Mhlontlo.

The leader of *amaCesane oMda* reminded him that Mhlontlo was no longer at Palmietfontein but had been transferred to Sterkspruit.

At dawn the next morning Malangana set his hovel on fire and hobbled away. It was what initiates did to their *bhoma*—their huts at the mountain initiation and circumcision school when the ritual was over and they were walking back to society as fully fledged men. He felt this was a transition for him too.

At Palmietfontein he met Inspector Dovey as he wanted to ascertain that Mhlontlo was the man in their custody. He was the Inspector of Native Locations of Number 2 Area in the District of Herschel which was headquartered at Palmietfontein so he was used to talking to natives and always keen to interview one in case he was a potential witness.

'Oh yes, the prisoner was Umhlonhlo all right,' he said. 'He was pointed out by one of my native men.'

He then reached for his record book and proudly read a statement he had written: '"He was arrested at a spot 120 yards on the Herschel side of the Telle River, in the Herschel District of the Cape Colony." He was in our jurisdiction all right. We didn't kidnap him in Basutoland as they are now claiming. No, siree, he was right here in our jurisdiction and we got him. He is at Sterkspruit now, has been charged with the murder of Hope, Warren and Henman of Qumbu.'

'I want to see him with my own eyes,' said Malangana.

Dovey said he could not see him because he had already handed him over to the Cape Mounted Riflemen stationed at Palmietfontein who had escorted him to Sterkspruit.

'And there I already gave evidence against him,' said Dovey. 'I don't think you'll find him there but I think you should still go. You might be an important witness. Yes, they might find you useful there. Go straight to the police station. Tell them old Dovey sent you.'

Sterkspruit was the administrative town of Herschel. Dovey hoped that if Malangana became a useful witness in nailing Mhlontlo then it would count in his favour for a promotion since he had made the arrest and the case against Mhlontlo had run into problems at Sterkspruit for lack of evidence. But he didn't say any of this to Malangana.

Malangana went back to old Feyiya at eKra and borrowed two horses and a herdboy who would return with them. He was so proud that the geldings they were riding to Sterkspruit had been sired by Xokindini.

Immediately Malangana arrived at Sterkspruit he went to the police station and demanded that he be arrested. The police wanted to know what crime he had committed.

'I am Malangana, son of Matiwane,' he announced, his hands ready for handcuffs.

'Yes, but what have you done?' asked the white sergeant. 'You've got to commit a crime for us to arrest you.'

'I am a wanted man,' said Malangana. He was losing his patience with this lot. 'Why do you think I was a refugee in Lesotho for more than twenty years?'

The white sergeant was impressed that he was able to communicate with him without an interpreter, though his English was shaky. The other policemen in the office, mostly black, found him quite funny and looked over the counter at the bundle of bones who was demanding to be locked up and sniggered and chuckled.

'*Tloho hosane, ntate. Re tla u ts'oara hosane,*' said a black policeman in Sesotho, condescendingly as if talking to a child. *Come tomorrow, sir. We'll arrest you tomorrow.*

'I demand to be locked up with my King Mhlontlo,' said Malangana. 'I was with him when the deed was done. I will be with him when you kill him.'

They broke into laughter when it became clearer to them what he was talking about.

'He is talking about the prisoner from Palmietfontein,'

said one of them.

'Dovey's prisoner! We didn't know what to do with him. We had no evidence against him,' said the sergeant.

Malangana was getting desperate.

'But Dovey sent me here,' he said. 'He said I should tell you so.'

'Dovey is a fool. He knows we had the case already on November 3rd before Acting Resident Magistrate David Eadie,' said the sergeant. And then he turned to the black policeman and said, 'Just explain to the man in his language.'

The black policeman took over and told Malangana in Sesotho that the trial was very brief. Dovey gave evidence to explain how he had arrested Mhlontlo. Mhlontlo's defence was that Dovey crossed the river to see him and grabbed him from Lesotho. The magistrate ruled that there was no evidence against Mhlontlo, but he would be remanded in custody while he sent a telegram to the Secretary of Law in Cape Town seeking advice on what to do with the prisoner. The telegram was duly sent and on November 4th the Secretary to the Law Department responded to the effect that the Warrant of Apprehension had been issued and that Mhlontlo had to be remanded to Umtata under strong escort. On November 5th the said prisoner, namely Mhlontlo, was transferred from Herschel to Umtata Jail.

Malangana insisted on responding in English and addressing the white sergeant. He said if Government had sent Mhlontlo to Umtata he was insisting that he be arrested and sent to Umtata as well since he was part of the same case. Mhlontlo could not be tried alone when he, Malangana, was also present when Hope was killed.

'Listen, we know nothing about that,' said the sergeant. 'It's not our case. Go and tell them there in Umtata.'

'You want me to use my money to go there? It is your job to arrest me and send me to Umtata,' said Malangana.

'Sorry, we are not interested,' said the sergeant. 'And we are busy.'

Another policeman waved some documents in front of him and said, 'Actually the prisoner is no longer in Umtata. He is in Kingwilliamstown. It says here the Secretary of the Law Department in Cape Town sent an urgent telegram on November 6th to the Chief Magistrate of Umtata telling him that they decided the preliminary examination would be in Kingwilliamstown and Mhlontlo had to be transferred to the Kingwilliamstown Jail for that purpose.'

The sergeant broke out laughing and said, 'We are not taking you to Kingwilliamstown either. So leave before things get nasty for you, my friend.'

The black policeman warned him that the sergeant was a very nice man and had been patient with him for far too long. He shouldn't test the kindly white man too much. He should leave in peace because no one was interested in arresting him. No one *would* arrest him. Instead they would beat him up and throw him out in the street.

Malangana stood there for a while and considered this advice. The policemen went on with their work and ignored him. He decided that perhaps it was wise to leave. As Malangana was stumbling out the white sergeant called him back.

'Somebody donate the old crutches lying in the store-room to this man,' he said. 'He looks like he's going to tumble down every time he walks.'

'I don't want your crutches,' shouted Malangana. 'I want to be a prisoner with Mhlontlo.'

Actually he needed those crutches. His gait was becoming strained and painful. He had not been doing much walking in Qomoqomong. He didn't realise that his joints had deteriorated to this extent.

He asked the herdboy to ride with him to Zastron in the Orange Free State where he took a train to Kingwilliamstown. The herdboy rode back to Qoboshane with the two geldings.

Now he was done with Kingwilliamstown. It was going to be months before there was a trial, they told him. And only Mhlontlo would be tried. Not anyone called Malangana, son of Matiwane. They did not know him, never heard of him, did not want to know him, and did not want to lock him up either. If he kept on pestering them they were going to blow his head off.

Government had no appreciation of his role in the War of Hope.

He walked to the ticket office and bought a train ticket to Umtata. From there he would see how to get to Qumbu.

TUESDAY MAY 17, 1904

He has taken to sitting outside his hovel on the slopes of the hill in the clearing that used to be a camp of the tree planters surveying those parts of the village within his view. He sees the puny villagers going about their business. He despises them all for their ignorance. The old residents whose blood he shares from the blue lakes of eMbo and the new residents who were placed there to lord over them as a reward for their loyalty after the War of Hope. They are all ignorant of him. And he is happy to leave them at that. And to play his drum.

Depending on the direction of the wind, the people of the village can hear the drum from time to time throughout the day. Sometimes it goes on for hours on end. Then it stops. The drummer is tired. He is not a strong man. He is skeletal. They are surprised he wakes up breathing and drumming every morning. Sometimes in the middle of the night they hear the drum. And sometimes when the drum is silent they see him hobbling down the hill to the village on his twisted crutches, with the heavy drum hanging on his back tied with a leather rope over one shoulder. He refuses when anyone offers to help him carry the drum.

He takes it with him when he has to go to the general

dealer's store. He dare not leave it at his hovel on the slope of the hill. What if someone comes and steals it? It is all he has left of Mthwakazi. He is no longer looking for her. All that *mkhondo* thing was nothing but shit. That is why ever since the day he walked to Sulenkama accompanied by stories of the past there has not been an inkling of it. It was strong all along the way but suddenly stopped when he entered Sulenkama. And yet Mthwakazi has lived here. Her traces are all over this village. Why is her *mkhondo* absent here then? One would easily believe some mischievous spirit was playing cruel games with him, yet everywhere there was a *mkhondo* there was always confirmation that indeed Mthwakazi had been there.

The chase has been fruitless. He has given up on Mthwakazi. All he is waiting for is death. He will die a happy man, with her drum in his arms. That is another reason it must always be with him everywhere he goes. Because the day and the hour are not known.

On other occasions the drum is silent because he is walking to the Sulenkama River for his ablutions. Sometimes when he has enough strength he walks right up to the confluence of Sulenkama and Gqukunqa and sits on the bank and dips his feet in the water and plays the drum.

The people of Sulenkama do not know that he despises them for their ignorance of him. They think they know him: he is the Madman of the Hill who used to claim to be a war hero but is now silent about it since he was exposed as a fake by itinerant tree-planting boys. Once in a while the Madman of the Hill gets fed up with people at the general dealer's store and shouts: 'I don't care what you say, my spear did taste his heart even though he was already dead.'

No one knows what he is talking about. This outburst happens when people are gathered around whoever has the news of the trial that day.

It is the only mad thing he expresses. That, and the beating of the drum. Everything else he utters sounds quite sane and reasonable. When people greet him he responds politely and is even able to conduct a civil conversation about the weather, and its being May, the end of the amaMpondomise year which is also the time of harvest; he comments about the brightness of Canopus at night and the promise of a good harvest this year. He seems to exude compassion and wisdom. Even the beating of the drum: those who are less mean-spirited consign it to *ukuthwasa* rather than madness—that is, perhaps he is being summoned by the ancestors to join one of the sacred orders of diviners.

He despises them, but they do not pay much attention to him. More exciting things are happening in Kingwilliamstown and each day has its new developments. Mhlontlo, who used to be a king, is on trial for a murder that happened more than twenty years ago. Whenever Malangana goes to the general dealer's store he stops to listen as the men congregate on the veranda around *amakhumsha* who came from Umtata or from Kingwilliamstown that day with the news of the trial. Some even read from the *East London Daily Dispatch*.

In the early days of the trial it seemed that the prosecutor was having difficulty getting evidence against Mhlontlo and people were saying it was because of his strong medicine. Who did not know that Mhlontlo was an *ixhwele* in his own right—a powerful medicine man who could work magic? Is the story not told that during the War of Hope he could make the bullets of the white man turn into water? Is he not the hero king who could fight on many war fronts at the same time on his magical horse Gcazimbane which could grow wings?

Malangana pays no attention to all this talk. Yes, he stands, listens, shows no emotion, and then moves on with his heavy burden on his back. He sits down whenever he gets tired and beats the drum.

Some days the trial produces new details and people ask themselves what they have to do with Hope's murder. They hear that a witness has revealed that Mhlontlo was being paid a Government stipend of sixty pounds per annum or that Mhlontlo sent Hamilton Hope's horse to a Mr Mqikela after the murder but he refused to keep it; he sent it back to Mhlontlo instead. When Malangana hears this last one his usually indifferent demeanour changes for a few seconds and he giggles like a child who is being tickled. To those who see him it merely confirms the communal diagnoses of the man.

Sometimes a woman—and it is always a woman who wants to make friendly conversation—asks the Madman of the Hill what he thinks of the trial today; does he think Mhlontlo will get away with it? He smiles and politely asks, 'Have you ever wondered why *amaKroza* stand on their head, *dadethu*?' The woman being referred to as 'my sister' wonders how *amaKroza*, *Orion's Belt*, has anything to do with her question. But Malangana continues regardless, 'We teach our children not to point at *amaKroza* with their dirty fingers because on those stars there are three sacred dwelling places:

one for the grave where the bones of our ancestors are peacefully resting; the second is where their spirits are roaming free; and the third is the dwelling place of the big man himself, uQamata.'

Then he walks away, leaving the questioner confused. Perhaps these theological outbursts are a residue of the influence of the days he spent at Ibandla-likaNtu.

But sometimes when he is in a hurry and the drum has taken its toll on his weak back, his answer is very brief: 'The great rains had returned after a long drought.'

Today is like other days. He has no special expectations. It is in the afternoon when he approaches the general dealer's store and *omathand'indaba*—the lovers of news—are already gathered around an *ikhumsha* gentleman, who is the local primary school teacher. He is reading details in the previous day's newspaper: *Both the prosecutor, Mr Rose-Innes, and the lawyers for the defence, Messrs H.S. Smith and H.W. Gush, have made their summations before the presiding officer, the Acting Resident Magistrate of Kingwilliamstown, Mr Robert James Dick. The defence emphasised that all the witnesses pointed out that the accused was not present when Hamilton Hope was murdered; he was out conferring with Mr Alfred Davis. Not a single witness linked him to a conspiracy. The accused stated that he knew nothing about any plan to kill Mr Hope and the Crown failed to prove otherwise.*

At that moment a horseman comes galloping, waving a piece of paper.

'It is from the telegraph office in Qumbu. In the case *Rex v. Mhlontlo*, the accused was found not guilty!' the horseman shouts, still waving the telegram, with the horse jogging around the crowd.

There is an instant outburst of applause and yells and screams and ululations.

The only thought that comes to Malangana is: that telegraph office, we set it on fire, didn't we? I personally lit the fire; but none of these despicable people will believe me. So, they built it up again?

He walks away. Along the path people have heard the news. Obviously news travels faster than Malangana can walk. One can conclude who among them are amaMpondomise from their mood. Other nations may not necessarily have any ill-feeling towards Mhlontlo but may not be overly excited. Yet more and more people these days are becoming increasingly united and would like to see themselves as one black nation, as the *ikhumsha* teacher who was reading *Izwi Labantu* was telling the people the other day. They have seen what the white man can do to them when they are many separate kingdoms.

He meets a group of young men and women singing: 'At last our king is coming back. We'll get our land back.'

Malangana tries to summon the memory of the king that is coming. The image is blurry; the king sees nothing and hears nothing for he is preoccupied with counting beads on a rosary. The singers try to encourage Malangana to join them in song even if he can't dance because of his crutches and the load on his back. He ignores them and stumbles away.

One of the singers stops and looks at him, and then asks, 'Why are you so sad, old man? Are you one of those who fought against him?'

He does not stop to respond.

The river is the place to go, even though he was there early in the morning for his ablutions. This time he will walk as far as the confluence of Sulenkama and Gqukunqa. As he shambles along the bank he is struck by a new observation: this river he has been calling a river even in his dreams is not a river at all. It is just a stream. How did it manage to pass itself off as more imposing than it really is for all these years? And what film has been removed from his eyes so that now he can see it for what it is, in all its emaciated nakedness?

The water still sounds the same. But now the familiar sound is intermingled with a cacophony of hooting and screeching. And then he sees the source. Strange birds grazing on the grass like sheep. Quite big too. Among them he sees their shepherd. Very close to the confluence of the two rivers. The two streams, for that's what they have become, after their lie has been exposed today. As he walks closer to the shepherd, he notices that the shepherd is not a shepherd at all. She is a woman.

She walks towards him, smiling.

'What took you so long?' she asks, her eyes squinting and her grin toothless.

He recognises her immediately.

Mthwakazi!

She's grown old and her face is wrinkled and her eyes surrounded by crow's feet, but she's undoubtedly his Mthwakazi. Her ears are adorned with earrings of gold. He does not notice them though they are quite conspicuous. She is not wearing the tanned-hide skirt or front-and-back apron of the abaThwa people that she used to wear in the olden days. She is in a brown European skirt and yellow blouse but she is barefoot. The clothes are not ill-fitting like the last European attire he saw her in, the red-and-white floral silk dress the bulk of which she had to carry over her shoulders.

He looks at the geese. It is not a friendly stare.

'What are these strange birds?'

'They're Rhudulu's geese.'

'You're herding his geese?'

She nods.

'They're noisy.' That is all he can think of saying.

She only sniggers.

'And they're ugly,' he adds. 'I don't think they taste so wonderful either.'

She looks at him curiously, and then at the geese. She turns back to him.

'I waited for you,' she says again. 'What kept you so long?'

'A war happened.'

'I can see it took its toll on you. And the load you carry is too heavy for you.'

'It's your drum,' he says, and he unloads it and places it between them.

She looks at it for a long time as if trying very hard to remember it.

'It's the drum you stole. You are only returning it now? You can keep it; I am no longer a diviner.'

'We'll keep it still,' he says.

She smiles and shakes her head, displaying the golden earrings. Nothing registers in him. They are standing to attention, facing each other with the drum on the ground between them. The twisted *umsintsi* crutches support his frail body. She shakes her head again; she wants him to notice the earrings and say something. He is looking at her face, mesmerised.

'Don't you remember them?'

'Remember what?'

'These earrings? You're so stupid! I wore them all these years so that you could remember them.'

'I remember the suns, though,' he says. 'There are many of them. Not just one.'

'There is only one sun,' she says with much enthusiasm. 'I was right all along. *Amakhumsha* tell us that the world is round and it moves around the sun. It is the same sun that we see every day.'

For the first time in a long time Malangana laughs. It is real laughter from the guts. This is the real Mthwakazi, the woman who makes him laugh.

'What do *amakhumsha* know? Look up in the sky on a cloudless night. What do you think those twinkling things are?'

'Stars, of course.'

'Stars are little suns.'

She cackles. She has lost some of her teeth, but she is still Mthwakazi.

They look to the hill that becomes a mountain after dark. The hill on which stars grow at night.

The end is always a journey.

EPILOGUE
THURSDAY DECEMBER 12, 1912

Mhlontlo dies a commoner at Caba Location, Qumbu.

Though he had been found not guilty of Hamilton Hope's murder he had been stripped of the status of 'Paramount Chief' by the Cape Colony Government and had been banished to Kingwilliamstown and later transferred to Willowvale, and was only allowed to live at Caba in Qumbu in 1906 when he was old and sickly. His heir Charles was not allowed to succeed either, since the intention of the colonial Government was to end the kingdom of amaMpondomise once and for all.

(Joe H. Majija, a descendant of one of the junior Houses of Mhlontlo, writes in his Dark Clouds at Sulenkama *that his body lies buried in a well-kept family cemetery at the Great Place of Ntabankulu. 'His grave is a source of inspiration to many Pondomises who normally visit it to get spiritual guidance and protection.')*

Malangana is not there to bid him farewell. He is still on a journey with his Mthwakazi.

The end is always a journey.

ACKNOWLEDGEMENTS

In this historical novel a fictional love story weaves itself into the true history of the assassination of Hamilton Hope, a British magistrate in the 19th-century Cape Colony, and the exile of members of my family under the leadership of Mhlontlo ka Matiwane from Qumbu to Lesotho, and later to Herschel on the Cape Colony side of the Lesotho border. I am grateful first to my grandfather, Charles Gxumekelane (A! Zenzile) Mda, who was born in 1880 and was a baby when the War of Hope broke out, and whose father, Feyiya, was a member of one of the Houses of Matiwane. Feyiya and his family were part of that migration from Qumbu to Lesotho with Mhlontlo. I am grateful for the stories he used to tell us, his grandchildren, about our origin. I am also grateful to the late Robert Mda of the Lesotho Mdas, who used to cross the Telle River to his Cousin Charles' homestead in Qobo-shane when I was a little boy. He never ran out of stories about the exploits of Mhlontlo—much embellished and full of magic; for instance, he could turn the white man's bullets into water. I was amazed when I was researching this novel to find a lot of consistencies (among minor inconsistencies) in Charles' and Robert's oral histories and the stories that other praise poets of amaMpondomise from different parts of the Eastern Cape, as the region is now called, tell about the origins of amaMpondomise from Sibiside of abaMbo right up to the change of fortunes as a result of the killing of Hamilton Hope. The most detailed of these narratives was left for posterity by the late Mdukiswa Tyabashe who lived at Cuthbert's Location and used to be King Lutshoto's praise poet, and whose oral history was one of those collected by Harold Scheub and published in *The Tongue is Fire: South African Storytellers and Apartheid* (Madison: The University of Wisconsin Press, 1990). I am grateful to Harold Scheub for this collection. Of course, I did not only depend on the oral tradition for my sources. Historical record, both primary and secondary sources, was crucial. Joe H. Majija of Mthatha, a descendant of one of the junior Houses of Mhlontlo, directed me to a lot of archival documents from the trove he used in his self-published booklet, *Dark Clouds at Sulenkama*. Here I must thank Wonga Qina, a Grahamstown teacher, who helped me track down Mr Majija and also took me to libraries and archives in Grahamstown. Ken Heath of Kingwilliamstown was a relative of William Charles Henman, one of the two white men killed with Hope. I thank him for the information he provided. I rediscovered Mhlontlo as a high school student in Lesotho in Sesotho praise poetry, 'Lithoko tsa Lerotholi', in historian Mosebi Damane's *Marath'a Lilepe* (Morija: Morija Sesuto Book Depot, 1960). The Basotho called him 'Mamalo. I was proud that I, a refugee boy, had a great-grandfather who featured in the praise poetry of Lesotho kings. Other materials that were useful were: Clifton Crais, 'The Death of Hope' in *The Politics of Evil: Magic, State Power and the Political Imagination in South Africa* (Cambridge: Cambridge University Press, 2002); and J.S. Kotze, 'CounterInsurgency in the Cape Colony, 1872–1882' in *Scientia Militaria: South African Journal of Military Studies* Vol. 31, No. 2 (2003) http://scientiamilitaria.journals.ac.za/pub/article/ view/152.

I hardly ever thank the two lovely women in my writing life: Pam Thornley, my long-time editor, and Isobel Dixon, my agent. It is high time I did so.

All the research for *Little Suns* was done, the initial chapters were written and the plan for the whole novel was executed during my sojourn as Artist-in-Residence at the Stellenbosch Institute for Advanced Study (STIAS), Wallenberg Research Centre at Stellenbosch University, Marais Street, Stellenbosch, 7600, South Africa.

ABOUT THE AUTHOR

Zakes Mda is writer, painter, composer and film maker. He commutes between South Africa and the U.S., as professor of creative writing at Ohio University, beekeeper in the Eastern Cape, patron of the Market Theatre, Johannesburg, and a director of the Southern African Multimedia AIDS Trust. He is the author of ten novels and a memoir, including *Rachel's Blue*, longlisted for the International IMPAC Dublin Literary Awards 2016, *Cion*, shortlisted for the Commonwealth Writers' Prize 2008, and *The Heart of Redness*, Winner of the Hurston/Wright Legacy Award 2003.